Willoughby's Return

A TALE OF ALMOST IRRESISTIBLE TEMPTATION

JANE ODIWE

SOURCEBOOKS LANDMARK™
AN IMPRINT OF SOURCEBOOKS, INC.®
NAPERVILLE, ILLINOIS

Published by Sourcebooks Landmark, an imprint of Sourcebooks, Inc.
P.O. Box 4410, Naperville, Illinois 60567-4410
(630) 961-3900
FAX: (630) 961-2168
www.sourcebooks.com

Library of Congress Cataloging-in-Publication Data

Odiwe, Jane.
   Willoughby's return : a tale of almost irresistible temptation / Jane Odiwe.
      p. cm.
   1.   Gentry--England--Fiction. 2.   England--Social life and customs--19th century--
Fiction. 3.   Married people--Fiction. 4.   West Country (England)--Fiction. 5.   Domestic
fiction. I. Austen, Jane, 1775-1817. Sense and sensibility. II. Title.
   PR6115.D55W56 2009
   823'.92--dc22

                              2009029776

            Printed and bound in the United States of America
                VP 10 9 8 7 6 5 4 3 2 1

For Romanus,
You pierce my soul

Chapter 1

MARIANNE BRANDON WAS BURSTING with news to tell her sister and was so excited at the report that her husband had divulged at breakfast before leaving for Lyme that morning, that she did not consider there to be time enough to don her bonnet. With her chestnut curls escaping from her coiffure to dance in the wind and her scarlet cloak billowing like a great sail behind her, she almost ran down the lane to the parsonage. Knowing that Elinor would probably scold her for not bringing the chaise, she nevertheless had not wanted to be bothered with the inconvenience of having to wait for it. Muddying her boots and the hem of her gown, she took the shortcut across the fields to the lane that separated the two sisters. Yesterday's storm had left the ground wet but there was the promise of a most delight-ful day, the autumnal sunshine kissing her cheeks with a blush. Marianne had not wanted to say goodbye to her husband but was resigned to his departure. There was nothing she could say or do to change the situation; she knew that from experience. Glad to be outside in the fresh air, she looked about with contented pleasure, waltzing through the familiar countryside that she was delighted to call her home. Delaford House in the county of Dorset was as dear to her as the former family seat at Norland had been. Marianne knew in her heart that she was a most fortunate young woman.

Elinor was delighted to see her as always, although she was a little surprised at her sister's slightly dishevelled appearance. "Goodness me, Marianne. Is ought amiss? You look rather harried. Where is little James? Is he well? Anna will be most upset not to see her cousin this morning."

"How is my darling Anna? I long to kiss her! And where is little Georgie? I must have a cuddle!" Marianne handed her cloak into the arms of a waiting maidservant before arranging herself with much elegance on the sofa in the comfortable sitting room. "I could not bring James with me, as he was not yet dressed, and in any case I just had to get out into the sunshine. Besides, he wants to look into every hedgerow and chase the falling leaves, and I couldn't wait to tell you my news. However, before I left I promised he would see his cousin soon. I have had an idea. Anna and James enjoy one another's company so much, as does our dear mama. What say you to a shopping trip in Exeter the day after tomorrow? It would be such fun. My nursemaid can take our babies in the carriage to Barton Cottage and after you and I have handed them over with our greetings we shall go out in the box barouche!"

Elinor looked at Marianne in disbelief. She wondered if she would ever grow up or if she would for once consider others before she set about on some scheme or other. Colonel William Brandon, Elinor thought, had done much to improve her sister's character. She was more settled in her habits, more tranquil than she had ever been, and was not quite so prone to as many flights of fancy or as many fits of sensibility as she had been in the past. But three years of married life had done little to really change her. Marianne still had an impetuous nature, she still retained a desire for impulse and enterprises undertaken on the spur of the moment. The Colonel, Elinor felt, indulged Marianne's whims far too frequently.

"Marianne, you know that would be impossible. I have far too much to do here at present and I do not think Mama will be as pleased as you think to have all her grandchildren at once. Besides, she may have other plans."

"But Margaret is there, kicking her heels with nothing to do. I am sure she would only be delighted to see her niece and nephews. And I would love to tell Mama and Margaret my news."

Elinor was firm. "I would love to go shopping on another day, but I really cannot go at the moment. Now, is that what you came to tell me in such a hurry?"

Marianne watched Elinor's maid set down a tray of lemonade and ratafia biscuits. She could hardly wait for Susan's starched white cap to disappear through the door before she made her announcement.

"Henry Lawrence is coming home—William's nephew," she added, taking in Elinor's puzzled expression.

"Oh, yes," Elinor exclaimed, her face breaking into a smile. "I remember hearing about him from Mrs Jennings. He has just completed his studies at Oxford, has he not?"

"Yes, and by all accounts he is not only very handsome but is also a very eligible young man, for he will inherit Whitwell. I have never met him, but I must admit, I am most curious to see him."

"Whitwell is a very handsome estate; William's sister made an excellent marriage."

"She did indeed, though her health has never been good. That is why they stayed in Southern France and Italy for so long, I believe. Hannah tells me that the air and the climate are very well suited to invalids, and is always at pains to point out her abhorrence of the damp atmosphere to be found in the West Country. William worries about his sister so much, but all I can observe is that the Dorsetshire rain does not improve her disposition." Marianne paused before looking directly into her sister's eyes. "I have a mind to say that there seems little that would divert a constitution so intent on being ill. I have never seen her without some ailment and I admit it is fortunate that we are not such close neighbours. I have never heard her discuss any subject other than that of herself, and then it is only to complain."

"Perhaps she suffers more than you know, Marianne."

"That we all suffer in her company is a certainty. You have not met with her above twice in your life and I believe you mistakenly felt that she was quite charming on both occasions. But then, you are not her intimate relation and I suspect you have been taken in."

"I daresay the entire neighbourhood will be throwing their girls in Mr Lawrence's path," said Elinor, changing the course of the conversation. "I expect Miss Strowbridge will have her eye on him before long."

"Miss Strowbridge, nonsense! He will be entirely suitable for Margaret, do you not think? You must admit there have been few young men to excite the romantic sensibilities of our dear sister to date. Charles Carey was never really suitable, and in any case he has gone to sea. I feel most excited at the prospect.

William says Henry was partly educated in France and that he speaks French quite like a native. Not only is he a character of romance but he is also conversant in art, literature, and poetry, preferring our own beloved Cowper. He is quite perfect for Margaret, I should say."

"Is it wise, dear sister, to be making matches in this way, before the two people in question have even set eyes on one another? Indeed, if his mother is the person you describe, I wonder that you are so keen for Margaret to make such an alliance."

"Oh, there is no need for our sister to worry. Sir Edgar will adore Margaret; I know he will make certain there are no impediments to a match."

"Do you not think that the Lawrences will already have a girl in mind, one who may possess a larger dowry than Margaret can claim?"

"I do not think that Margaret's chances with a fitting suitor are any less than most girls. Despite the lack of money, she is a very handsome girl. She will steal Henry's heart the moment he looks at her."

"I imagine that there will not be many opportunities for them to meet however, especially if you are desirous of avoiding your relatives," added Elinor with a laugh.

"I've already thought hard on that particular problem and for Margaret's happiness I am prepared to make sacrifices. I have decided that we must have a round of social events. Firstly, we will throw a party to welcome him. Nay, a ball, nothing but a ball will do! I shall invite the Wiltons and the Courtneys."

"And not invite the Strowbridges!"

"I suppose I shall have to invite them, though I know that young minx Selina will do nothing but flaunt herself before

Mr Lawrence. Never mind, I shall take Margaret shopping; she shall have a new gown and our ardent suitor will not be able to resist her."

"I hope all your efforts will not be in vain, Marianne. I suppose you have reflected on the possibility of the lovers detesting one another on sight. And I do hope Henry's good looks match up to the gossip, which no doubt has exaggerated the fairness of every feature."

"Elinor, it will not be so, I promise you. Margaret will be in love with a very handsome man before the end of the month!"

"How is William?" asked Elinor, keen to move on to another discussion.

"He's well enough, though he left for Lyme this morning without even touching his breakfast. He has gone to see you-know-who, so I expect I shall not see him until the day after tomorrow."

"How are Miss Williams and the child?"

"Eliza Williams is another who is always fancying herself unwell and now it seems she has taught her daughter to be sickly also," answered Marianne, knowing she was being more than a little unkind. She replaced her glass on the table none too quietly. "A begging note and off Brandon runs to attend to his little family. I know I sound churlish, but sometimes, Elinor, it is too hard to bear."

"Marianne, the Colonel has an obligation to his ward and her daughter. He has never forgiven himself for the death of her mother; you know he could not leave them in distress."

"I am aware more than anyone that he has not forgotten Eliza's mother. She is always there, a spectre from the past who will never go away. Well, we all know that she was his first great attachment and for all the fuss he makes of her descendants, I have lately concluded that she was probably his one true love."

"Oh, Marianne, you are being a little fanciful now. Anyone can see how much you are adored by William."

"Am I adored, Elinor? Am I really loved for myself alone or because I resemble his first love so much? I sometimes think if it were possible for her to return from the grave I would never see him again."

"Come now, Marianne, you should not say such things. You are a little upset. Think of what you are saying."

"I cannot help myself. Elinor, I love him so much and I cannot bear the thought of William spending all that time with a young woman who surely must resemble her mother to perfection."

"Why do you not visit them together?" Elinor asked, refilling Marianne's glass as she spoke. "I'm sure if you saw her and her situation you would realise how unfounded your worries must be."

"I never want to visit them, you know that is impossible," came her sister's reply. "Oh, Elinor, however could I see them knowing what happened between Eliza Williams and… the truth is, I could not bear to see the child." Marianne broke off, unable to carry on.

Elinor looked at her sister's expression and knew it was useless to continue. An aura of anguish like a ghostly shroud seemed to settle upon her sister's shoulders. Marianne's dark eyes flashed, her distress plain to see.

Elinor was vastly relieved when the conversation was interrupted in the next second by the arrival of her children, accompanied by their nurse. Anna, who favoured her aunt so much in looks, chose to break free from her nurse's restraining hand. She immediately tottered over to her aunt on unsteady legs with outstretched arms. Marianne's temper was instantly soothed. She laughed, kissed the top of her dark head, and fetched her up onto her lap. There was only a month between Anna and Marianne's boy, James, and they were as friendly as any two-year-olds could be. Marianne loved her niece and baby nephew very much, though she often thought that her sister curbed and controlled Anna's behaviour far more than was necessary.

Elinor, on the other hand, who similarly doted on Marianne's son, felt that her sister was far too liberal with him. If James were spoiled much more, she was sure Marianne would have her hands full. She had often tried to advise her sister with little success and had decided that in the interests of friendly relations between the sisters, it might be prudent to forgo airing her misgivings in future.

The sisters parted before the afternoon was over, promising to meet soon. Elinor tried to insist on her sister having her chaise to take her home but Marianne would not hear of it. She took the same path back but allowed herself to dawdle this time, drinking in the breathtaking views all around. The colours of the leaves on trees and hedgerows were turning to drifts of copper, bronze, and vermillion, a most beautiful sight. The fresh winds shook the leaves from the trees, which rained down on her head like gold coins at a country wedding. Marianne liked to take a walk most days, as it helped her to think, to sort out her thoughts and troubles. She had few material problems; her devoted husband saw that she wanted for nothing. Mrs Brandon was very grateful to the Colonel, who had taken such pains to court her and bring her to Delaford as his wife. Theirs had been an unusual romance, a second attachment on both sides. She had grown to love him with the slow sweetness of enduring affection, sharing his life with the son whom she could not imagine being without. Yet, she could not entirely shake off the feeling that in her husband's eyes she would always be deemed second best and that the love he bore for her would never match that of the grand passion he had shared with his first love. On occasion Marianne's feelings of agitation on these considerations distilled into a sense of dissatisfaction that no intervention nor entertainment would remove. These moods usually coincided with her husband's travels, especially when he went off visiting his ward. In this frame of mind she would take herself off to walk about the estate, finding that the combination of the exercise and the splendour of her surroundings was usually enough to shake off any feeling of unease. Marianne was devoted to her duties as a wife and mother, which came as naturally to her as breathing the perfume of white Campion in the hedgerows, but on certain days, such as this one, when the heat of summer was giving way to the sweet mellow days of autumn, her restlessness was apt to return. She was reminded of the girl she had been before her marriage, a creature she now felt was a figment of distant memory.

"Marriage has altered me, I know that to be true," she thought. "Indeed, I wonder why I never noticed before that change seems to be an inevitable truth shared by all the married women I know. Our husbands' lives carry on in much the same way as they did before they tied the marital knot. William has another life apart from the one he shares with our child and me. How I envy his freedom, his interactions with the world, but most of all I resent those other distractions on which I dread to dwell. I hate him being gone from home to attend to these responsibilities, obligations that belong to a distant age and another woman. I never thought before our marriage that

I would feel so jealous and envious of a girl I have never met. In my heart I feel truly sorry for all that happened to Eliza, yet despite what Elinor says nothing will dispel the loneliness or private fears when William is away. Being married has its delights and disappointments. Tied by love and duty, to serve our men and children, I now recognise too well how marriage transforms the female situation."

She walked along in the sunshine, every scent and sound recalling earlier times, bringing forth the inevitable bitter sweetness of memories. Bending to pick a bunch of blue buttons, the last of the wildflowers from the meadow, she was instantly reminded of a posy once given to her in that first season of happiness, now dry and faded. Held together by a strip of frayed silk ribbon, staining the pages of a favourite poetry book, they belonged to the past.

"John Willoughby," she said out loud.

Marianne allowed herself to repeat his name, but instantly admonished herself for dwelling on the remembrance of former times. Willoughby had used her very ill. At the time she had believed that he was in love with her yet still he had chosen to marry another. He had been her first love and therein rested the problem. If she could not entirely forget Willoughby, who had injured her, how could Brandon ever be freed from the memory of his first love, the woman who had been taken from him by circumstances beyond his control?

"I want to blot Willoughby from my mind, even to hate him," she said to herself, "yet I know that he will always be a part of my conscious mind that I can do nothing about. I do not want to think of him but I cannot help myself. I love my husband more than life itself, but am I not as guilty as I declare him to be if I allow thoughts from the past to haunt me?"

And she understood why he crept stealthily like a phantom into her thoughts once more. Willoughby was inextricably linked with the Brandons and her husband's concerns in a way that could never be erased or forgotten by Marianne.

Besides all that, this business of Henry Lawrence coming home was occupying her daydreams more than she would admit. Henry and Margaret were two young people with like minds, she was sure. Perhaps first attachments could end in happiness, without the complications that second ones entailed. A girl with so similar a disposition to her own must be allowed to follow her heart, and Marianne was determined to help her.

Edward Ferrars returned from his parish duties to the comfort of Delaford Parsonage where his wife Elinor was busy supervising the children at tea. The door of the nursery was open and he crept upon the pleasant domestic scene unobserved, to lean against the doorframe and smile at his good fortune. He had loved Elinor the moment he had set eyes on her and, having overcome all the difficulties that had threatened to forestall their happiness, had succeeded in claiming her as his wife. He observed the happy scene. His daughter Anna was chattering to her mother in a most endearing way, whilst George looked about him, cradled in his mother's arms.

"I expect he will be just like me before he is much older," Edward thought, "happy to sit back and observe his surroundings, letting the conversation flow with little attempt at joining in."

Elinor was cutting up slices of cake with her free hand and appeared rather pensive, though to all intents and purposes, was engaged in attending to her little girl. He could always tell when she was immersed in her thoughts, because her eyes darted from one place to another and her brows knitted together. Edward wondered what she could be worrying about.

"Papapapapa," shouted Anna, who had suddenly spied her father and pointed at him with a chubby finger.

Elinor rose immediately to greet him, the ribbons fluttering on her cap in her haste to reach his side, a smile replacing her frown.

"Edward, you are just in time for tea. I will ask Susan to fetch some more tea things. Come, sit down and tell us all about your day. How are Mrs Thomas and all her family? I do hope she enjoyed your basket of vegetables and the bread and honey. I did not imagine on my marriage that I would be blessed with both a gardener and a bee charmer for a husband, but then I know I should never be surprised at your talents, my dear."

"Mrs Thomas enjoyed her bread and honey very much, Elinor," he replied, dropping a kiss on Anna's curly head before picking her up in his arms. "She is feeling much better and now the weather has improved she expects to be very cheerful."

"Well, that is good news." Elinor paused. She wanted to tell Edward about Marianne's visit, to admit her misgivings about her sibling's present state of mind. She had not seen her sister's spirits so unsettled for a while and she was concerned. She knew perfectly well what was behind it all and could only guess at what other fancies disturbed the balance of Marianne's mind. Elinor decided she would say nothing of her fears for the present. "Marianne has been to visit us today and told us that Henry Lawrence of Whitwell is coming home at last."

Edward hardly attended. He had Anna on his knee and she was demanding the clapping game she loved so much. "I am glad you had your sister for company," came his reply.

Chapter 2

MARGARET DASHWOOD SAT BEFORE the glass in her room, gazing pensively at her reflection, unaware of the plans that were being made on her behalf. She tugged at her gleaming locks, pulling out the pins that restrained her curls, letting her hair fall down her back.

"How shall I ever leave home or lead an independent life?" she asked as she stared at the girl in the glass. "And as for my dreams of travelling to the far corners of the world, I do not know why I torture myself with such ideas. How, indeed, could a girl like myself even manage to travel on my own from one end of the country to the other, let alone another land?"

She imagined she would always live with her mother. Marriage seemed to be the only chance she might have to fulfil her desires, but she knew without a dowry her chances for finding a suitor were slim. Not only was there the problem of having no money, but there was also the delicate matter of a suitable match. There was not a young man in Devonshire whom she found in the least attractive or who could tempt her to marry.

Not that she had received any firm offers to refuse. At eighteen, she had already decided that she would end an old maid with no prospect of fortune or adventure. Besides, there was another reason. How could she leave her mother all alone?

Mrs Dashwood had made it quite clear that she required no company and would not stand in the way of Margaret's happiness. "I do not wish to be a burden to my children. I am perfectly comfortable in my cottage and here I will stay until the good Lord sees fit to do otherwise. No, thank you, Margaret, it is not my wish to become a dependent relative, interfering in my daughters' lives and frightening away their husbands."

"Mama, I will never leave you. I cannot bear to think of you spending your days all alone."

"Why, I shan't be alone, I have all the company I need in my cousin, Sir John, and his family at Barton Park. As well you know, we have often wished that our lives could be half so quiet. There will always be company enough for me in that household, I can assure you, when you are gone to make a new life for yourself."

Despite these assurances, Margaret was inclined to worry about her future and that of her mother whom she was sure could not really relish the prospect of living out her days alone at Barton Cottage. Mrs Dashwood would be returning from the village at any moment. Margaret bit her lip and pinched the colour back into her cheeks, before she grimaced with resignation and went downstairs.

"I have a letter from Marianne," Mrs Dashwood announced as she came through the door a minute later, putting down her basket but omitting to remove her cloak and bonnet before she sat down. She loved to hear Marianne's news and with impatient fingers undid the seal.

"Dearest Mama and Margaret," she read out loud, "I hope this letter finds you well, as we all are here. I know you will be as excited as I am to hear William's good news. His nephew, Henry Lawrence, is coming home to Whitwell at last. William is anxious to welcome him and has suggested that we invite Henry and all the Lawrences to Delaford with a view to reacquainting him with our family. Is that not good news? I have heard that he is a very pleasant, handsome young man, Margaret."

"Am I never to be free from Marianne's schemes for match-making?" groaned Margaret. "There is not a man alive in Devonshire or Dorsetshire who has not been made to stand up with me by my sister. Nor is there one who has yet lived up to my expectations from descriptions exaggerated by old friends and neighbours. How many handsome young men do we hear thus chronicled, who have nonetheless turned out to be very far from pleasing to the eye and years past their youth?"

"Come, Margaret, you are a little hard on your friends. I am sure you thought Charles Carey quite handsome enough at one time. He was very smitten with you, I know, and I daresay that is why he has gone off to sea. You have quite broken his heart."

"Mother! Charles is a dear friend, but that is all. There never was the romance you suspect. For one thing, he is too practical, too prudent for my taste. For another, he does not like poetry, scoffing at any mention of Cowper's cool colonnades or Wordsworth's dizzy raptures."

"I always thought Marianne the one with the most romantic sensibility, but I think I have been mistaken. And whilst I admire a lofty crag or babbling rill as much as the next person, I do not know if it is wise to cast off eligible young men simply because they do not wax lyrical on a sofa or shady dell."

"Mama, you love to tease me but I will never compromise. Perhaps I should not say so, but there has only ever been one man who matched my idea of manly perfection. But his name is never uttered here now and I know you will be cross if I so much as mention him."

"I cannot think to whom you refer, Margaret—James Whitaker perhaps?"

She gave a sideways glance at her mother. "No, he is not the man. It is John Willoughby."

"John Willoughby!" her mother exclaimed. She studied Margaret's face, folding the letter and setting it down upon the table.

Margaret took a deep breath before speaking her thoughts out loud. "I know I was hardly fourteen years of age when he came to court my sister, but John Willoughby stole my heart as well as hers, though I am sure no one suspected as much. There, I have dared to say his name."

"Well, do not speak it again, I beg you. I do not know what you can be thinking, Margaret, after the way he treated Marianne. I have forgiven him in my own way of course, and indeed have felt quite sorry for him, but I hope I shall never set eyes on him ever again, nor have cause to wonder about him in any way. I am quite ashamed of you."

"What else does Marianne say?" Margaret asked, turning the subject back to the letter's contents as quickly as she could.

"And I am glad to say that I have never seen Mr Willoughby in these parts," her mother replied, completely ignoring her. "He has not visited Allenham often, I believe, since his marriage to Miss Grey, though by all accounts I hear old Mrs Smith is to leave the estate to him after all. Lucky for him that I have not bumped into him in Barton on his trips into Devonshire!"

"I doubt he has ventured as near as Barton, Mama, nor would he wish to, for fear of encountering Mrs Jennings. I believe she gave him a piece of her mind when she ran into him at Yeovil when she was visiting her daughter."

"Yes, Charlotte Palmer delights in relating that tale whenever we see her," Mrs Dashwood sighed, untying the strings of her bonnet, "and to anyone who will care to listen. One would imagine from her tone that she is quite upset not to have made an acquaintance of Mrs Willoughby. She says she has not been able to completely ignore the Willoughbys' presence at Combe Magna, as they are practically neighbours, and has even once had them to dine."

"Do not distress yourself, Mama. Although Mr Palmer is an M.P. in the opposition, I expect it was because of some political matter that they were forced to entertain them. As for them being neighbours, I am sure I heard Mr Palmer say that the Willoughbys live at least ten miles away."

"Well, it is no concern of ours, I am sure." Mrs Dashwood removed her bonnet and smoothed back her hair before picking up the forgotten letter again. She resumed reading.

"I have persuaded William that we should host a ball, to be held on Friday se'ennight. There is nothing like dancing to put us all at ease with our neighbours. To be frank, if we are all up on the floor, there will be less reason for me to have to converse too often with my sister-in-law!"

Mrs Dashwood paused in consideration. "Marianne never did suffer fools, and though they do not meet often, I know Hannah Lawrence has not always been on the friendliest terms with our own dear girl. I have always suspected her to be jealous of Marianne's youth, beauty, and good health. But perhaps we should not be too quick to misjudge Lady Lawrence, I believe she is often ill with nervous complaints and has to take to her bed."

"I would enjoy a ball. I love to dance, and it would be fun to see my Delaford friends. I haven't seen Anne Courtney since June when Marianne gave a picnic in the park," cried Margaret.

Mrs Dashwood continued with the letter. "Margaret need not worry that I shall forget her; if she can be ready by eleven o'clock on Thursday morning, I will collect her in the chaise and we will go to Exeter to choose a muslin for the occasion. We have plenty of time for it to be made up before the night of the ball." Mrs Dashwood smiled. "Marianne is so generous, is she not, Margaret?"

"She is a true-hearted sister, though I cannot help feeling she has reasons for wanting to make the most of my appearance; motives which are not only to do with her generous nature."

"How can you be so suspicious?"

"Because I know Marianne almost as I do myself," said Margaret, laughing. "However, I am prepared to overlook her grand designs for me because I will admit that I find the prospect of a new gown and a dance most diverting. As for Mr Lawrence, I daresay he will fall in love with me as soon as our eyes lock across the crowded ballroom. Alas, it will all be in vain. He should be warned, there is not a man who can live up to my ideals of perfection and until that man comes to claim me, I shall remain single."

Chapter 3

COLONEL BRANDON LOOKED SURREPTITIOUSLY at his wife over the breakfast table. Three years on from the day they had wed had hardly changed his feelings toward her, although as he sat in secret contemplation on the matter, he swiftly acknowledged his regard for Marianne was altered in every way completely. His love for her was deeper and more passionately felt than it ever had been, he decided, and his covert glances at her over the coffee pot confirmed this in his look of sheer admiration. He watched her as she buttered a slice of toast and stirred her chocolate, before licking the fragrant cocoa from the silver spoon, her eyes closed to savour the moment.

"Marianne Brandon is a very attractive woman," he thought, "her complexion as brilliant as when first my eyes beheld her, her smile still as sweet, and in those dark eyes, her spirit and eagerness are as discernable as ever. Even the most disenchanted soul would call her a beauty."

She looked quite contented as she daydreamed. Yet, he was disturbed by a sense that Marianne, for all her animation, was not as happy as she ought to be. Sometimes, as he watched her, he was aware that she was lost in her own thoughts, seeming to be somewhere else far away. He occasionally detected a want of spirits, discerning the escaping breath of a sigh from her lips; a sound so slight as to be hardly there at all, only perceptible to him. Any enquiries he made, however, as to her welfare, always had the immediate effect on Marianne's composure, bringing a bright smile to her countenance once more. But there was something on her mind, he was certain. Ever since he had returned from Lyme there had been a feeling of slight distance between them but he knew she hated to talk about Eliza and Lizzy, or to hear about their life, so he had kept his silence on the subject.

"He hasn't mentioned a word about his trip," thought Marianne as she scraped the remains of chocolate from the bottom of her cup. "He does not wish to communicate his true interest in his other life, the one he shares with those who possess such a claim on his affections. I wish I knew how Miss Williams looks, if she is like her mother's painting. And the child; she must be almost five years old now. Does she favour her mother or her father? But I cannot ask Brandon; I must pretend that I do not care about either of them. He would think me such an unworthy person if he could read my mind and know how I despise them for taking him away from me so often. But Elinor is right; I must bear it for his sake. And I must try harder not to think about his time spent with them and keep my counsel on the subject. After the last time when I said so much that I did not really mean, when I saw the look of hurt in his eyes, I cannot be so outspoken again."

William longed to ask his wife on what she was reflecting. Indeed, any conversation would have been welcome. He wished he could talk to her about his fears for little Lizzy's health, but the last thing he wished was to upset her with any conversation of Lyme. He tried to catch her eye but failed. His reverie was disturbed by a knock at the door. James, accompanied by the nursemaid Kitty, ran into the room to jump upon his father's knee. Marianne laughed, catching William's eye at the same moment. He held her gaze in his and the look of love that passed between them brought a blush to Marianne's cheek. She looked down to smooth the tablecloth with her slender fingers, aware of his lingering expression and feeling immense happiness that at last she had gained William's full attention.

"Your mama is in very good looks today," pronounced the Colonel to his little son, as if expecting him to understand his every word.

"William, do not tease so," Marianne admonished with a smile, raising her eyes to his again, to be caught once more by a look that spoke of his most earnest feelings.

"I have never been more sincere," he added, blowing a kiss to his wife over the top of his baby's head. "I am wondering if the mistress of Delaford has any plans for today?"

"Why, yes, I have made arrangements to see my sister," said Marianne, dabbing at her mouth with a napkin to remove the last traces of chocolate. "I am to take the carriage to Barton and then Margaret and I are to travel on to Exeter to visit the shops. I have promised her a new gown for the ball. She must look her best. I daresay Henry Lawrence has seen many a young French fancy in his time, but he is going to fall in love with a beautiful English rose. Margaret has a bloom as fine as any flower."

"You and your schemes for matchmaking. Does Margaret know what is in store for her? Or more to the point, should I be warning my nephew of your plans? Do be careful, Marianne, it is a dangerous game you are playing."

"Psh, dangerous, it is not. Exciting, thrilling, and stimulating are the words I would use to describe the game of love. In any case, a little flirtation is vital for our young people. How else might they find their partner in life, the soul most suited to theirs?"

"I do wonder if it is a good thing to be filling Margaret's head with these ideas. Hannah will have plans for Henry, I am sure, and getting married at his tender age is not necessarily going to be one of them."

"When he becomes smitten with my sister, as he surely will, his mother will have to change her plans."

"Marianne…" started the Colonel, but he noted the expression on his wife's face, as a most becoming flush spread from her slender white neck to suffuse her cheeks with spots of pink, and he knew it was useless to continue.

Her mouth was set in a firm line; she was quite determined. "I will of course have to stay overnight at the cottage. The journey is too fatiguing to be going and coming back in one day, and I am sure I shall be quite worn out enough by Margaret's shopping excursions." Marianne knew she was being petulant, but she wanted very badly at this moment to irritate her husband and show him that she could be quite as independent as he.

William saw no fault in her behaviour. He could not bear to have her upset and see her retract from him. "Of course, my love, and two manservants to accompany you." He reached inside his jacket. "James," he continued, "come, I have a little errand for you. Could you give this little token to your mother?"

Marianne's attention was engaged once more, her face breaking into a beaming smile as James toddled over to present her with a tiny box, a divine confection of silk and ribbon. With trembling fingers Marianne peeled back the wrappings to reveal a small, hinged leather box. She looked to William, who nodded with encouragement as she opened it. Nestled on a silk cushion was the most exquisite heart-shaped diamond, fashioned onto a ring of gold.

"I have not forgotten to mark the occasion, my love," said William softly. "I hope you like it."

"Like it! I love it!" Marianne exclaimed, sweeping James into her arms and jumping to her feet to run and hug her husband, bestowing kisses on them both.

William took her hand and placed the ring on her finger. He pulled her towards him. "Will you marry me?"

"I would, kind sir," she answered with a curtsey, "but I have to tell you that I am already married, three years this day, and to the most wonderful and generous-hearted man in the whole world!" she cried, laughing at their gaiety.

James caught his parents' playful mood and clapped his hands in excitement, begging to be let down. He skipped around the room, whooping and shouting with delight, until the sight of the nursemaid reappearing at the door to lead him away to the nursery quieted his heightened spirits for the time being.

"I think you must get yourself ready, my dear," William announced, reluctant to let go her hand, "or Margaret will think she has been forgotten." He glanced at his wife with a half hope that she might change her mind and stay with him. He would not tell her about the private dinner he had arranged as a surprise or about the Bridport musicians he had booked to play for them as they ate. He would postpone his schemes. Instead, he reproached himself for not thinking to ask about her arrangements, but in truth, he had assumed she would be free to spend the day with him.

"Why, yes, I had best not be late. If I know Margaret she will be standing at the gate as I speak, in anticipation. But first…" Marianne bent her head to tenderly kiss her husband and whisper in his ear. "You will have to wait until later, very much later for your anniversary gift, my dearest one," she smiled. Her smiles turned to laughter once more as she caught William's expression. He was blushing like a bride and quite as eager. Without a backward glance, Marianne swept out of the room and ran to her chamber to don her travelling clothes. She glimpsed her reflection in the looking glass and was quite satisfied with all she saw. Her handsome ring looked very well on her hand, but what a pity it was to have to cover the sight of such beauty with a glove!

Pausing on the stairs as she rushed down to the awaiting carriage, she looked up at the painting, which of all the works hanging in the hall, never failed to arrest her. It was of a woman, who had by some strange twist of fate a close resemblance to herself. The young lady was standing arm in arm with a man, who had a look of Brandon, only this painted version had a leaner face with a distinctly cruel mouth. At least, Marianne thought his mouth brutal in appearance, especially knowing that it belonged to Brandon's brother who had borne no love for the wealthy wife who was to save the family home from ruin. Eliza Brandon, captured so elegantly in oils, wearing a gown fashionable twenty or more years ago, was Brandon's sweetheart from his youth, yet forced against her will to marry his brother. Here depicted on her fateful wedding day, forever smiling in pink silk against a background of verdant landscape, perpetual happiness was displayed in her pretty smile. But on closer examination Marianne saw that the smile did not quite reach her eyes, and further observation suggested that her slim fingers betrayed her true feelings, as they barely rested on the arm of the bridegroom who had eventually divorced and abandoned her.

Marianne was struck once more by the uncanny likeness. "She is like my mirror image," she thought, "and yet, Eliza looks taller, more statuesque, and I must admit, more beautiful than I could ever hope to be. Is her daughter such a vision of loveliness also, I wonder?"

Eliza's eyes seemed to gaze back at her in return as if telling her that she would only be capable of bearing a divine child. In Marianne's imagination she saw the two women, Eliza Brandon and her daughter Eliza Williams, looking down at her with the same glittering eyes, both bound to William with a hold she felt incapable of challenging or surmounting.

"But what of little Lizzy?" she asked herself about the child whose very existence caused Marianne's heart to ache. Did she favour her mother and grandmother before her? Did she have the same dark grey eyes or was there a stronger resemblance in a pair of black eyes of her own, to match those of her father, John Willoughby?

Chapter 4

THE JOURNEY TO BARTON was accomplished in good time; there being fine weather, a good toll road, and an enthusiastic coachman, making it all the more possible. Marianne spent her travelling time gazing out at the fast flying scenery, lost in her thoughts. The lush green valleys and chalky hillsides of the neighbouring villages soon gave way to the drama of the rugged Devonshire countryside that she knew so well. It was strange to think that she had now lived at Delaford longer than she had lived at Barton, and she could not immediately account for the intense feelings of nostalgia that overcame her as they neared their destination. Marianne began to think about her days at Barton living with her mother and sisters, reminiscing about the carefree girl she had once been, when she had had no responsibilities or worries about husbands and their duties.

Her journey was nearing its end, the horses and the moving landscape slowed as they turned into the familiar lane. With her head held high and a smile in place, she looked eagerly for her mother and Margaret as the carriage drew up outside the small green court and wicket gate of Barton Cottage.

"Marianne, my dearest, how good it is to see you," cried Mrs Dashwood, running out to greet her with open arms. "Come inside and tell me all your news. How are the Colonel and my dear grandchild? What a pity you could not bring James with you."

"I will bring him soon, Mama, I promise, but this trip is all for Margaret's benefit. I wish to take my sister in hand and prepare her for the ball with care. That will take time and considerable effort on all our parts if we are to make the most of her attractions."

"Goodness me, Marianne, you had best not let Margaret hear you run on so. She will never allow such an intervention. Do be careful how you proceed. If she imagines for one moment half of your designs for her, she will not submit, I am certain."

"Where is she? I thought she would be waiting with impatience for my arrival."

"She is eager to go shopping, believe me," answered Mrs Dashwood, her voice dropping to a low whisper, "but I think anxious not to appear as if her life depends upon the outcome of it."

Margaret rose to greet her sister as mother and daughter entered the sitting room. "Marianne, it is so kind of you to take me shopping. You are not too fatigued, I hope, after your journey. Mama has a little nuncheon prepared and then we shall make haste to town."

Marianne hugged Margaret, exclaiming after her good looks, and took a seat upon the sofa. She looked round the room, at all the familiar objects: the bookcase with their old volumes of poetry; Elinor's drawings, elegantly framed and fixed to the walls;

and lastly, at her old pianoforte, still occupying the corner of the room. Of course, she had a much finer instrument at Delaford Park, a Broadwood Grand, and volumes of printed sheet music that William had purchased when they were courting. But she looked fondly at the place where she had sat for many an hour, in raptures and in melancholy. Margaret's sheet music lay propped above the keys. There was no sign of the manuscripts that had once been written out for her. She was sure her mother would have burned any music copied out by Willoughby's hand, long ago.

The tea things were brought in by Betsy, who made such a fuss on seeing Marianne at last, that she felt quite distraught at not remembering to bring her a small gift. There was a pot of tea with cake and scones, piled high on a plate of her mother's best china.

"We are to dine at the Park this evening, Marianne," Margaret continued. "Mrs Jennings arrived yesterday to stay with Sir John and Lady Middleton and they are all anxious to see you."

"Oh no, please, Mama, say it is not so," groaned Marianne, helping herself to a scone and jam. "Can we not have a nice, quiet evening here all by ourselves? It is so long since I have seen you."

"I thought we had agreed not to say anything on the matter yet, at least until Marianne had got back her breath after her journey," Mrs Dashwood admonished, casting a frown in Margaret's direction as she poured tea from a steaming silver pot. "Mrs Jennings called early this morning with Sir John and they were most insistent. Oh, you know how it is, Marianne. They would brook no refusal."

Marianne could not help but feel pity for her mother whom she was sure still felt indebted to Sir John for his kindness to them. When the Dashwoods had been forced to leave their ancestral home at Norland in Sussex on the occasion of their stepbrother's inheritance, Sir John Middleton, Mrs Dashwood's cousin, had stepped in and offered them a cottage on his Barton estate. Marianne was certain that her mother wished she were in a position to decline their invitations more often but felt obliged to accept them. As a dependent relative, her own desires were not taken into consideration.

"I suppose we have no choice, but Mrs Jennings will have me worn out before the evening is begun," sighed Marianne.

"Do not be so unkind," her mother answered. "Remember that old lady has been immensely good to us in more ways than I can ever repay."

Mrs Dashwood referred, Marianne knew, to the time after her great disappointment with Willoughby when Mrs Jennings had nursed and looked after Marianne as if she were her own child. Mrs Dashwood was eternally grateful to the lady, though the reasons for that gratitude were hardly ever mentioned now or discussed at Barton Cottage. The unspoken words hung in the air above their heads like grey spectres, together with the recollections of all that had passed to make her former love's name an anathema. John Willoughby's crimes were never discussed.

Margaret had excused herself shortly after this exchange to make ready for their expedition, returning moments later in a blue kerseymere pelisse with a bonnet of the same, trimmed with ribbon. She made a pleasing picture. Margaret was not as dark as her elder sister; she had a fair complexion and light brown curls to frame her countenance. Her eyes were the blue of April forget-me-nots but still there was something of her sister's spirit in them. The contrast, however, was like ice and fire: against the black gypsy eyes of Marianne, Margaret's were frozen shards of sapphire.

"My little sister, you are growing into a fine young lady!" Marianne exclaimed at the sight of her. "Come, we must hasten to the chaise or there shall not be a decent muslin left in all of Exeter."

"Do take care, my darlings," cried Mrs Dashwood as she waved them off at the door. She could not help but be pleased and proud as she watched the carriage bowl away, the sight of her pretty daughters enough to produce a lump in her throat and a tear in her eye.

Chapter 5

THEY WERE SET DOWN by the square of the New London
Inn, so that they could work their way down the High Street
and not miss a single shop or market stall. Exeter was teeming
with people and carriages, all seemingly unaware of the other as
they set about their determined business. There were so many
stalls with traders thrusting their wares under the girls' noses
as they attempted to pass, that there was scarcely any room to
manoeuvre. Trays of sticky buns, held head high, wafted tempting smells of freshly baked treats. Panniers of ruby apples and yellow pears, swaying from the hips of ruddy-cheeked girls, scented
the air with the perfume of a September orchard, whilst tiers
of orange pumpkins arranged along the wayside impeded their
every step. Waggons and carts rumbled down the street, piled
high with sacks, boxes, barrels, and packages. A flock of sheep
were being shepherded by two small boys wielding sticks, along
with a barking dog who leaped and snapped if any chanced to
stray too far. Geese and ducks waddled in formation down the
central thoroughfare as though they owned the road, as a young

girl with a basket of eggs called out to passersby to try her goods. Marianne and Margaret wove their way through the teeming tapestry of market town life, calling to one another to look in a particular shop window or laugh at some amusing sight. They soon found themselves on the corner of Queen Street, close by their favourite linen drapers. On entering the shop, they found it to be as busy inside as out. Every mother and daughter in Exeter, it appeared, had chosen to arrive at the same time, all jostling for a chance to view the latest muslin, lutestring, and satin.

"Margaret, what do you think of that one?" Marianne asked, pointing to a fine white mull draped in the window, embroidered with gold thread, which glimmered in the sunlight.

"It is very beautiful," sighed Margaret, "but I fear it will cost the earth!"

"I have not brought you here to discuss finances," Marianne scolded, "I have promised you a ball gown of the highest quality, and that is what you shall have!"

"But there is a very good white satin laid out on the counter which would make a very pretty gown. And though I must admit the mull is quite the most divine gauze I have ever seen, I could do very well with the other."

Margaret could see the shopkeeper deep in conversation with a very smartly dressed young woman who was ordering yards of the glossy fabric which waved like the sea over the counter, rippling over the edge onto the floor. The elegant plumes on her grey hat were nodding as she talked. There was quite a queue forming, the mother before them muttering under her breath at the time it would take to get to the front, as her daughter complained that there would be no satin left if the lady preceding them was any indication to go on. Another assistant appeared to alleviate the restless crowd and at last they moved forward.

"Let me indulge you this once, Margaret," Marianne insisted. "Henry Lawrence will be used to seeing women of his acquaintance attired in the very finest clothes; I cannot have you look anything but your very best."

"Very well," laughed Margaret, "so long as you promise not to speak of that man again. I am well aware you have married me off to him and I am certain that he and I will never suit."

"How can you say such a thing? I have heard he is a very handsome man, cultured and charming. Every report declares him to be just the sort of gentleman you like."

"There has never been a man yet who has had the power to engage my heart." Margaret picked up a pair of long kid evening gloves from the display by the window. She turned them over but was not really examining them at all. She was lost in thought, wondering if she should confess her folly to her sister. Marianne was engrossed on the other side, in admiration of a bolt of crimson velvet, but declared it as being too dark for such young skin.

"Actually, that is not entirely true," Margaret persisted, although not understanding quite why she was willing to confess her old, childish fantasies.

Marianne turned, all astonishment. "Tell me, Margaret, who is this paragon, this nonesuch, this nonpareil?"

"Do you promise not to reprimand me if I dare tell?" Margaret looked into her sister's eyes, and then sighed. "Oh, it is so silly, I wish I had not said a word. It was just a youthful infatuation. What will you think of me? You will be very cross with me."

"My goodness, Margaret, you are serious. I detect a broken heart. Whoever this gentleman is, I hope he knows of your feelings. And why should I reproach you? Margaret, it is no secret that I have been very foolish in the past and gave my heart where I ought not."

The mother and daughter who stood directly in front of them chose this moment to give up and strut out of the shop, complaining in loud voices that they were forced to go else-where. Marianne sighed with relief. They were now directly behind the lady dressed in grey and she looked to be almost finished. The back of her pelisse pronounced a most elegant cut and expensive taste. The shopkeeper asked for directions to send her parcels and Marianne heard her announce in a loud voice, so that everyone should take note of it, that all packages should be delivered to Devonshire House, West Southernhay.

"Did you hear that?" whispered Marianne. "The very smartest part of town. No wonder she is so keen for the whole shop to hear of it! Now, where were we? Ah, yes, you were about to reveal your lover's name."

"I cannot tell you," Margaret insisted. "It was so thought-less of me to have mentioned him at all. You will think me a perfect dolt."

"Well, in that case, I think a spotted muslin will do after all," snapped Marianne, but she looked sideways at her sister and Margaret noted the amusement in her eyes.

"Very well," cried Margaret, determined to get his name out before very much more time had elapsed. She lowered her voice to a whisper. "John Willoughby is his name."

"John Willoughby!" cried Marianne out loud. "You were in love with John Willoughby!"

Marianne had never learnt the art of being discreet; she spoke as she found and whatever happened to be in her head popped out of her mouth with little reserve. As Marianne cried out in amazement, the whole shop seemed to quieten and everyone turned to gaze at the woman who had mentioned a gentleman who was known by name to many in the vicinity. For not only had she shouted out his name but she had linked it with a word that was guaranteed to excite universal interest. There were not many other words capable of arousing such a reaction as that of love, especially when it connected itself to a married man. Margaret instantly reddened, realising not for the first time the great stupidity in relating such an ill-timed confidence. The entire shop was agog and none more so than the lady in grey before them who turned to stare with more than a hostile glance.

Marianne blushed as scarlet as her cloak as the woman in front looked her up and down. A flicker of recognition passed across the lady's countenance and trembled in the lilac plumes waving above her bonnet, to vanish just as quickly in the next second. Marianne took in the features of the handsome, well-dressed woman who stood looking down at her as though confronted by a vagrant. She lost the power of speech, her heart hammered, and all she could think about was getting herself and Margaret as far away from the place as possible.

"Will that be all, Mrs Willoughby?" demanded the shop-keeper of his customer, anxious to regain her attention and move on to the next awaiting person. "I will have the carrier deliver immediately. Southernhay is the address, you say?"

Mrs Willoughby, dressed to match her former name, turned to the counter once more, as reserved and calm as she had been moments ago, to confirm that she was residing in that most fashionable of districts.

Marianne grabbed Margaret's arm to march her outside. "We cannot stay here. Come, we must go!"

Her sister protested vehemently, declaring that she would never take Marianne into her confidence again. As she was steered down the street at a pace, she caught her foot on a pyramid of pumpkins, scattering them across the path of everyone who passed by, sending them rolling into the gutter. A woman bundled in shawls shouted and raised her fist, before running off after the golden globes as they trundled down the street.

"What on earth is the matter with you?" shouted Margaret as she limped along. "Are you ill?"

"We must go home," cried Marianne. "She cannot be here on her own. I do not want to bump into him."

"Who cannot be here on her own? Whom are you talking about?" Margaret was losing patience with her sister.

"Did you not hear? That lady, the one so beautifully dressed and looking as elegant as ever, was Mrs John Willoughby," cried Marianne. "Sophia Grey as was. Did you not recognise her?"

"I have never seen Mrs Willoughby in my life before," exclaimed Margaret. "I would not know her if I fell over her in the street. Besides, I was only thinking about what I had said and was afraid you would be cross with me. Oh, Marianne, I am so sorry, I should never have said a word."

"It was not your fault. I shouted out his name. How could I have done it?" Marianne's eyes welled and tears threatened to spill down her cheeks.

"It is over now, it does not matter," Margaret pleaded, producing a pocket-handkerchief just in time and dabbing Marianne's face. "We shall not see her again. Let us go home, you are so upset. Mama will have tea prepared and make you better."

Marianne stopped. She stood still, leaning on Margaret's arm as her breath slowly steadied itself. They could not go home. Mrs Dashwood would have to be told about what had happened, and Marianne did not want to relate the sorry tale to another soul, least of all her mother. She was determined they would return home with their shopping spoils as intended. "No, we will not go home," she affirmed, taking the kerchief and blowing her nose. "I have promised you a new gown and even if we should run into an entire neighbourhood of Willoughbys, I will not be swayed. The shock disturbed me, but I am well now. We will enter the shop again in a quarter of an hour, by which time anyone who witnessed the little scene will have left."

"But are you quite sure, Marianne? You do look most ill."

"Of course, I was so silly to react in that schoolgirl manner. I am quite composed now. Come, we will partake of some refreshment in the coffee house just over there by the Guildhall. I do not want to go any lower into the town, if I can help it."

"You look as though you were in shock still," said Margaret as they took their seats at a table inside.

"Oh, do not worry about me," Marianne assured her sister, ordering strong coffee and a dish of sweetmeats to be brought immediately. "I am well enough."

"Have you not seen Mr and Mrs Willoughby since they married?" ventured Margaret, unconvinced by Marianne's protestations.

Marianne looked out through the window. The rain had started in drips and drops and soon gathered pace running in large, wet rivulets, down the windowpane. She watched two raindrops slide down the glass, one chasing the other but never quite catching up. "I did see them once," she replied in a quiet voice. "The Colonel and I were just married and had gone to

London for the season. We spent the entire time together of course, but on one particular day, William had some business in town, of a nature that I was not to be a party to, and so it was arranged that we should meet in Berkeley Square, at Gunter's tea shop."

"How romantic! Are the ices as wonderful as they say?" demanded Margaret, taking a bite from a marzipan sweet, modelled like a cherry.

Marianne smiled. "They are, though I have to admit that on that occasion I was not to taste them. I had decided to walk to the tea shop; it was a fine day and even in London I prefer to walk about on foot. I knew William would be bound to be there before me, so I should not have to worry about being unescorted for long. But I could see no sign of him as I approached, though I looked everywhere, and then my attention was caught by the sight of a couple I recognised, seated in an open carriage underneath the maple trees. The autumnal day was very fine; the sun was shining and dappled light fell in golden shafts, like the colour of the turning leaves. Sophia Willoughby looked very happy swathed in sunshine with her husband at her side."

"Did she see you?" asked Margaret, hardly daring to interrupt in case Marianne ended her tale too soon.

"I think she did, enough at least to wonder who I was. She stared long and hard until his curiosity was aroused. He looked round, Mr Willoughby raised his hat I remember, but I pretended I had not seen them and as soon as I could I turned the corner. William soon came alongside in the carriage; he had been going round and round looking for me. He had observed them from the window and very fortunately guessed I had taken a turn elsewhere."

"How did you feel?" asked Margaret. She was very curious about the whole business between her sister and Mr Willoughby. She was very fond of Marianne's husband, but her childish sensibility tended to dwell on the romanticism of the lovelorn, rather than on any pragmatic consideration. She had never been convinced that Marianne's love for the Colonel was the same as it had been for Mr Willoughby and was impassioned by what she considered to be the tragedy of their situation. How could Marianne ever recover? She was sure she could not. And as for herself, she still felt a pang whenever she remembered Willoughby.

Marianne looked at her sister and immediately changed the subject. "You have not yet explained yourself. Whatever did you mean when you said you were in love with John Willoughby?"

Margaret stirred her coffee thoughtfully. "I do not suppose it was real love. I was very young, I know. But from the very first time we met him on High-Church Down, I was smitten. All my childish fantasies involved being carried aloft in John Willoughby's arms. I am surprised you did not notice. I did not make such a nuisance of myself to be your chaperone, you know. I hung on his every word and when he looked in my direction or spoke to me, I thought I should die."

Marianne sighed. "He certainly had an effect on every lady who came into contact with him. On some more than others," she added ruefully.

"How is Miss Williams?" Margaret asked. She was aware of the history shared by the Colonel's ward and Mr Willoughby, that they had run away together from Bath and of how he had abandoned her. She knew that Brandon had challenged Willoughby to a duel, though both had escaped the ordeal unscathed. And Margaret was fascinated by the idea that

Willoughby had an illegitimate daughter who would by now be nearly five years of age.

"I have little to tell you except that William is very attentive to all their needs. I am afraid I know very little about them apart from the fact that they are settled at Wolfeton Fitzpaine, just out of Lyme. The Colonel is reluctant to speak on the matter and I am reticent to ask. I do not want to know about them, I assure you."

"Are you not a little curious?" Margaret knew she was being terribly intrusive, but she could not resist asking the question.

"What do I need to know that I am not already familiar with? They are banished to some quiet part of the country where I believe Miss Williams supplements her income by netting purses and the like. She must be a changed character, I think."

"Do you not wonder about her daughter?" Margaret persisted tentatively, thinking that at any moment Marianne would cease her confidences and become a closed book on the subject.

Marianne paused to bite into a marchpane strawberry. She nibbled at it absently before abandoning the rest, dropping it onto her plate in agitation. "I confess that I do. William once told me that she bears a striking resemblance to her grand-mother, as does her mother before her. The three Elizas: no doubt this one will be as troublesome as the other two! I am sure if I were Brandon, I would not be spending so much time and money on such undeserving creatures. No indeed; I should not abandon my own family so much for someone else's."

Margaret thought it might be wise to change the subject. Her sister was becoming most cross, and Margaret surmised that Marianne's perceived indifference to the subject of the Williams's household was not as impartial as she professed. She was clearly envious of any favour bestowed in Eliza's direction.

Marianne did not like being reminded of Miss Williams's existence. There were times when she was totally convinced of her husband's love, when at last she thought she had triumphed over Eliza, but having since witnessed his expression as he fondly doted upon the painting hanging above the stairwell, she had no doubt that he still harboured longings for his lost love.

"Come, if you have finished your coffee we will go back to the shop and select the finest embroidered muslin, spangled with tinsel and I know not what," Marianne announced brightly, determined not to linger on such thoughts. They gathered their belongings, wrapped themselves up against the weather and made for the door.

As Marianne reached for the handle, the bell clanged and the door was opened with full force, making her leap nimbly back to avoid being knocked over and injured in the process. Aware that whosoever was standing within the doorway was making no attempt to step forward or back to let her pass, Marianne quickly recovered herself to acknowledge the person. However, her composure was lost the instant she recognised the tall and imposing gentleman who stood before her.

Chapter 6

IT WAS JOHN WILLOUGHBY! A thousand feelings rushed upon Marianne, who acknowledged his bowing form and met his earnest gaze with as little hesitation as she was able. The years had not changed him for the worse in her eyes. He was, if possible, more handsome than ever and he made a striking figure. Everything about him suggested and reflected easy wealth, from the styling of his hair to the cut of his blue coat.

He was the first to speak. "Mrs Brandon, how do you do?" His elegant appearance matched his cool manner; he spoke as if they were used to meeting every day in just this way, and Marianne hoped that her troubled feelings would not betray her. He bowed toward Margaret. "Miss Dashwood."

Margaret became tongue-tied and hoped Marianne would find the strength to speak for them both.

"How do you do, Mr Willoughby?" Marianne answered at last. Her voice remained steady and though she wanted to run away that very moment, she knew she could not. This was a meeting she had always known would eventually transpire, and one that she had half suspected might take place before the day was out.

He stepped aside and raised his hat in a gesture that dismissed them both. Marianne, eager to leave, took Margaret's arm in hers and swept through the doorway without another word or look. She wanted to look back, to see if he observed them still, though she was sure she could feel his eyes burning into her back as they forged ahead. They walked back up the road towards the linen draper's in shocked silence. Marianne hardly knew what she was feeling.

"The worst is over," she said to herself. "We have met and should we do so again, I shall be able to bear all with feelings of equanimity."

"Oh, let us go home now," Margaret begged. "I have no more desire to look at muslins than I wish to tramp about Exeter bumping into personages from the past. We will bump into Mrs Jennings next and the day will be complete."

This last made Marianne smile. "Do not worry on my account, Margaret, I could not care if I should collide with a murderer along the High Street. I am perfectly able to conduct myself; I am not perturbed by the experience of seeing Mr Willoughby though I have to say he certainly seemed rather distraught to have seen me. And did you see his face? All lines and wrinkles, my goodness, time is ravaging to some countenances, is it not? Well, if you learn to rate your pocket book above all else, I daresay that is the penalty. Having too much money to squander does nothing for one's complexion, especially if one is outdoors too often. I suspect his wife is keen for him to follow his pursuits and encourages him to be out hunting constantly. And I expect he is keen to be gone too, when he has to look at Mrs Willoughby's countenance every day over the breakfast things."

So Marianne ran on without a pause, until Margaret quite despaired. It was very clear to her that, no matter how much her sister protested that she was as self-possessed as ever, declaring that her encounter with Mr Willoughby had had no effect, she was most upset.

However, all conversation on the affair had to cease for the present as they soon arrived back at the shop, Marianne insisting that the most expensive fabrics were displayed and cogitated over. The beautiful mull they had seen in the window was decided on at last: to be worn over white satin of the highest quality. Marianne was sure Lady Middleton's dressmaker would be able to fashion the most wonderful creation for Margaret in time for the ball at Delaford. Despite herself, Margaret was delighted. She did not want to admit how much she was looking forward to the ball. It would only encourage Marianne to tease her about Mr Lawrence. She was looking forward to seeing her friends and showing Henry a thing or two about English country dancing.

Laden with their purchases, they made the short distance back to the New London Inn where Marianne had instructed the coachman to attend them, anxious that they leave as soon as possible in order to get home before darkness fell. Fortunately, the sun decided to make another appearance, and they travelled home in good light. The two young ladies were quiet and thoughtful.

Marianne gazed out of the window; she could not help re-enacting in her mind all that had passed that afternoon. "Oh, the shame I feel at the idea of Sophia Willoughby listening to us discussing her husband in that way," she thought. "I will never forget the look of utter disdain that reproached and humiliated me. What possibilities can explain their presence here in Exeter? Perhaps they are visiting friends. But if that is the case, why are they not staying with Mr Willoughby's benefactor, Mrs Smith?"

As if she read her thoughts, Margaret spoke, breaking the subdued solitude of their ponderings and the rhythmic sound of the horses' hooves, as they splashed through mud and thundered over turf.

"What do you think they are doing here?" asked Margaret, turning to face her sister, to scrutinise her expression.

"I suppose they must be on a visit to see Mrs Smith," Marianne replied, "though it seems a little odd that they are not staying at Allenham itself, do you not think?"

"They have not visited these parts for a long time, I am sure," Margaret added. "At least, they have never been here for any significant length of time or I am certain we should have heard about it. The Middletons would surely have had some news of them being in the vicinity, and there has not been a mention of them. And even if Lady Middleton were only being discreet, fearing to mention them in front of Mama, her mother certainly would not have held back. Indeed, Mrs Jennings has only ever spoken his name to declare that he must be the cold-hearted creature she always assumed, to leave poor Mrs Smith alone, for years on end."

"How dare she presume to know anything about him," Marianne exclaimed in irritation.

"I believe she only attacked him for the way he treated you in the past," urged Margaret, placing her hand over her sister's to reassure her. In this mood, she knew Marianne could erupt like a volcano or simmer away like a hissing kettle on a low flame, depending on how she was handled. Margaret was determined to keep her on an even keel if she could.

"You must not mention a word about what happened this afternoon," Marianne burst out. "News of their arrival in Exeter will be certain to reach Barton Park sooner or later, and for my own part, I would wish it to be a lot later. Let us hope it is a fleeting visit, though I am sure this cannot be the case. They would not have taken a house in Southernhay if they were only here for a day or two. I cannot bear to think what Mrs Jennings will have to say when their proximity is discovered. Thank heaven I shall be gone back to Delaford tomorrow. If only this carriage had wings and could fly, I should give my excuses and be gone this very evening. How I dread going up to the Park and being scrutinised by them all."

"Oh, it is not so very bad, I am quite used to it," Margaret answered, a little put out that Marianne had no feelings for her situation. Going to dine at the Park was a trial she had to endure several times a week. "All the attention will be on me, I suspect, with all the talk of Henry Lawrence and the Delaford Ball. I do not see why you are so worried. I shall be the butt of all Mrs Jennings's jokes and merciless teasing. Lady Middleton will comment on how I have grown and say how much I have improved, glancing in my direction once I suspect, as she does not have time for anyone but her children. Sir John will be as jovial as ever and force us all to be lively. You do not consider anyone's feelings but your own, Marianne. You forget; I am forced to rely on these very people for most of my entertainment. You are let off very lightly, I think. I wish I could hide away with a husband and a child who love me."

"I am sorry, Margaret, please forgive me," Marianne begged. "I do not suppose that I have ever considered what your daily life must be. But I have known Mrs Jennings longer than you, and if you think I shall be let off her inquisitions, you are deluding yourself. However, I promise I shall steer our conversation round to that of muslins and fripperies and away from young men."

"If you really think you shall succeed with that line of talk, then you are very much mistaken, my dear sister," Margaret retorted. "Have you really forgotten her passion for gossip? I cannot believe it!"

Marianne sighed with resignation. They were passing the sign-post for Allenham, the narrow, winding valley a mile and a half from Barton Cottage. Seeing Willoughby again had disturbed her mind, and now she was travelling through countryside she could only ever associate with him. Pulling down the window to breathe the cool air, she could not help being reminded of a time, five years ago, of a season just like this one. She tried to dismiss her thoughts, but they crowded in on her until she was forced to remember a particularly golden, autumnal day, when she had first been taken to see Allenham Court, which John Willoughby would inherit one day. The dwelling he had hinted would also be her future home was the place where he had first stolen more than a lock of her hair.

It was at his suggestion that he show her over the house. They travelled alone in an open carriage, bowling at speed down the green lanes, so fast that Marianne was forced to cling to his arm for fear of being thrown abroad.

He was so pleased and proud to show it off. "Do you like the house?" he asked, taking her hand and helping her down from the carriage. "Would it suit Miss Dashwood to live in a house like this?"

Marianne's excitement knew no bounds. "This house would suit anyone, Mr Willoughby," came her fervent response, gazing up at the charming edifice.

He took her into the garden first. They strolled away from the house and into a leafy walkway. The fragrance of damp earth and the musk scent of leaves like amber jewels above her head in the arbour were smells she would associate forevermore with those feelings of longing and love. He crooked her arm in his and they wandered through thorned archways, gleaming scarlet with rose hips, embroidered with the lace of jewelled spider's webs. It seemed like a dream come true to Marianne, and the thought that this might be her retreat some day brought on such ecstasies of happiness that she was lost for words. They walked in silence. All she heard were the leaves rustling under her feet, the birds in the trees calling out to one another. Her only desire was to link his arm in hers, and to feel the nearness of his face, his breath so close as to stir her curls. She could not have imagined greater felicity.

After going all round the grounds, he took her inside. They crept about for fear of disturbing Mrs Smith, who slumbered in her chair in the drawing room, quite unaware of their presence. He took her hand as they crept up the stairs with stifled giggles. The ancient oak door opened with a creak into a darkened room, the heavy, old-fashioned drapes drawn against the morning sun to protect the furniture.

Marianne's eyes were not able to adjust to the gloom after the brightness outside. "I cannot see," she whispered.

He caught both of her hands in his and whispered in reply, "Let me be your guide, Miss Marianne." He pulled her to him, draping her arms about his neck, before he bent to kiss her lips. She made no attempt to stop him; it all seemed so fitting, the perfect end to a wonderful morning. "I think the sofa will be your favourite spot, I see you in my mind's eye, on that day when you can claim it as your own. I will sit beside you and steal as many kisses as I wish. But for now, I wish to see you reclining there in all your beauty." He picked her up and deposited her there, before drawing back the curtains and opening the shutters, to flood the room in sunshine, returning to her side where he claimed her heart once and for all.

She had imagined herself living there many times, seated in the corner of that pretty upstairs sitting room, between two windows, unable to decide whether the view of the bowling green and hanging wood were preferable to that of the church and village with the hills beyond. Both views were indelibly etched on her mind, along with every emotion and feeling that would be forever married with every stick of furniture, every object in that quaint, old-fashioned room. No detail of that room or of any of the others she had glimpsed that morning had ever been forgotten. She had made plans for them all in her daydreams, having been so sure that she was to be mistress of Allenham. Indeed, she surely had been mistress, if only for one day, as she had lain in her lover's arms. But time and fate had been cruel in their treatment of Marianne; the days passed by and with them any possibility of those first dreams becoming a reality. Such was the wicked pain of memories she thought were buried forever. They had a habit of returning to haunt her mind as vividly as ever.

Marianne wondered what schemes Mrs Willoughby might one day entertain for its refurbishment with her fifty thousand pounds.

"I bet she will be spending considerably more than the two hundred pounds John Willoughby had suggested might be enough to cheer up the place," she thought. "I would never confess that despite my situation, living in what anyone would call a superior abode, I am secretly filled with jealousy at the prospect of anyone else undertaking the job I once thought rightfully mine. How foolish I am," she thought. Marianne removed her gloves and delved into the reticule beside her on the buttoned seat for her handkerchief. A spear of sunlight caught the ring upon her finger, and flashes of diamond sparkles spotted the interior of the carriage. Colonel Brandon's face, his admiring eyes and sweet expression, were immediately brought to mind. "My beloved William; how lost I would be without him." Yet, the battle she fought within herself seemed impossible to resolve. If only she could be certain that he loved her alone, she would conquer her feelings, she was sure.

Mrs Dashwood was waiting for them at the gate, waving with relief as they arrived. Dusk was giving way to the dark of the evening as they stepped down from the carriage. A weary Marianne gave orders to the coachman, who was staying in the village that evening, to collect her first thing in the morning. Her thoughts turned to home. She wished that William were here with all her heart. She missed him and longed to feel his reassuring presence.

With a heavy heart did Marianne dress herself for the evening's entertainment. She did not wish to admit to herself that she was quite shaken by the episode of the afternoon, but she did acknowledge that the last occupation she needed was to spend any length of time with Lady Middleton's inquisitive mother, Mrs Jennings. She heard Sir John's carriage draw to a standstill outside in the lane, the horses whinnying with impatience to be off again. Marianne adjusted the pearls at her throat and stroked the diamond on her finger as though touching it would bring William nearer to her. If only he were to accompany her to the Park. She knew he would have steered the conversation away from any subject that Marianne did not care to discuss. One look from her was usually enough and he would come to her rescue, but he was not here and she would have to make the best of it. Mrs Dashwood's voice calling her to come down broke her reverie; she picked up her gloves and slowly descended the staircase.

The reception that greeted them all was as welcoming as it could be. Sir John Middleton, a gentleman in his mid forties, was as good looking and as congenial as ever, apologising for the lack of bodies to divert them, saying that had there been more notice of Mrs Brandon's visit he would have secured a much larger party to dine with them. Lady Middleton, an elegant woman of two and thirty, was as reserved as her husband was frank and as cold in her manner as she had ever been on former visits. If she spoke more than a dozen words together for the entire evening, Marianne decided she would have been surprised. In complete contrast to this lady, her elderly mother was affable and merry, talking nonstop, never pausing to take a breath before she ran on to some other subject. She was a tease, full of jokes, and to Marianne's mind was still rather vulgar. However, this aspect of Mrs Jennings's character Marianne was prepared to forgive for the most part, for she had never forgotten the old lady's kindness. Mrs Jennings dominated the conversation from the start and was convinced that Margaret must have a secret beau because of the way she had dressed her hair. She pretended that she had prior knowledge of his name, even when it was quite apparent to everyone else that this could not possibly be the case.

Mrs Jennings's conversation took a turn for the worse, being made up of impertinent questions that more than hinted at her idea of Marianne being in a particular situation on account of the fact that she had detected a want of appetite at dinner. "I daresay I am correct, Mrs Brandon, am I not? I see you blush. Tell me, James is over two years old now, that's right, isn't it? And I am sure it is about time for him to look forward to having another baby to play with."

Marianne was as cross as she could be and could not think how to divert the course of the old lady's banter. She soon formed a plan to amuse the whole company and give her an excuse to leave Mrs Jennings's side. She would offer to play the pianoforte. But before she had the chance to speak or remove herself, she heard Lady Middleton suggest that her mother relate the news that she had heard in Barton village that very afternoon.

"Why, yes, I was coming to that, only I have not seen Mrs Brandon for a twelve month and we had important intelligence to divulge to one another first. Now, having got that out of the way, I must tell you I happened to see Mrs Whitaker this afternoon in the village. Poor soul, she is plagued with such ailments, it is a wonder she can walk at all. Her eldest daughter, Elizabeth, who by the bye was at school with my daughter Charlotte, was never expected to marry, what with her being such a plain sort of girl and always so very shy, but is confined and expecting her ninth child as I speak. By all accounts she is not so very timid now…" Mrs Jennings paused to laugh out loud, nudging Marianne with her elbow followed by a theatrical wink. "Do not mind me, Miss Margaret," she added with a nod towards her direction, "but I daresay we married ladies know to what I surmise…"

Marianne winced with embarrassment and glowered at her mother. She desperately wanted to go back to the cottage and retire to bed. Mrs Dashwood averted her eyes. Mrs Jennings's voice droned on in the background and Marianne hardly attended to a word she said. Her thoughts turned to Delaford. She wondered what William was doing. James would, no doubt, be tucked up in bed now; his dark curls tumbling over the pillow, his cherubic face flushed with sleep. It was hateful not to have said good night to him and she was missing him terribly. William would be in his study, reading his favourite poems, perhaps. She was quite lost in thought.

"...And Mrs Whitaker said that she is very dangerously ill, with only her faithful servants to nurse her," Mrs Jennings continued. "Poor lady, no children of her own and no sign of the one who is to inherit. He who shall be nameless! You know to whom I refer, Mrs Dashwood."

Marianne's ears pricked up at the last declaration and guessed that the lady she spoke of was none other than Mrs Smith of Allenham Court, Mr Willoughby's benefactor. Now Mrs Jennings was running through the list of Mrs Smith's ailments and announcing, as if she were the apothecary herself, that it was certain she would be dead before the week was out. Allenham would be empty, a very sad business, or so she had thought at first. "Then I bumped into Mrs Carey, whose cousin had been shopping in Exeter this afternoon. Mary Carey had seen them with her own eyes!"

"I wish you would explain with a little more comprehension, mother. Whom did Mary Carey see in Exeter this afternoon?" begged Lady Middleton, who despite affecting disinterest was clearly anxious to hear a full report.

"Mr and Mrs John Willoughby, of course!"

Mrs Dashwood coloured on hearing this information and cast a glance at her daughter. Marianne was clearly mortified and her mother grieved for her. How could Mrs Jennings be so insensitive?

"Did you not happen to see them yourselves?" the old lady enquired, directing her attention at Marianne, whose blushes were now visible to even the most unobservant of the party. Mrs Jennings looked searchingly into Marianne's countenance, which betrayed every emotion she was feeling, though her voice spoke her hot denial. Margaret was scrutinised next but the latter was unable to speak at all, so afraid was she of betraying the truth of the matter and upsetting her sister further.

"Well, what I want to know is why they are not up at the Court attending their cousin, said I, to Mrs Carey," Mrs Jennings blundered on, "though I intimated that he had always been somewhat of a character not to be trusted and a very cold fish to boot. And this is not all, Lord bless me. Mrs Carey said that her cousin had been in the linen draper's just half an hour later when she not only heard the reason why the Willoughbys are refusing to be put up at Allenham, but also received the most shocking news of all!"

Marianne faltered. She felt faint and thought she might pass out at any moment.

"Apparently, Sophia Willoughby was talking to an acquaintance as she was going out of the shop, someone whom it appeared must be a near relation. She heard Mrs Willoughby saying that it was insupportable that they should stay at the Court, that the place needed completely fitting up from top to bottom and that she would not step inside it, let alone stay in the place, until all was done to her satisfaction. She finished by saying that with luck, they would be able to start work within a fortnight. Now, what do you think to that? The house is to be occupied by the Willoughbys, who will no doubt make it their family home. Not that there is yet any issue from that marriage to date!"

Marianne knew this to be true. The Willoughbys had not been blessed with any children in the four years they had been married. She wondered what John felt about it all, if he ever thought about the daughter he had never seen. She knew she would never have been able to bear the idea of a child of hers being brought up in the world without any acknowledgement of her existence. Perhaps John Willoughby was the cold fish Mrs Jennings described, though in her heart she protested at such an idea. She did not think him completely reprehensible. After all, he had once tried to explain his past actions to Elinor, for which he had seemed truly sorry.

Sir John broke in immediately, striking up an animated discourse on the weather, declaring that the excellence of such fine days always produced the very best sport. He was well aware of Marianne's discomfort; though not a gentleman to be described as intuitive, he had known the sufferings of both parties, witnessing Marianne and Willoughby's romance from its earliest beginnings to its miserable end. It was entirely due to him that Mr Willoughby had ridden in haste to Cleveland, Charlotte Palmer's home, where Marianne had lain in a grave state. She had become extremely ill not long after discovering Willoughby's engagement to Miss Grey. Elinor had waited until she was out of danger before she had related the gist of what he had confessed. Marianne was told that he had loved her after all, and that he had proclaimed that his heart had never been inconstant. However, it appeared all his motives had been selfish ones. When Mrs Smith had discovered the truth about Eliza Williams, Willoughby, and the resulting child, she had disinherited him on the very day he was to have asked Marianne to marry him. As a consequence, he had secured Sophia Grey's hand for her fifty thousand pounds, knowing that he was more attached to Marianne than ever. John Willoughby had admitted to Elinor that he was sure he would never find domestic happiness. Marianne could not but help wonder if this was still the case.

Lady Middleton was heard to murmur something in response to her husband, but their combined efforts were not enough to dissuade Mrs Jennings from speaking.

"Mrs Brandon," she pronounced, "we are all looking forward to your ball at Delaford. And Miss Margaret, I expect you will be very interested to meet a certain person who by all accounts is described as a prodigiously handsome young man."

Margaret could not hide her confusion.

"Come now, Miss Dashwood," the old lady teased, "do not pretend that you do not know of whom I am talking. I daresay you have set your heart on Mr Lawrence, having heard he likes a poem as well as you do."

Margaret tried her best to smile and think of something to say. She was anxious to steer the conversation away from the Willoughbys and felt compassion for Marianne, who was looking quite mortified. "I am looking forward to the ball very much, Mrs Jennings," she replied brightly, "and I am hoping to see many of my acquaintances at Delaford. Mr Lawrence will be lucky if I find five minutes to be introduced to him, you know.

Anne Courtney and Jane Wilton are to come, with all their brothers and sisters. I have not seen them since the summer and there will be so much to catch up on."

Sir John could be as teasing as his mother-in-law. "I know when you young girls protest so much against such a thing that it usually means quite the reverse. I expect you'll be setting your cap at a certain Mr Lawrence before the evening is out."

"Oh, indeed," cried Mrs Jennings, joining in, "it would not do to let Miss Wilton and Miss Courtney get in first. And it will be most fitting as the sister of the hostess, that you will first be engaged to stand up with the guest of honour."

Margaret submitted quietly to all these abuses. Marianne flashed a smile toward her in recognition of the sacrifice her sister was making on her behalf. The evening continued in much the same vein, though Marianne was relieved that the subject of Allenham and the Willoughbys was not raised again.

Chapter 7

MARIANNE THREW HERSELF INTO the preparations for
the Delaford Ball as soon as she returned home next day. There
was a noisy reunion with James and a tender hug from William
who declared his love, telling her how much he had missed her
before promptly disappearing for the rest of the day. After a
joyful hour or two of play with James, it was time for the work
to begin. Invitation lists were checked against a tottering pile
of replies that had come in since she had been from home. A
hundred people had replied already with letters of acceptance
and that number again was expected to attend. There were
menus to discuss with Mrs Spencer the housekeeper; arrangements made for musicians to play, and instructions given for
seeing that the room for dancing was emptied of all unnecessary
chairs and tables.

She was ready to put her feet up by the close of the afternoon and was on her way to her room to accomplish this very act
when she was handed a note from her maid, who looked at her
with a smirk, as though she were party to a huge joke. "Colonel

Brandon asked me to pass on this note to you, my lady," she said, dropping a curtsey as she spoke. "I am to wait for an answer."

Marianne frowned and tried to catch Sally's eye, but her maid instantly looked up to the ceiling where she appeared to take great interest in the mouldings above. Marianne undid the seal and read.

> My *dearest Marianne*,
> *It will be my pleasure if you could meet me in the dining room at five. Come alone.*
>
> > *Your loving husband,*
> > *William Brandon*

The maid looked at her mistress enquiringly.

"What is going on, Sally?" Mrs Brandon asked.

"I am not at liberty to say, ma'am. I must await your answer only."

Marianne smiled in secret anticipation. She was quite used to the Colonel arranging little treats for her and she was certain that his hasty removal after breakfast confirmed that he had been up to mischief. "In that case," she replied, "tell Colonel Brandon it will be my pleasure to do as he instructs and, Sally, could you please attend me when you are finished? You may help me to choose a suitable gown."

With little time left before her assignation, she hastened to her room to change, grabbing armfuls of dresses from the closet and throwing them across the chaise longue, to form a veritable rainbow of rich fabric. She wanted to look her best. More than anything in the world, Marianne loved the adoration of her husband; her greatest pleasure was to feel him succumb wholly to her charms.

Sally appeared not ten minutes later, just as Marianne was despairing over her final choice between blue silk or diaphanous muslin. Sally proposed that she should wear the latter, saying that the sheer, white muslin would complement Mrs Brandon's dark complexion to greatest advantage. She was soon dressed and sat before the looking glass adjusting the last-minute touches to her appearance. She fixed on a pair of long diamond earrings to set off her new ring, as Sally tied a length of white silk ribbon around her dark hair. It was caught up at the front and sides but tumbled down her neck at the back in luxuriant, glossy curls. "You look a picture, Mrs Brandon," Sally declared in admiration, stepping back.

Marianne studied her reflection and saw a young woman who glowed with vitality and beauty. Would William think she was beautiful? Marianne hoped that she would be all he desired. "Thank you, Sally," she answered, "and if you will not confide what I am sure you must know, I shall leave you." But an indulgent hug communicated Mrs Brandon's pleasure in the whole joke, along with the laughter that echoed from the corridor as she rushed away.

The doors of the dining room were very firmly shut as she approached, and she was hesitant as to what to do next. Should she wait for William or should she just walk in? Marianne placed her ear to the door. There were sounds coming from within but she could not hear Brandon's voice. A light step from behind alerted her to the recognisable footfall of her husband. But before she had a chance to turn, however, she felt her eyes being covered by his long fingers, which blotted out everything but the sense of him being very close. She felt the warmth of his breath and his lips pressing against the scented skin of her soft, white neck.

"You must promise to keep your eyes shut," he implored.

Marianne giggled, nodding her head and shutting her eyes tight. Leading her into the room, William's guiding hand directed her till she was asked to stay quite still. Only when he was persuaded that all seemed satisfactory was she allowed to look. What a sight met her eyes! The table in the middle of the room was garlanded with greenery, looped through with wild Michaelmas daisies and lilac ribbons. A centrepiece of the same was graced on either side by ivory candles in silver candlesticks. William had thought of everything: the cook had produced a menu fit for a queen with half a dozen dishes of delectable variety all placed with decorative precision. The musicians having been in residence for the best part of the afternoon, all smartly attired in elegant dress for the occasion, had set themselves up in a corner of the room, where they were close enough to be heard but not so much as to be intrusive. At a nod from the Colonel, they started to play a favourite melody of Marianne's, a country dance which had been played at their wedding. The violins, horns, and pianoforte were united in perfect harmony to her ears and tears sprang to her eyes.

"I missed you so much!" she cried, turning to him and taking his arm as they stood together listening to the music. "Oh, thank you, my darling!"

William raised her hand to his lips and had no need to reply. Every gesture, all that lay before them said everything she needed to know. At that moment she felt secure in his love. He escorted her to the table and with a mock bow, proceeded to wait on her every want, her every command.

"I cannot tell you what a trial I endured at Barton Park," she admitted as they sat contentedly over their meal. She spoke without thinking, regretting the words as soon as she uttered them, knowing that she would have to explain or at least expand on what she had just said.

William looked at her impassively, waiting for her to continue. Marianne did not want to relate all that had passed during her trip, and frantic thoughts raced through her mind as to how she could carry on without revealing the fact that she had encountered Mr Willoughby and his wife in Exeter. Mr Willoughby was a name that was never mentioned at Delaford Park. If it were ever repeated by anyone, the Colonel would retreat into himself and become taciturn. He was not a man to suffer moods, but on these rare occasions his character seemed quite altered to his wife's ideas, his disposition changeable and his spirits low. She did not want to upset him now, especially when they were having such a lovely time. However, Marianne was certain that sooner or later the Willoughbys' arrival in Exeter would be discovered and the likelihood of further avoidance on that topic would be impossible.

Colonel Brandon broke the silence. "How is my dear friend, Sir John?" he asked. "I've not seen him for a fortnight at least, not since our last shoot together. I daresay he enlivened your party and made the visit more bearable."

"Oh yes, Sir John is as affable as ever," Marianne agreed, pausing to choose for a moment between a dish of chicken fricasée and a platter of beef steaks. "If only the same could be said of his lady and mother-in-law."

"I suspect from your tone that Lady Middleton was as preoccupied as ever and that Mrs Jennings spent the evening in a teasing mood," said William, taking a steak from the plate his wife held out to him.

Marianne could not help but smile from his astute summation. "Mrs Jennings is as impertinent as ever, hinting at confinements and babies and I know not what. Poor Margaret suffered just as much. The old lady is such a gossip that no one for twenty miles around can escape her inquisitive nose."

"But she means no harm, I am sure," stressed Brandon, "and if there is anything of great import to discover in the neighbourhood, she is sure to know of it." He paused as if waiting for her to speak and when she did not, he continued to defend Mrs Jennings. "You are a little harsh, Marianne. She has a kind heart and makes it her business to act on her discoveries, most often to one's advantage."

"Mrs Smith of Allenham is dying," Marianne blurted out, before he had quite finished, feeling that the sooner the subject was aired and begun, the sooner it would be over.

William's face clouded, his plate was pushed aside, as he looked searchingly into Marianne's countenance. "Mrs Jennings informed you of this fact, I suppose," he added, avoiding her eye and staring into his glass, the colour of its contents matching the flaming cheeks of Marianne. "I suppose she told you that the Willoughbys are in Exeter, too. It is a wonder that you did not bump into them."

Marianne felt his eyes on her again but this time she could not meet his gaze. She felt her face flush deeper and grow warm. Why could she not admit that she had seen the Willoughbys, that she had not only encountered John Willoughby but that she had acknowledged him? She could not speak it out loud and turned her head, pretending to be fascinated by the music. Why did she suspect that William knew she had met him? But he could not have known, she was sure, although by whose intelligence his prior knowledge had come about, she could not immediately guess.

"Mrs Jennings wrote to me this morning," he admitted, as if reading her thoughts.

Marianne caught her breath. "What does Mrs Jennings mean by writing to you? This news about the Willoughbys being in Exeter should not concern us particularly. Why is she bothering you with it?" Marianne was angry. How could Mrs Jennings interfere so?

William Brandon looked at his wife and knew with certainty that she had seen Willoughby after all. He had not surmised for a moment that there was anything suspicious about her activities in Exeter, but he had only to witness her agitation to have their meeting confirmed. The Colonel believed that Mrs Jennings's letter had been sent out of concern for them both. She had thought that Brandon should be informed, anticipating that Marianne might find the subject difficult to communicate. For all her provoking ways, she did indeed have a generous heart; the Brandons were especial favourites of hers and she wished to spare them unnecessary anxiety. Mrs Jennings had filled her letter with news about her family and her plans whilst visiting in the vicinity, expressing a hope that the Colonel would be able to call on them all at Barton soon. Allenham and the Willoughbys were only mentioned at the last, as an aside, written in such a way as an old acquaintance might send to another of long standing. But William knew very well the intentions behind it. Marianne had been upset by her trip to Exeter, that was clear, and he must now find a way to restore the equilibrium. Hopefully, the coming ball would be enough to divert Marianne's attention and it would be some time before either of them needed to go as near as Barton or Exeter. There would be no opportunity for meeting the Willoughbys, for which Colonel Brandon felt much relieved.

"We are to drive over to Whitwell tomorrow, at Hannah's invitation," he began, glad for an opportunity of a new subject for discussion and one he thought would intrigue his wife enough to divert her attention entirely. "She would like us to be introduced to Henry before the ball. I have accepted on our behalf."

Marianne was pleased that the conversation had moved on. She smiled her assent far more readily than she would have done in normal circumstances, feeling quite mollified towards her sister-in-law, and was almost generous in her praise of that lady, proclaiming she was most desirous to see her again.

They were coming to the end of their meal; the musicians performed their last song to rapturous applause from their audience and retired from the scene, leaving Marianne and her Colonel in the soft gloom of the evening. They sat in silence. The candles on the table cast their golden haloes over Marianne's creamy skin, lighting up her eyes to twinkle like nuggets of black jet. Marianne studied William's countenance. He still looked grave and appeared to be somewhere else, lost in thought.

"He looks so sad," she thought, "but he has always had a melancholy air about him. Mrs Jennings used to say it was because of his broken heart, though at one time I really believed that I had mended the break. Perhaps he regrets not running a sword through Willoughby when he had the chance. I do not know, but I wish he would come back to me."

She stared at him, forcing him to look at her, and when she was sure that she held his permanent regard, she laughed in her most endearing way, before promptly blowing out the candles. Rising deftly, she went to stand before him, so that she could be admired with greater ease. Marianne bent toward him to whisper in his ear. "I have a present for you, my love," she whispered, "but, alas, I am very remiss. I have forgotten to bring it with me. Do you think you could bear the inconvenience of accompanying me to my chamber to receive it?" She stroked his face with her slender fingers and caressed the curls at the nape of his neck. "Would you oblige me, my darling?"

Colonel Brandon did not answer. He was as captivated and ready to comply as a soul bewitched. He rose, enfolded her in his arms, and felt the pleasure of his wife submit to his sweetest kisses.

Chapter 8

AFTER BREAKFAST NEXT MORNING, the Brandon family made ready to travel the short journey to Whitwell. Marianne did not really wish to go despite her curiosity to see Henry and meet him at last. Hannah Lawrence always did her best to discompose Marianne, and no matter how hard she tried her sister-in-law rebuffed any attempts to be congenial. At least Sir Edgar was kind and always appeared to be glad to see her. So it was that just over half an hour later they were bowling up the drive of Sir Edgar Lawrence's country estate, to come to a standstill before the grand Palladian mansion known as Whitwell House.

James's behaviour had been reasonably subdued during the journey, but once out of the coach he found his energy and liveliness once more. Between Marianne and the nursemaid they managed to ascend the many steps with some semblance of order. The Brandons were shown into a large salon, filled with the most beautiful fittings and furniture. The style was French, the room ornate with gilded chairs, pier glasses, and chandeliers of the finest crystal. The silk-covered walls glowed with coral shades and iridescent hues of shell pink, further illuminating the room in flowing drapes at the floor-length windows, in the decorative ceiling, and in the Aubusson rug, which burgeoned with fat summer roses and green leaf garlands.

Lady Lawrence sat upon a velvet sofa, bolstered with pads and rolls, guarded by golden lion heads on either arm, which seemed ready to spring into life and leap out at anyone who might come to disturb her apparent idle repose. Despite the warmth of the day, she was covered to her waist by a heavy coverlet fringed with gold braid. She did not get up when they entered but excused herself, claiming that the damp of the day was responsible for her inability to stand.

William marched quickly to his sister's side, all concern, expressing his pleasure in seeing her again. "My dear Hannah, it has been too long. I am sorry to see you so indisposed. It is not your old trouble again, I hope?"

Hannah Lawrence, Marianne decided, was a woman of faded beauty. She imagined that at one time she would have been considered extremely attractive, but that a combination of ill temper and indolence had taken their toll. Lady Lawrence stretched out her hand to Marianne but did not meet her eyes when she took it. The lady ignored her and continued to address William as if she was not even in the room.

"Oh, William, you always understand. You are such a comfort to me, that I know I shall feel quite enlivened and ready to face whatever may befall me by the close of the day. Come, sit with me and tell me your news."

James, who had become very quiet in the presence of his aunt, now left the nurse's side and came to stand by his mother, as though he were quite aware of the unspoken rebuke.

He was soon noticed, however much he tried to hide behind Marianne's skirts.

"James, come here and let me look at you," commanded Lady Lawrence. "There is no need to be so shy. Dear me, I never saw such timidity in a child. Come forward, I say. Mrs Brandon, how do you countenance such behaviour?"

Marianne noted the embarrassed expression on William's face as he also failed to cajole James into greeting his aunt. Marianne whispered encouragingly into James's ear and the child stepped forward.

Fortunately, at that precise moment, Sir Edgar walked in and Marianne's spirits were lifted. His attitude and manner were as far from his wife's as it was possible to be. He was an athletic man of five and forty, with a figure and disposition that would convince the majority of those who met him on first acquaintance, of being at least ten years younger than his real age and at least half that of his spouse. He had the talent, which his wife did not possess, of making Marianne feel instantly at home.

"My dear Mrs Brandon, how charming it is to see you again. But where is your baby? For this young man cannot be the bairn I met last time!"

James beamed, running instantly to Sir Edgar's side and holding up his hand to him. He had not forgotten this kind gentleman, though it must be several months or more since he had seen him last. Before long the little boy was sat on his uncle's knee, pulling at his whiskers, emptying his pockets, and making such a commotion that Marianne was forced to intercede and call Kitty over. Disapproving clucks were heard from Lady Lawrence, and Marianne wished she could be anywhere else but under the scrutiny of that forbidding lady. A coin produced from

Sir Edgar's pockets and a pat on the head was a clear signal as far as nurse Kitty was concerned. James was taken away for a walk round the grounds, but not before a promise was extracted from Sir Edgar that he should play with him again later.

Marianne was very pleased that he urged her to sit next to him. "Now then, my dear sister," he said, turning to her after he had made his enquiries to the Colonel, "I expect you are wondering where young Henry has got to and why he is not here to introduce himself as was promised. He will be along in just a little while but he has been delayed. We have had a visitor this morning. He arrived quite unexpectedly, a cousin of an old school fellow of Henry's, I believe. They've been out shooting, but I'm expecting them back at any moment. He appears to be a capital fellow, and a very respectable gentleman by Henry's account. I am pleased he has some acquaintance in these parts."

"All young men love to have a little sport," cried Marianne. "And on such a day as this I am sure Henry can find no better employment. It will be pleasant for him to have the company of another young fellow."

"Aye, you are quite right and that very idea brings me to something else. I've a mind to ask our guest to stay on for a while. It seems he might be able to put a decent property in Henry's way, and you know what young men are for increasing their fortunes, Mrs Brandon. I've a mind he wants to mess about on an estate of his own; I am keen to help him for he will not wish to wait until I am in my grave before he has a home of his own." He chuckled at this idea.

"Oh, Sir Edgar," cried Marianne, "do not talk of such a dreadful event!"

"Nay, my dear, well it will come to us all, sooner or later." He fiddled with the fob at his waistcoat and pulled at his stock with some agitation. He looked as if he might be going to stand, then changed his mind and turning to face her, beamed with all his usual cordiality. "May I ask a great favour, Mrs Brandon?" he said at last.

"Why, of course, Sir Edgar, it would be my pleasure to bestow upon you any favour you desire," Marianne declared.

"It is a favour I ask on Henry's behalf. He is most anxious that the sale of the property I mentioned will be seen to completion. Would it be too much to ask that if this young man could be persuaded to stay on, that he be included in our small circle? I do not know that he has many friends in the area, and an invitation to your ball at Delaford would make Henry happy, I know."

"Well, of course, I should be delighted to invite Henry's friend. Indeed, invite whosoever you like, the more the merrier," laughed Marianne. "I am sure we would all enjoy the society of a pleasant young man and though the young ladies will hate me for saying so, I am certain every one under the age of twenty-five will be anxious to meet him."

"Well, that's settled then. Thank you, my dear, I knew you would understand."

"What are you discussing, my dear?" Lady Lawrence was heard to say from across the room. She was sitting up with more animation, clearly anxious to hear all that was being said on any subject that she was not a party to.

"I was just telling Mrs Brandon about Henry's plans," admitted the jovial gentleman, "and have just extracted an invitation to attend the ball for his young friend. I do hope that is acceptable to you, Brandon, old chap."

Colonel Brandon nodded. "Of course, we would welcome any friends of yours, Sir Edgar."

"Just what your wife said, only more prettily," chuckled Sir Edgar. "The thing is, Brandon, Henry is after a pretty property of his own and this young man has one to sell. Dash it all, what's his name, Hannah? I should forget my own name if it wasn't scribed in the family bible!"

"Why, it's Willoughby," his wife answered, "Mr John Willoughby. I could not forget the name of such a gallant and handsome young man." She laughed and patted her curls in a girlish manner.

Marianne caught her husband's expression and their eyes met across the room. There could not be two John Willoughbys in this part of the world. Brandon looked most uncomfortable. He opened his mouth to speak and then closed it again.

His sister continued. "Henry wishes to increase his prospects, you understand, and such an opportunity could not be turned down. I believe the property needs a little attention but I am sure if Henry and Edgar can secure it, he will enjoy making the improvements."

Marianne's heart was beating so fast she was sure it could be heard. Was Willoughby to sell Allenham Court? This did not fit with the intelligence from Mrs Jennings, who had intimated that the Willoughbys themselves were to live there and that plans had already been drawn up for major works to be started. One thing was certain. It was very clear to Marianne that Hannah Lawrence had no prior knowledge about John Willoughby and that her brother's shared history with that gentleman, or indeed her own, were quite unknown. Relief of a kind washed over her, only to be replaced by the thought that

Sir Edgar had informed them that Henry and his friend would soon be making an appearance.

As if her thoughts were transpired into reality, there came sounds from without the salon doors. Voices, talking loudly, were soon followed by the doors being flung wide open, to reveal a tall, handsome, fair-haired man whom Marianne had never seen before, waving the servant away. A younger version of Sir Edgar stood before them, bowing and smiling, but there was no sign of his companion, for which Marianne felt grateful.

"Henry! You are come at last," cried his mother. "Come in and say how do you do to your uncle. He is most anxious to see you again. William, here is my dearest son, Henry."

Marianne was sensible of the slight made against her for a second time that morning and did not know where to look. Henry Lawrence, however, as charming as he seemed, nodded towards Brandon but then presented himself before her. He bowed and held out his hand in greeting. "No one told me I had such a beautiful aunt, Mrs Brandon. It is an honour to meet you."

Marianne was enchanted and could not help smiling at this rather forward gentleman. She guessed they were of a similar age to one another, and it amused her to think that he was indeed her nephew.

He crossed the room next, to shake Brandon's hand. "It is good to see you, Uncle William; it is some time since I saw you last. I have not forgotten the wonderful times we had, how you taught me to ride and to fish."

"Of course, the summer before you left for France, I remember it well. You were determined you should be able to ride before you got to Avignon and if I recall, you succeeded, too," William answered.

"I was determined I should show those French boys how to ride the fiercest stallion with panache," he cried. "And I did, too, thanks to you."

"Is Mr Willoughby with you?" asked Lady Lawrence, cutting in with no regard for anyone else.

"Oh, he begged to leave his apologies, Mama, but he had business to attend to in Exeter this afternoon," Henry replied. "He said he had put us out quite enough already and did not want to disturb us further. I told him my Uncle William was here for a visit, so he did not expect to be included."

"I was hoping we might persuade him to stay," Sir Edgar added.

"Oh no, his wife is in Exeter waiting for him. They have taken a house in Southernhay, I believe."

"I did not realise that Mr Willoughby is a married gentleman," Sir Edgar went on. "Well, Mrs Brandon here has invited your friend to the ball at Delaford, and I daresay his wife will be most welcome too. Isn't that capital?"

"Have you really, Mrs Brandon?" Henry cried, turning and bowing with a full flourish. "You really are the kindest aunt any nephew ever had!"

Marianne could not decide whether he was teasing her until she caught him winking at her surreptitiously a moment later. She tried to be cross with him but his ways were so endearing it was not possible. She wondered how Henry had been introduced to his friend and could not resist making enquiries. "Have you known Mr Willoughby long?" she asked, knowing her husband was observing her and listening to every word, despite the fact that his sister kept talking over the top of anyone who chose to start a conversation.

"No, not for long," said he. "Mr Willoughby is a cousin of a chap I was at school with; we met at a house party that Charles's parents were giving last summer, when I was down from Oxford. He is a great rattle, you know, and he loves to hunt as much as I do, so we got on well from the very first. Never met his wife though. I understand they spend quite a time apart. Still, I expect if he accepts your kind invitation, I shall meet her at the ball."

Marianne very fortunately did not have to reply as they were all interrupted by the timely arrival of James, who came skipping through the door, followed rapidly by Kitty at his heels. The small boy timidly presented his aunt with a sweet bunch of wildflowers he had picked from the park. Such a pretty gesture delivered with a bow should have melted the hardest heart.

"If you had wanted to pick a posy, James," Lady Lawrence admonished, "Dawkins would have directed your nurse to the hothouses. These are wild and will fade before the day is out, but I suppose you may take them home if you wish."

Marianne was distraught to see the crestfallen countenance of her little boy, especially when he was heard to whisper to his miserable aunt, "For you."

It was time to go home.

Chapter 9

ON THE FOLLOWING TUESDAY afternoon, Elinor and Marianne were sitting in the latter's favourite room at Delaford, a small parlour with windows that looked toward the orchard and the mellow brick garden walls that enclosed it. The apple trees, heavy with fruit, gleamed crimson in the October sunshine, and the twisted mulberry tree, in one corner, associated forever in Marianne's mind with those star-crossed lovers, Pyramus and Thisbe, was abundant with swelling purple berries.

The ladies were sat over tea and the conversation had taken a turn to the subject of Mr Willoughby, and all that had recently passed at Barton and Whitwell. Elinor was shocked to hear that he and his wife were in Exeter, but when Mrs Brandon confided that he was on terms of intimacy with Henry Lawrence also and that she had unwittingly invited him to the Delaford Ball, her sister was, for a moment, quite incapable of speech.

"I was coerced into inviting the Willoughbys to help Henry. I believe Mr Willoughby means to sell Allenham Court from what Sir Edgar hinted," Marianne explained, "though Mrs Jennings's intelligence is that Mrs Willoughby is ready to move in as soon as the alterations are done. Mama has written to me this morning, saying that poor Mrs Smith has only been buried these three days, but that there are already workmen inside the house, reports of furniture piled high outside and bonfire smoke over the village, like a funeral pyre!"

"My goodness me," Elinor replied, her eyes round with astonishment, "they have not wasted any time. But surely Mr Willoughby has no need to sell Allenham? His wife is very rich, is she not?"

"Who can say? Sir Edgar did not specify Allenham, now I come to think on it," Marianne continued. "Perhaps he wishes to sell Combe Magna." She had not thought of it before, but she realised she could not bear the thought of John Willoughby living so closely to Barton. Was he really so insensitive? Had he been able to forget all that had happened between them, so much so that he did not care whether or not he lived on her mother's doorstep?

"Surely he will not come to live so close to Barton," said Elinor, as her thoughts mirrored Marianne's own. "Whatever has dear William had to say on the matter?"

"It was so difficult to converse at first that we did not discuss what had gone on at Whitwell until yesterday," Marianne sighed, shaking her head in remembrance. "William's demeanour, so grave and aloof, frightened me, Elinor. I have never seen him in such an ill humour. Finally, it could be avoided no longer. I asked him if his sister knew anything of Mr Willoughby's history, but of course he replied that Hannah and Edgar had been in France on their way to Italy when the first knowledge of Miss Williams's predicament had arisen. Of course Brandon does not refer to myself in connection with Mr Willoughby; it is never discussed nor mentioned. It is as though the whole affair never happened."

"Well, that is understandable," Elinor said softly. "What does he intend to do now? Will he warn the Lawrences of Mr Willoughby's character?"

"He says he cannot. William insists that this whole matter must be hushed up. He reasons that five years have passed since the unfortunate affair and that, as nothing further has been heard against the character of Mr Willoughby, that he is not in any position to besmirch it. William is too much the gentleman to behave in any other way, and besides, if he can be of use to Henry, he will do all he can."

They were both lost in their own thoughts for a moment and then Marianne spoke again. "I believe Hannah to have been at school at the time when William and his first love attempted an elopement. Lady Lawrence is ignorant of that lady's complete history after her abandonment, even if she does know of the existence of William's ward. But William did not see that there was anything to be gained by his sister having any knowledge of Eliza Williams's seduction by Mr Willoughby or the subsequent birth of the child. Of course Hannah and her husband were on the continent for many years at that time."

"But surely William must think of his nephew Henry, and what if you are thrown together in circumstances not of your own making? What then?"

"William believes that when Willoughby realises the connection, which is probably done already, he is certain he will not show his face. His dealings with my nephew and his father are of a business nature; we will not have to meet socially."

"I do not share your confidence, Marianne," Elinor went on, "I think he will brazen out any meeting; he has already shown he is capable of such. And is William sure that Henry Lawrence can trust Willoughby in his business matters? I do not think he is to be relied upon."

"We can hardly be his judge," snapped Marianne, "we have had no dealings with him for the past four years. He is older and possibly wiser. Mr Willoughby is a man of consequence and respectably married. No one's character is fixed for life, Elinor; perhaps we should give him the benefit of the doubt."

Elinor did not know what to say. She was disturbed by the fact that Marianne was prepared to defend him in such a voluble manner. "Have you given some thought as to whether he is likely to accept your invitation?"

"Mr Willoughby will never show his face at Delaford Park, of that circumstance I am as certain as of the sun rising in the morning," pronounced Marianne with feeling.

Elinor remained unconvinced. She had an awful feeling of foreboding, which no amount of reasoning could do away.

It was arranged that Marianne would drive over to Barton on Wednesday, two days prior to the ball, in order to collect her mother and sister. Margaret, who was in high spirits, had expressed her excitement about their invitation in a letter that had arrived on the very morning Marianne was to head into Devonshire. This news did not come as a surprise, but the remaining content of the letter disconcerted Marianne to a greater extent.

Barton Cottage,
October 7th
Dearest Marianne,

I can hardly believe that the day of the ball is almost upon us. I look forward to seeing my friends at Delaford. The prospect is too exciting! My gown arrived yesterday morning. Marianne, you will not believe how beautiful it looks; it has surpassed all my expectations. It fits me quite perfectly and Mrs Jennings has sent some silver ribbon and silk flowers for my hair that she bought in London and has been saving for such an occasion as this. Wasn't that kind?

You will never guess whom I bumped into in Barton village yesterday when I went to collect the post. John Willoughby himself! He was very gentleman-like and kind, not in the least brusque as he was when we saw him in Exeter. He asked me how I did and enquired after Mother. He said he was sorry he had not been able to converse more when he saw us in Exeter but that the surprise of seeing us had taken away his power of speech. He especially asked to be remembered to you. I did not know that Mr Willoughby was acquainted with Henry Lawrence, and it was a great surprise when he said that he was very pleased to have been invited to the Delaford Ball. Can this be true? Has Colonel Brandon forgiven Mr Willoughby? I must admit that I was very surprised to hear about his invitation, but it did seem as if he was very keen to attend. I have not mentioned this to my mother or to Mrs Jennings, as it seemed so very strange to me that you have not written of this in any communication regarding the ball. I thought I should mention it, however,

*but in any case I shall see you before you have time to pen
a reply.*

> *Believe me to be,*
> *Your loving sister,*
> *Margaret Dashwood*

Marianne folded the letter carefully. "I will not think about its contents now," she thought, placing it inside her reticule, "I must concentrate on getting ready to make the trip to Barton. William must not know about this; it will not make any difference whether he knows of Margaret's meeting with Willoughby or not. Neither will it be a good idea to have him worried about the matter before I set off and, with this news, he might even prevent me from going. No, some things are better left unsaid."

She pulled on her bonnet and fastened her cloak about her shoulders, busying herself with the final preparations and instructions to the coachman. But despite all this activity, she could not eradicate certain parts of Margaret's letter from her mind. "So Willoughby was sorry he had not been able to converse more when we saw one another in Exeter and he had asked especially to be remembered to me. I cannot help but smile at the thought that his manner was not quite as it had appeared." She took her seat in the carriage and gave the signal to move off. The journey to Barton seemed to take an age. The settled weather of the last week had given way to rain and wind, and the roads were muddy and the lanes become as dirt tracks. The coachman and his boy had to step down twice to push the carriage out of the mire and had made a wrong turning before they reached Honiton. Marianne felt unsettled by Margaret's letter and though she could not believe that Willoughby had any intention of coming to Delaford to attend the ball, a part of her imagined that he might, after all, brazen it out. "But will he really wish to embarrass his wife? Surely Mrs Willoughby will refuse to attend when she understands the connection. It is not worth worrying about. I cannot think of such an unlikely event as the Willoughbys attending a ball at Delaford Park."

They had just passed the turning for Stoke Canon and were within a half-mile of Allenham when Marianne first saw the pall of dark mist, rising in undulating columns. Even in the rain, the plumes of black smoke could be seen rising up above the grey clouds where torrents of water poured from the heavens. Seized by a sense of longing, Marianne experienced a feeling of great curiosity that was impossible to override: consumed by questions that would not go away. She must and would take a look at the house. Urging the coachman to take the turn, the carriage set off down the lane, flanked on either side by tall, dripping hedgerows, whose overhanging branches clawed and scratched the glass windows. She felt no alarm; after all, she had been down this bridleway a hundred times before. Trees, contorted into the grotesque by the gales, twisted and entangled their boughs to form a dim tunnel over their heads. They made slow progress through the mud, which splashed the carriage up to the windows and the horses to the tops of their tails. At last the track widened to reveal a pair of ornate gates opened to the road like inviting arms, to swallow the coach as it rumbled to a standstill several yards from the house, the ancient manor which even now had the power to arrest Marianne's heart. There, to one side by the outbuildings, were a series of huge bonfires, as had been reported, piled high with all manner of items. Several trees worth of wooden planking, panelling, painted doors, and redundant furniture, blistering in the heat, were being consumed by the fire, licked to the bare bones by the rapacious flames. Beyond the haze and smoke the house itself looked shut up, the shuttered windows like unseeing eyes, closed and drawn. Only the main doors were ajar but there was no sign of life. Marianne felt it was the saddest scene she had ever contemplated: the violation of a home with her precious memories buried at its heart. She did not think she could stay longer to witness such destruction. Banging on the roof to alert the coachman, the wheels turned her carriage towards the gates once more before she looked back, as if in final salute. A shutter moved. Someone looked down from an upstairs window. The unmistakable silhouette of a gentleman threw back the remaining screen. Their eyes met and connected with lingering recognition. Then he was gone. Marianne started; kneeling up on her seat to look out through the window behind her, straining to see what she imagined might only have been in her head. She heard the coachman's cry; he cracked his whip in frustration as they slowly rounded the last bend. The house grew small. And then he appeared, running hard, his greatcoat flapping behind him, as though he wished to catch her up. Should she stop the coach? She did not know what to do and was on the point of calling out when she saw that he had stopped to close the gates. John Willoughby stood, motionless, like a ghost. Marianne watched until he was out of sight, a lone figure staring after her.

Chapter 10

MRS DASHWOOD AND MARGARET were ready to travel immediately. They had enough boxes and trunks piled up in the hall as if they were going for half a year instead of a few weeks. Marianne felt weary after her journey and was pleased to rest in front of a cheerful fire in the sitting room and glad, despite the eagerness of the other women, that they would not be travelling until the morrow. She was also grateful that on this occasion there was no mention of going up to the Park to see the Middletons and Mrs Jennings. She would be seeing them quite soon enough, she felt, for they were to come for a visit to Delaford, arriving on the eve of the ball and stopping a fortnight. Still, it could not be helped, and she hoped that it would all be to Margaret's benefit.

Marianne had not expected to relate anything of the goings-on at Allenham Court or for the subject to be raised at all, so she was greatly surprised when Mrs Dashwood brought up the topic; not only of the poor deceased Mrs Smith but of Mr Willoughby himself.

"I wrote to you about Mrs Smith, did I not, Marianne?" Mrs Dashwood fussed about with the cushions on a chair, patting and plumping them and setting them straight.

Marianne noted that her mother did not look at her directly as she spoke. She waited to hear more.

"We had a visitor early this morning," Mrs Dashwood said, pausing to take up her needlework to stitch furiously along a seam. Marianne could not help notice her mother's agitation, or the colouring about her throat.

"Mr Willoughby came here," said Margaret.

Still Marianne remained silent.

"I was determined to snub him for your sake, Marianne," Mrs Dashwood continued, "but I think when I tell you all, you will see that it was quite impossible for me to be so unkind."

"He was very charming," Margaret added with enthusiasm. "Please don't be cross, Marianne. He came to make amends."

"What did he say?"

"Well, we were sitting after breakfast as we always do," interrupted Mrs Dashwood, "and Tom came in to say Mr Willoughby had called. He said he was most anxious to see me. I could not refuse to see him but I was prepared to give him a piece of my mind. Well, he came in, looking quite as handsome as ever, in a dark brown coat to mirror those dark eyes to perfection and I was a lost cause from the moment he entered the room. Oh, Marianne, forgive me, but the years melted away and though I can never forgive him for his conduct toward you, please let me say this. He has suffered, truly suffered, for his crimes. I believe he has regretted you since the day he severed the connection."

"Did he say as much?" Marianne asked, rather astonished that such an intimacy had been established on so soon a reacquaintance.

"Not in so many words," admitted her mother. "At least that was the impression he gave most earnestly. What did he say, Margaret?"

Marianne sighed. Her mother was always easily charmed and no doubt Mr Willoughby had eased his way back into her good books with little effort. Smiles and compliments had been his most likely method, thought she.

"He said that now he was coming back to the neighbourhood, he was sure that we would meet from time to time and he was most concerned that his past behaviour to our family might rightly prejudice us against him. He wanted to ask our forgiveness and apologise most profusely for what had happened. He said he knew there was probably little hope that we would ever accept him back as the friend he had once been, but that his dearest wish was to be able to meet with cordiality. However, he would be content if he could at least greet us in the street as we passed by. I think that was about the drift of it, wasn't it, Mama?"

Mrs Dashwood nodded and her eyes appealed to Marianne for Willoughby's forgiveness.

"He asked after you and wanted to know if you were happy," Margaret added.

"I told him you were very happy, Marianne," said Mrs Dashwood. "Indeed, because you are so settled and everything has turned out so much better for you, I did not think you would mind if he called on us occasionally. I did not have the heart to be cruel to the man. He seemed so genuinely to regret losing our friendship. I suggested he might call again and perhaps bring Mrs Willoughby."

"Mother! How could you do such a thing," Marianne shouted. "I cannot believe you could be so thoughtless. Have you forgotten William in all of this, and the other business of Brandon's ward?" Marianne could not bring herself to say Eliza's name out loud. "You know how William detests Willoughby. He would have killed him when they met to duel if he had been able. Have you forgotten Eliza Williams and her child?"

"Mr Willoughby is keen to make amends to his natural child. He told me as much."

"And William will never allow it," Marianne cried, standing up and pacing to the window. "It is as well that we are going to Delaford in the morning." She stared out at the landscape, the rolling hills and green valleys undulating before them. "Oh, goodness," she started, "whatever will I do if he presents himself at the ball?"

"That is highly unlikely, Marianne. Why on earth should Willoughby do that?" Mrs Dashwood walked over to her daughter and put out her hand to stroke her arm in an affectionate gesture.

"I haven't said a word on the matter, sister," cried Margaret, observing her mother's expression of puzzlement and alarm at these words.

"Because he is an acquaintance of Henry Lawrence," Marianne announced, turning to look her mother in the eye, "and because I have invited him!"

The whole story came out, about how she had unwittingly invited Willoughby to the ball, about how Sir Edgar Lawrence was interested in buying a property for Henry that Willoughby had to sell. "I was certain that he would not come once he found out that the ball was at Delaford, but now you have given him so much encouragement, Mama, I cannot be sure. There will be trouble, I know it."

"There is no point worrying about it now, Marianne," her mother soothed, taking her arm in her own and leading her back to the sofa. "We must hope for the best. And if he does come, we will deal with that too, if and when it happens. Now, come along, let us have no more on such a distressing subject. You must calm yourself or you will be ill."

But Marianne could not be calmed, she would not eat any dinner and excused herself as soon as she could, saying that she had a headache from the journey and that she wanted an early night. "We will set off as soon as we rise, Mama," she said. "James is so looking forward to seeing you both and William will be anxious until we reach home. I will feel better in the morning, but I must rest now. Good night." She did not add that she wished to be as far away from Barton as soon as she could be, for fear of running into a certain gentleman who had promised would call again before long.

A merry party, caught up in the mood of the celebrations to come, were sat in the dining room at Delaford Park over breakfast, early on Saturday morning. Colonel Brandon presided over the company, eager to see that his guests had every comfort at his disposal. The Middletons and Mrs Jennings had arrived the day before, accompanied by all six Middleton children in two carriages. The ladies from Barton Cottage had arrived just before them and greeted the other Devonshire family, as though they had not seen them for a month at least. Elinor and Edward Ferrars had arrived early in the morning from the parsonage with their little ones; Anna now sat with her Brandon cousin. Marianne smiled at the noisy scene; it was impossible to feel anything but pleasure at such conviviality. Everyone was talking at once as vast quantities of bread rolls, cake, and chocolate disappeared into hungry mouths.

"My dear, Mrs Ferrars," said Mrs Jennings, breaking a soft white roll and buttering it liberally, "it is such a delight to meet with you again, your dear husband and the little F's. It still tickles me to think of the time when I used to joke you about Mr F. Oh, I knew how it would be, even when it was discovered that my cousin Lucy was secretly engaged to him. I did not say so at the time but I was never convinced that Lucy and Mr F would make a match. You two were such a perfect couple. And here you are now, as proof to that testament, with a growing family and more to come, I daresay."

Elinor smiled but did not quite know how to answer. If her memory served her well, Mrs Jennings had been convinced that Elinor had been all set to marry Colonel Brandon. However, Mrs Jennings always meant well and had a kind heart, but it was imperative that she should divert the lady's conversation away from herself. Elinor did not want to be drawn into answering her impertinent questions and so encouraged her companion to talk of herself, a favourite subject with that lady. "How are you, Mrs Jennings? How is your daughter Charlotte?"

"I'm very well, my dear. Charlotte is nursing baby number four at Cleveland at present and hoping to be fit enough to come to London a little later on. I shall be going to my house too and will see them all there."

"You have a fine set of grandchildren, Mrs Jennings. Lady Middleton has six children now, does she not?" Elinor politely stated.

"What a number of grandchildren I have, Mrs Ferrars, I cannot for the life of me remember all their names, I assure you. Ten of them, Lord bless me, though between you and me Mary seems to have slowed down a little at last. Good thing for her too, I say, this child rearing is a tiring business."

"Yes, indeed, ma'am," Elinor nodded in agreement.

"Will we be seeing you in town this winter, Mrs Ferrars?" Mrs Jennings went on. "Mr Palmer has to be in town of course for the opening of Parliament, so we will all be going. Being an M.P. takes up so much time, you cannot imagine. Charlotte says she hardly sees her husband from one week's end to the next, when they go to town, though between you and me, I think Mr Palmer spends as much time sitting in his club as he does in the House! We would be very pleased to see you there. I expect your sister will be going, will she not? The Colonel never misses a trip to town, and I daresay young Margaret would be keen to go too, especially when the Lawrences are likely to take a house. I hear young Henry Lawrence may be the very young man Miss Margaret has been waiting for!" Mrs Jennings chuckled at this last retort and as Margaret's ears caught the mention of her name, her expression betrayed the anxiety she felt at having it bandied about by the former in such a jocular fashion.

Edward Ferrars came to the rescue by asking Mrs Jennings when she intended to travel. She soon glossed over that subject to make her enquiries after his brother, Robert, who was married to the Lucy with whom Edward had once been secretly engaged. It had been an engagement made when they were both very young. Edward had consequently fallen in love with Elinor but had been prepared to honour his promise to Lucy. Luckily for them both, Lucy had turned her affections toward Robert when she discovered the latter had been favoured with Edward's inheritance. Fortunately for Edward and Elinor, as their visits to

London were very infrequent, they did not have to meet Robert and Lucy very often.

"My brother and sister are very well, I believe," Edward replied. "They will be expecting to see you when you are in London, Mrs Jennings. Lucy begged me to apologise for not having written lately but she has had much to do with their removal to Russell Square."

"Aye, I expect she has, though it has to be said that she has become a very poor letter writer since she married and has no need to beg my company. Well, well, youth was ever thus, unthinking and plaguing in the extreme. Old folks like me lose their attractions with every passing year. I daresay she is spending all her time fitting up her new establishment and looking after that brood of naughty children. Lord, bless my soul, three children and another on the way, even quicker than my Charlotte or Mary."

"I believe the children do take up a lot of her time," Edward agreed.

A knock at the door interrupted the flow of conversation around that end of the table. The servant came in and proffered the salver toward Marianne, who took the letter and stared at the handwritten direction with a frown. She had barely opened the missive when it was hurriedly folded again. Marianne did not seem at ease as she looked around the table, but she could see the Colonel deep in conversation with Sir John Middleton at the other end and her expression lightened temporarily. Her discomposure was noted not only by Elinor, who guessed immediately from whence the letter came, but also by Mrs Jennings, who asked about it without hesitation.

"It is just an old acquaintance," Marianne stammered, colouring as she spoke and placing the letter in her pocket, pulled the strings firmly together. "If you will all excuse me, I need to speak to Mrs Spencer about some arrangements for this evening." Marianne rose from her chair abruptly and left the room without a backward glance.

"Well, that was all rather mysterious," cried Mrs Jennings, "I do hope it wasn't bad news. Mrs Brandon looked quite as if she had read something unpleasant. I wonder what it can have been about."

Edward responded to Elinor's gentle nudge under the table and proceeded to engage Mrs Jennings in a conversation about his mother, which he knew would divert the interests of his companion with little effort on his behalf. Elinor tried to look as though she was listening with concentration, but felt most concerned. She would have to wait to speak to Marianne later, but in any case, Mrs Ferrars had a suspicion that she knew to what subject the letter pertained.

In her room, Marianne fetched the letter out with trembling fingers. She had recognised the handwriting instantly and a whole rosewood box of memories came flooding into her mind, along with the recollection of three tear stained letters and a lock of hair that had once been returned to her.

Southernhay
October 8th
Dear Mrs Brandon,

It is with great pleasure that I accept your kind invitation to the Delaford Ball. Unfortunately, Mrs Willoughby is indisposed at present and will, therefore, be unable to accompany me, but I shall be attending with the Lawrence party, who I know are also looking forward very much to the evening's entertainment.

I have had the great fortune to reacquaint myself with your mother and youngest sister, for which, I am truly thankful. They have welcomed me into their home most willingly. I have only one wish that remains unfulfilled and that is to be given the opportunity to be on cordial terms with you again. I may ask too much, I know, but I beg we can be at the very least on a most civil footing.

I remain,
Your obedient servant,
John Willoughby of Allenham.

In fury, Marianne crushed the paper in her hands and tore it into pieces. She did not know what she should do. How she would be able to conduct herself through the evening's entertainment with this fore knowledge, she could not imagine. And how was she going to tell William that he was to play host to his old adversary and foe this very evening?

Chapter 11

DESPITE TELLING HERSELF THAT she did not care a jot about meeting Henry Lawrence, it was with great care and excitement that Margaret prepared for the evening's diversions. She loved staying at Delaford, and it was at William's suggestion that Margaret had been given the Bombay Room as her own, from her very first visit. The luxury of this chamber and dressing room were always hers to enjoy and she delighted in its opulence, from the tester bed brought from Mandalay, inlaid in gilt and mirror mosaic, to the painted chintz that adorned walls and windows, flowering with exotic trees and blooms. Indian craftsmen had carved the ebony chairs, brassware urns, and scented sandalwood boxes with rosettes and arabesques. Even the silver looking glass and lacquer boxes on her dressing table were from the East as were the perfumed oils smelling of rose and frangipani that she smoothed into her skin after her bath.

Sally came to help dress her hair, button her gown, and exclaim at her beauty. When she had gone, Margaret stood before the long glass and was surprised by her appearance.

Swathed in shimmering gauze and satin from head to foot, she did not recognise the sophisticated young lady who looked back at her. Sally had done her proud, her curls were swept up and caught into a ribbon at the back, through which the silver leaves Mrs Jennings had generously bestowed wreathed and glittered. Margaret's excitement rose. Mr Lawrence had better make his move instantly, she thought, or he might well be disappointed. She felt sure that she would have as many partners with which to dance as she chose tonight. The Courtney and Wilton brothers were all certain of attending. She particularly loved to dance with Anne's brother George and Jane's brother Thomas. There had never been anything more than a wish to dance with them; they were pleasant enough boys, but that was all. Neither had a romantic bone in their body and as far as Margaret was concerned, to be romantic was a prerequisite of a potential beau.

She had found and made friends quickly in Delaford. On her sister's marriage she had been invited almost immediately to stay at the Park and her mother had encouraged the visit in the hope that Margaret would be introduced to a larger society. She had soon met the families in the neighbouring villages, and a firm friendship had been established with their daughters: Anne Courtney from Delaford itself, Jane Wilton from Dalworthy, and Selina Strowbridge from Whitstock. Many a pleasant hour had been spent in these girls' company, as they confided all their secrets, whilst sitting in the old yew arbour behind the house, watching the carriages pass along. She had danced at the local assemblies with their brothers and she had been invited to their houses. Margaret's particular favourite was Anne, a level-headed yet lively girl who was always thoughtful and kind. She loved poetry as much as Margaret and they would sit together reciting their favourite passages from Cowper. Anne would never betray a confidence. Jane, however sweet of disposition, was inclined to be rather loose-tongued and spent too much time in Selina's company, of whom Margaret was not so fond. Selina was in the habit of flirting wildly with any young man who showed the smallest interest in Margaret. It seemed to the latter that Selina could not bear to be ignored by anyone, disregarding the young gentlemen who did take notice of her in favour of those who did not. She always wanted what she couldn't have, and Margaret wondered how Selina might behave this evening.

Margaret smoothed on her long, white kid gloves until there was not a wrinkle to be seen, picked up her fan, and went in search of her mama. Mrs Dashwood was putting the finishing touches to her appearance and the two ladies admired each other on sight. Margaret did think her mother looked very pretty and told her so.

"But the sight of you is so lovely to behold, Margaret," her mother declared, her voice cracking with emotion, "that it breaks my heart. How I wish your father could have lived to see what a beauty his daughter has turned out to be!"

"Oh, Mama, you are exaggerating, I'm sure, though I thank you for the compliment. Shall we go down now? Marianne wants us to be altogether when the Lawrences arrive. I think she is worried that Mr Willoughby may turn up after all."

"It is all such a worry to Marianne and the dear Colonel. And I am sure to say the wrong thing. If only your father were here to escort me, I am sure I would be equal to anything."

Margaret was anxious to divert the conversation away from the subject of her father, whose mention was apt to induce melancholy in her mother, who still mourned him with great sensibility. Miss Dashwood was in high spirits and knew she could with a little effort cajole her mother into being better humoured too. "Come along, Mama, I expect Admiral Strowbridge will want to claim the first dance. You are always a favourite with Selina's father."

"No more than with any of the other widowers in this county," Mrs Dashwood commented. "I daresay if I had a few more pounds to my name I should have had several offers by now, but as it is I have to content myself with being a favourite on the dance floor. In any case, I would not wish to marry again; I am perfectly content in my cottage."

"You should be careful, Mama, you never know where love might strike next!" cried Margaret with a laugh, taking her mother's arm and escorting her downstairs where the family was gathering.

The ballroom glittered with candlelight and jewels. The hum of chattering voices, the footfall of soft kid shoes pattering across the polished floor, sounds punctuated by merry peals of laughter, announced the expectation of the evening's entertainment. The musicians tuned their instruments to the swish of muslin and the waving of tall ivory feathers. Powdered and perfumed, poised and pretty, satins and silks shimmered on slender forms, admired by bucks, beaux, and brothers alike. Mamas and chaperones steered their offspring and charges into the paths of their unsuspecting targets with the graceful precision of an arrow fired from a crossbow. Every gleaming eye pursued its consort with the relentless vigour of a hound scenting a likely trail. The sport of husband hunting began.

Margaret and Mrs Dashwood took their seats with Elinor and Edward. The Lawrences were not to be seen anywhere yet, though most of the other guests had arrived. Margaret and her mother had been of the party that had greeted the guests in the hall. Marianne had seemed more than usually concerned when the Lawrences had not appeared, but Margaret guessed that her agitation was probably as a result of Mr Willoughby's impending arrival. Margaret wondered what could be keeping them and she was most curious to see that certain gentleman and how he might behave. The Middletons and Mrs Jennings were working through the crowds, finding old friends and relating all their news and gossip from Barton. Margaret was bewitched by all that she saw: the splendour of the men in black, the gaiety of the women like hothouse flowers with ivory petals or as brightly painted as exotic blossoms. She had not attended a ball of this magnitude at Delaford before. A little way off, she could see her sister Marianne, arm in arm with William, engaged in conversation with two gentlemen just arrived, one young and the other, who bore such a strong resemblance to the former that she quickly judged them to be father and son. The young man had an air of great confidence about him and a striking figure. She craned her neck to get a better view but it was so difficult, there were so many people threading their way across the room. A gap in the crowd presented her at last with a glimpse of his face; he seemed to be looking straight in her direction. Even from a distance she could see what an incredibly handsome young man he was, with a shock of very light, fair hair which waved back from his strong features. His eyes smiled at her though his mouth barely curved at the corners. The attraction was instant and Margaret was determined that she should be introduced before very much longer. Her heart began to hammer just a second later as she noted that her sister was urging the gentlemen in their

JANE ODIWE

direction. Both men had certainly had an effect on Marianne, who was chattering away and laughing in a very animated fashion. Margaret thought she had not seen her sister look quite so carefree for a while. She was more determined than ever to discover who these handsome men could be.

"Oh, look," said Mrs Dashwood, sitting up in her chair as she saw them approach. "I believe this must be Sir Edgar and his son, Henry."

"The Lawrences, Mama? No, it cannot be," declared Margaret, "they were to bring a large party with them. Besides, there is no lady with them; they would hardly have forgotten to bring Lady Lawrence. You are quite mistaken."

"Well, in that case, I cannot think who they must be," answered her mother. "Friends of Marianne's, I don't doubt. A rather handsome couple, do you not think, Margaret?"

Margaret remained silent on the matter. She did not want to divulge the fact that she had never seen anyone quite so worthy of her attention at a Delaford ball or any other, for that matter. She was quite intrigued.

Chapter 12

THE COLONEL AND MARIANNE were all beaming smiles as they presented their guests. "Sir Edgar Lawrence, may I introduce Mrs Dashwood and her daughter, Miss Margaret Dashwood," said William.

"I am delighted to meet you, my dears," Sir Edgar pronounced, taking their hands warmly, "I have heard so much about you. Please allow me to present my son, Henry, who has come home to Whitwell."

Margaret could not have been more surprised. Henry was not the coxcomb she was expecting. He took her hand and bowed, a ready smile on his lips. "I am delighted to meet you at last, Miss Dashwood," he said softly.

"I was just apologising to Mrs Brandon for the lateness of our appearance," cried Sir Edgar, "but I am afraid that my wife's constitution is not as strong as it should be and this afternoon, quite without any warning, she was taken with one of her dreadful attacks."

"Dear me," cried Mrs Dashwood, "I do hope Lady Lawrence is not ill."

"Poor Hannah is suffering, I am afraid, but she is used to these bouts which occur every now and then. The apothecary is with her now and so she is at ease. She insisted that Henry and I should come over to Delaford and as Mrs Willoughby suggested that she should keep her company, we decided that she could not be in better hands. Mrs Willoughby, you understand, is the wife of Henry's friend, Mr John Willoughby of Allenham. They have come to stay with us for a few days."

"Yes, Mrs Willoughby's name is known to me and I am acquainted with Mr Willoughby," stammered Mrs Dashwood, whose flustered manner betrayed her feelings. "His estate is not but two miles from Barton Cottage, where we live."

Sir Edgar turned to the Brandons. "Well, that is a surprise, fancy Mrs Dashwood being acquainted with Henry's friend. You have never met him yourself, William?"

"Ah, Mr Willoughby of Allenham," uttered the Colonel, as though recollecting a name he had forgotten. "I had not thought your Mr Willoughby was the same man."

"Then you do know him! Capital fellow. He's selling a property belonging to his wife, you know, Mrs Dashwood. She inherited it lately from an uncle and it seems they have enough to do with the upkeep of Combe Magna in Somerset and his place at Allenham to be much bothered with it. And my son Henry here is keen on it, very keen. He wants to be setting up his own place."

"And has Mr Willoughby stayed behind to keep company with Lady Lawrence, too?" asked Margaret who realised as soon as she had spoken that Marianne was glaring in her direction.

"Oh, no," cried Henry, "unfortunately, he was called away this morning to attend to some urgent matter over at Allenham where he is having a lot of work done to his house. There had been some dispute between the craftsmen working there, and he rode over after breakfast, assuring me that he would return later. A note arrived just before we left to say that he would be late but would come directly here as soon as he was able."

A look of sheer panic flashed across Marianne's face as it became clear that this information was completely new to her. Margaret guessed immediately that Marianne had assumed that Mr Willoughby would be too afraid to show his face and have no intention of coming to the ball. Now it was clear that she was not so sure.

Just at that moment, Mrs Jennings, accompanied by Sir John and Lady Middleton, joined the party and introductions were made all round. After this, the general lull in the conversation, coupled with the thoughtful silence of the Brandons, caused Mrs Jennings to speak out.

"Well, upon my soul, when is the dancing to start, Colonel? I expect young folk like these cannot wait to be on the floor, now can you?" she cried with a nod and a wink towards Margaret and Henry.

As if the conductor had heard her very words, the musicians started to play and with no time to feel further embarrassed by Mrs Jennings's insinuations, Margaret allowed herself to be swept off for the first dance of the evening, a rather stately minuet. The Brandons walked out to lead the dancing with the entire ballroom following suit. Indeed, there was hardly space to turn.

Margaret realised very quickly that all eyes were upon her and her ravishing partner. He, in his turn, seemed to delight in furthering her blushes by gazing far too often into her eyes. She did not know how he could see where he was going, so steady was his scrutiny. Margaret began to feel that perhaps there was something wrong with her face, had she a spot or a blemish she had not noticed? She was relieved when he started to speak.

"I do not think we shall disappoint the chaperones, Mrs Jennings in particular," he whispered into her hair.

Margaret looked at Henry with astonishment. "I'm sure I do not know what you mean, sir," she answered, stepping away from him, perfectly aware of his meaning.

"A handsome pair," he laughed, raising one eyebrow and speaking in imitation of the old lady, "he cannot take his eyes off her. How soon will they dance again and when can they be married?"

"Mr Lawrence, you are truly shocking!" Margaret exclaimed, but could not help laughing too.

"Come, Miss Dashwood, do you imagine they are discussing anything else, or for that matter is anyone discoursing on any other subject in the room? For instance, the two young ladies standing opposite us now with their respective partners have not uttered a word to them in the last five minutes. Would I be correct in assuming that they are friends of yours?"

Margaret saw, as she nodded her reply with great amusement, that Jane Wilton and Selina Strowbridge had been caught in mid conversation, talking over their respective partners, their eyes and mouths engaged on one subject. Margaret knew with certainty that the topic of their gossip was without any doubt that of she and her dancing partner.

"Let us give them something to talk about, Miss Dashwood," Henry continued, fixing her with earnest regard. "Look now into my eyes with feeling. Let us see how they react."

Margaret could not help but be amused by Henry; he was so charming, artless, and funny. She readily did as he asked. The outcome was as desired. Jane and Selina, not to mention half of the ladies who sat at the edges of the dance floor, were instantly animated in their speeches to one another.

"You will get me into trouble, Mr Lawrence. However shall I look my friends in the eye again?"

"I sincerely hope to make as much trouble as possible," he smirked as the dance came to an end, "and I hope and beg, Miss Dashwood, that you will partner me again before this evening is over. If we are to keep tongues wagging, I insist on at least the promise of two more turns, if not three."

Margaret was unable to answer. She could not have been more delighted. How she was to avoid the attentions of the likes of Mrs Jennings, however, she could not think and, whilst she had been flattered by Henry, she was not sure she was ready for the teasing she would have to bear. As they came off the floor, Jane and Selina bounded alongside to greet them, insisting in whispers on immediate introductions. They were joined a moment later by their other friend, Anne Courtney, who hung back until Margaret pulled her forward to meet their new acquaintance. He was very cordial in his manners if a little more reserved than when he had been with Margaret.

Selina was obviously most impressed and flirted with all the experience of a long practiced habit. "Let me introduce you to all our fine company, Mr Lawrence. You cannot guess what sort of a stir you've caused coming into the district, and I will tell you now that I hope you know it is your duty to dance with all eligible young ladies. If you have no one to dance with next, sir, I am most happy to oblige. I could never say no to a handsome man, Margaret will vouch for that!"

"It would be my pleasure, Miss Strowbridge," Henry gallantly answered. "I hope Miss Courtney and Miss Wilton will honour me with the two after that and then, Miss Dashwood, I think you desired the next two after that, did you not?"

Margaret was so shocked, she could not think what to say to him in immediate reply and by the time she had thought of a cutting retort he was gone, wrested away by Selina, who linked her arm in his and lost no time in making eyes at him.

"I think Mr Lawrence likes you very much to tease you in such a manner," said Anne with a wry smile.

"I assure you, I did not ask him to dance once, let alone twice," Margaret insisted. "Besides, I do not know what shall be said if I stand up with him for another two dances, indeed I do not! I think I shall refuse him!"

"Everyone will say you have set your cap at him, that's for sure," said Jane. "My brother Tom is hoping you will dance with him a little later."

"Well, I think you make a lovely couple and if you enjoy dancing with Henry Lawrence, then I think you should," said Anne. "Take no notice of the gossips, Margaret, they are only jealous."

"Sometimes it is prudent to listen to gossip," Jane went on. "I do not know that I shall be falling for the charms of Mr Lawrence, however teasing or handsome he may be. Charlotte Newby told me he is quite a wild young man. Her brother knows a friend of a friend of his cousin, who lives in Exeter. He says that Mr Lawrence and his friend, a Mr Willoughby, have been going about attending all-night card parties, roistering round the place at all hours with a noisy group of youths, racing their curricles down the High Street at midnight and across the sands at some seaside place."

"I hardly think Mr Lawrence has had time enough to partake in all that activity," cried Margaret, at once defending him. "I would not believe such a tale with so little proof of provenance. And even if he does like to drive fast, I do not think that makes him any different from most young men. I rather admire a gentleman with spirit!"

It was Anne's turn next on the arm of Mr Lawrence. Jane's brother Tom came to claim Margaret, and so for the time being she was forced to think of something and someone else.

Marianne's anxiety was such that she found it hard to fully enjoy herself, however well the evening's entertainment was progressing. She and William had not really had much of a chance to discuss the possibility of Willoughby's imminent appearance, apart from a few snatched words on the dance floor. Although they were both reconciled to think that there was a distinct possibility that he would come sooner or later, they had yet to relate to others in their party of his being known to the Lawrences and of the story that that involved. Colonel Brandon was inclined to think that it was best kept quiet until it became an absolute necessity to be divulged. Each privately knew there was little chance of keeping the affair secret, but were still clinging to false hope. Marianne could not think how she was to start to tell the Middletons or Mrs Jennings that Willoughby had been invited, but an instance arose sooner than she would have liked of it not being avoided. Sir Edgar Lawrence, being a jovial and sociable sort of fellow, had found a very willing partner in Mrs Jennings on all subjects of discourse. They had admired everything they saw about them, Mrs Jennings had talked at length on the subject of her daughters and grandchildren, and now it came to Sir Edgar's turn. He related all of his wife's history on her poor health, much to Mrs Jennings's great concern and curiosity, before he turned to the subject of Henry. The name of Willoughby soon being uttered could not escape the notice of Mrs Jennings, who spoke out with great alarm.

"My goodness, nay, it cannot be. Mr John Willoughby. Lord, bless me, are we talking of the same Mr Willoughby? He is to come here this evening, to Delaford? Are you quite sure? Does the Colonel know about this?"

Before Sir Edgar had a chance to reply, Marianne, who had been observing this contretemps from a little distance, stepped up. "Excuse me, Mrs Jennings, I am so sorry to butt in, but I have come to claim my dance and I will brook no refusal. Sir Edgar, you will break my heart if you do not keep your promise." She took his arm immediately and led him off, leaving Mrs Jennings, her jaw slack and her mouth open. Marianne saw her stare after them and watched her turn instantly to her daughter, Lady Middleton. Thankfully, William was there to charm Mrs Jennings into accepting a turn about the dance floor and, having taken in all that had passed between her and Sir Edgar, removed her from her daughter's side. Brandon soon took Mrs Jennings into his confidence, relating the tale of Sir Edgar's house buying and Henry's connection with the Willoughbys, whilst extracting a promise of her silence on the subject. Of course Mrs Jennings could not resist dropping a few hints to Marianne later that she knew all about the episode, adding that she would be confidentiality itself, excepting any occasion where that good-for-nothing fellow might show his true colours. Upon witnessing such a scenario, she would not hold back to give him a piece of her mind. Needless to say, Marianne did not feel consoled by these reassurances.

In the meantime, Margaret enjoyed her two dances with Henry and had passed from feeling a little cross with him for his teasing ways to have elevated him in her mind to the most wildly romantic suitor she had ever known. He insisted on dancing with her again and this time she made no attempt to refuse him. She thought her fondness for dancing with Henry had gone unnoticed, but Elinor was waiting for her with an expression that told her she had observed all three consecutive dances.

"Margaret, I am very pleased to see that you are making Mr Lawrence feel welcome, but I think perhaps you are taking your duties as a hostess a little too enthusiastically. It is not seemly, dear, to dance with a gentleman three times in a row. Besides, there are many young ladies here tonight who I am sure would like to take their turn."

"Oh, Elinor, I would not have done so but he insisted," declared Margaret. "I would hate Mr Lawrence to think I am rude and that I did not enjoy his company. What else could a girl do?"

"You could have declined him gracefully," Elinor admonished. "A gentleman, one worth pursuing, would not put a young girl in such a situation. People will talk, you know."

"Oh, let them talk," Margaret declared. "I do not care about the opinions of old ladies with nothing better to do than sit and spread malicious falsehood about others. And understand this; I am not pursuing Mr Lawrence, whatever you might think. I hardly know the man!"

Margaret turned on her heel, leaving Elinor to sigh and wonder at the similarity between her sisters, both hotheads, both determined to have their way in everything and utterly insensible of the devastation they caused around them. Well, there was hope, Elinor thought, when she considered how Marianne had improved since her marriage. Though it was impossible not to feel concerned at this moment. Marianne looked as if she had just seen a ghost. Elinor thought she had never seen her looking so drawn and pale. Perhaps she should talk to her at supper and find out if anything was amiss.

The gong rang out, calling the weary dancers to rest awhile and replenish their energy. All the guests hurried off to the dining room, where tables were set, groaning under the weight of a magnificent spread. The musicians laid aside their instruments and dashed to the servant's hall for a glass of negus and a bowl of soup. Colonel Brandon ushered his guests, Sir Edgar and Henry Lawrence, to his table, where much to her great delight, Margaret already sat, with her mother, the Middletons, and Mrs Jennings. There was such a hubbub and frenzied bustle about the room as people found their chairs and struck up conversation. Every little party was talking nineteen to the dozen, piling plates with cold meat and hot pies, sweets and sorbets, filling glasses with ice cold wine. Everyone had so much to say and wanted to say it all at once. The sound of chattering, braying, prattling, and screeching, punctuated by howling laughter or tittering giggles, added to the delirious atmosphere.

Henry took his seat next to Margaret. "This evening is surpassing all my expectations," he whispered, smiling into her eyes. "This is so much fun, do you not agree, Miss Dashwood?"

"I do, indeed, Mr Lawrence," she replied. "I am enjoying myself very much, though I would more so if I felt we were not under so much scrutiny. Do not look now, but we are being observed."

"Let me guess, Miss Dashwood," he responded, "Lady Middleton and her sweet mother are watching us and, no doubt, trying to catch the essence of our conversation. Hmm, let me see. I must give them something on which to ponder and discuss."

He selected a dish of pink, heart-shaped marchpane and, taking one between thumb and forefinger, proffered it toward her, proclaiming in an audible voice for all to hear, "Miss Dashwood, may I offer my heart? Pray, do not leave me in suspense, I beg you. Do not break it, but take it and devour it whole!"

Margaret felt mortified, especially when she saw Lady Middleton exchange knowing glances with Mrs Jennings. Everyone laughed when Margaret refused to take the heart and even more so when Henry begged again and it was only when Mrs Jennings spoke that the table fell silent.

"Colonel Brandon, where is your dear wife? Has she not come in to supper? I cannot think where she can be and for that matter, I cannot recall when I saw her last. I hope she is not ailing; she did look a trifle pale after the last dance. Bless my soul, but I must say it is probably wiser that she sit down more often."

Margaret looked about the room and, in so doing, caught her sister Elinor's solemn expression. They had each perceived the hints that Mrs Jennings was making and knew their sister would be far from pleased. But apart from that neither of them could see Marianne and both recognised the solicitous mien in the other.

Chapter 13

JUST BEFORE THE SUPPER bell had sounded, sending the throng swarming like hornets to the dining room, Marianne had been waylaid by her butler.

"There is a gentleman asking to speak with you, my lady," he said in a low voice, "a Mr John Willoughby. He wishes a private interview with you. Shall I send him away or summon the Colonel?"

Marianne had felt very tempted by the offer to send for help but knew that she would have to be the one to grant him an interview. She owed him that much at least, and she was gratified by his conduct. He had not come waltzing through the door expecting to be greeted with open arms.

"No, that will not be necessary, Thompkins, I will come right away," she answered, smoothing her gown and pushing back a strand of hair that had escaped from her headdress.

"Very well, madam, he is waiting in the small parlour." Thompkins led his mistress away, leaving her at the door of the room but remaining outside in case he was needed. He did not like the idea of gentlemen conducting audiences with Mrs Brandon in the middle of the night. He felt that the Colonel ought to have been with his wife or seen him himself, especially as the gentleman had been so adamant that he should talk only to Mrs Brandon. It was not right.

John Willoughby was standing, leaning against the mantlepiece when she entered the room. He turned with a bow and as he did so, Marianne tried to compose her feelings. She imagined that she must look no more sophisticated or grown up than when they had first met. Finding it difficult to look upon his countenance, she was unable to meet his gaze when at last she found the courage to raise her eyes. Why did she have so little confidence when faced with his impeccable figure? He looked more imposing than ever as he towered before her, dressed for the evening in a black coat that turned his eyes into dark stones of glistening granite. She tried to tell herself that she should not be afraid, that she could withstand any meeting. After all, she was the mistress of Delaford, with this grand house and her noble husband behind her. But as he spoke, all those feelings fragmented and vanished like the vapour frosting the windows. She was seventeen again and just as gauche.

"I had intended to come to the ball this evening at your invitation and indeed, the Lawrences are expecting me, Mrs Brandon," he said with some agitation.

"Yes, Mr Willoughby, I am aware of that fact," was all Marianne managed to say.

"I do not imagine, however, that my presence here is really desired," he continued, pacing across the room to stand within inches of her.

"I do not understand, Mr Willoughby," Marianne replied, drawing courage from the fact that he seemed far more ill at ease than she. "If that is what you have suspected or surmised, then I cannot think why you are here or why you would wish to have it confirmed."

"I suppose I hoped, in a small way," he asserted, "that you might really have decided to forgive me and welcome me into your home. I realise it was a vain hope. I can see by your very expression that I shall not find a welcome here from you. I hardly expected to find one from your husband, but I hoped to find forgiveness in you."

"Mr Willoughby, it is not as simple as you make it appear; it is not a question of forgiveness. Cannot you see my situation or that of my husband?"

"I see that I have little choice in the matter," he sighed.

"Well, now you have come to that conclusion, I will leave you to make your decision," Marianne declared, feeling quite strong and concluding that she had the better of him, despite the violence of her heart beating in her chest. "You must decide whether it would be prudent to stay, to join your friends and face my husband, or whether it might be an altogether better idea to go back to Exeter or wherever you are residing at present."

"Why did you come to Allenham that day?" he said, fixing her with his dark eyes.

Marianne looked away. She could not tell him the truth and she knew if she allowed him to look too closely, he would know her innermost sensations. "I thought your house was on fire, I could see plumes of smoke," she lied, picking up a book from the table and examining its cover closely. She breathed deeply and met his eyes. "I came out of curiosity."

"And were you curious to see what had become of Allenham?" he begged.

"I do not know why you are asking these questions, Mr Willoughby," Marianne cried with exasperation, slamming the book down again on the table. "You should know that Allenham holds no interest whatsoever, as far as I am concerned. Now, tell me, Mr Willoughby, what is your decision?"

"Please answer my questions, Mrs Brandon. Would you have me stay? Do you wish me to go? I will do as you bid. I do not want to cause undue suffering. If my presence will be an embarrassment, and I fear it must, I am ready to depart. But I will not go until I have heard it from your lips."

Marianne hesitated for only a second before she heard her voice proclaiming her wishes, with clarity and determination. "Then go, Mr Willoughby. I wish you to leave Delaford immediately."

He stood, his head bent in contemplation before he looked up at her. Marianne could barely witness the sorrow in his eyes. He looked as though he had been struck and his expression was like that of a wounded animal, whose eyes begged compassion. Wanting to tell him that he could stay, that she wished to offer him her hand in friendship, she remained silent and bit her lip. Staying, she knew, was not an option she could place at his disposal.

"If it pleases you, madam, I shall take my leave," Mr Willoughby cried, making a low sweep and walking out without a backward glance.

Marianne returned to the dining room as soon as she was able. Telling William about their visitor was a priority, but if she could avoid doing so just yet, she would. She was relieved that there had been no scene and most of all, that Willoughby had desired no confrontation with William. Her spirits rose. Moving about the supper tables, she chatted and laughed as though she hadn't a care and by the time she came under Mrs Jennings's scrutiny, she gaily dismissed her enquiries with a pretty tale about having to speak to the housekeeper on important matters. But she had to tell someone of her ordeal and as supper came to an end and the whole room flocked back to the ballroom, she was able to commandeer her sisters, who listened with much sympathy. As she came to the conclusion of her story, who should appear before them but Henry Lawrence, eager to dance with Margaret once again. As Margaret accepted readily and skipped off to the dance floor, Marianne could not help but notice Elinor's countenance.

"What is the matter, Elinor? I know that expression of old, you do not look at all happy. Do you think that I should have said more to Mr Willoughby?"

"No, Marianne, it is our sister I have my concerns about," Elinor replied, watching Margaret and Henry eagerly taking their places in the set. "She has danced too many times with that young man. He is rather too enthusiastic for my liking. And I cannot say that I am at all happy about Mr Lawrence's connection with Mr Willoughby, whatever might be said on the latter now being a respectable character."

"Henry is utterly charming, Elinor. He is just like his father. And his connection with Willoughby is not really based in friendship but in business. I am sure that Henry's desire for a house of his own is at the heart of their association."

"Nevertheless, Margaret should not be throwing herself at him like that!" Elinor gestured toward the floor where the happy couple danced, apparently with eyes and ears for no one else. Margaret was gazing up at Henry with a face shining with adoration. Marianne observed the picture they made with feelings of pleasure. Margaret's animated dancing, her sparkling eyes, and vivacity told her all she needed to know. Her sister might deny it in the morning, but Marianne was convinced that Margaret was falling in love. Everything was working out exactly as she had planned. "Elinor, you are being too silly for words. It is clear he is as smitten as she. What a match it will be!"

Elinor opened her mouth to respond once again, when the sisters were both joined by Sir Edgar, beaming from ear to ear. "Why, it does my old heart good to see such splendid dancing. What a handsome couple they make."

"They do indeed, Sir Edgar," Marianne heartily agreed, nudging her sister to make a response. Elinor smiled and nodded her assent, though Marianne knew that her warm acknowledgement belied her true feelings.

"I think Mr Willoughby must have run into problems at Allenham. What a pity, he was looking forward to joining our party. I expect he is most upset," said Sir Edgar. "But Henry has been so occupied that I do not think he has even noticed his absence," he went on. "He certainly seems to be enjoying Miss Margaret's company."

"Indeed, I would venture to say that the delight appears to be on both sides," Marianne replied with a laugh.

"I have been forming a little plan," Sir Edgar continued, "a little scheme which I hope will be to all our liking. The Goose Fair at Colystone is to be held next Saturday and I wonder if it is the sort of amusement that you might both enjoy, Mrs Brandon, Mrs Ferrars. I would be honoured if you would join us to make a party to attend the Fair, with the Colonel, Mr Ferrars, and all your other guests, of course. I am sure Henry would like it above all things if Miss Margaret were to come, too."

"I should love that, Sir Edgar," declared Marianne with excitement. "And I can speak for the Colonel, too. I know he will love to come. I'm sure such an outing will be more than agreeable to Margaret, also. I cannot speak for my mother, the Middletons, or Mrs Jennings of course, but we will be delighted to come!"

"Unfortunately, Mr Ferrars and I are otherwise engaged," answered Elinor in a serious tone. "We have our visiting to do on Saturday and one of our parishioners, Mrs Thomas, is quite unwell at present. She looks forward to our calling on her so much that I would hate to disappoint the poor old lady."

"Surely you could miss Mrs Thomas's visit just once, Elinor. We will have such fun!" Marianne entreated.

"No, I could not upset the dear lady, and she is not the only one who relies on us, you know. There are many in the village that look forward to seeing Edward. He would not miss his duties, Marianne."

"Well, my dear," Sir Edgar butted in, "I hope you shall visit us up at Whitwell on another occasion. Bring your children too, I always love to hear the sound of laughter in the house, and now Henry is grown it is not the same. Still, we can always hope that the place will be filled with grandchildren, one of these days. Let us hope it will not be too long before that happy event, eh, Mrs Brandon?" Sir Edgar winked at Marianne, who could not help smirking also. He excused himself with a bow, saying he would mention his thoughts and ideas to Henry, and then left them.

"See, Sir Edgar thinks they are as smitten as I do," Marianne announced with triumph.

"Oh, Marianne, it is too soon to be making such judgements. They have only just met and we know nothing of his character. His family may be good but that is not enough for a suitable marriage in my opinion. I do not understand how you can be marrying off our sister before you know anything about Henry Lawrence."

"I have seen enough to make my judgement and if Margaret loves him, that is good enough for me," Marianne retorted. "And now, if it is not too late, I shall go and claim the last dance of the evening with my dear husband. Come, Elinor, where is Edward? Let us make merry!"

Chapter 14

EVERYONE DECLARED THE BALL had been a great success. All were merry at breakfast, none more so than Margaret, who seemed to take great enjoyment in dropping Henry's name into the conversation at every opportunity. She didn't even appear to mind when teased by Mrs Jennings, who pronounced that she was sure Henry would call before the day was out.

Marianne was subdued and lost in her own thoughts. She had been going to tell William what had passed with Mr Willoughby when they had at last gone to bed in the small hours, but the time for confession had never seemed to be quite right. In the morning, there had been so much to think about and organise for all their guests, that again the moment for relating the exchange between her and Willoughby did not take place. Marianne began to think that there was little point in upsetting William unnecessarily. Perhaps it would be wise not to mention the fact that he had called; after all, there was nothing to be gained by troubling her husband. And it was certain that the knowledge of his wife being privy to a private interview with that gentleman would, without doubt, distress Colonel Brandon. Marianne decided she would not mention it.

The menfolk took themselves off to go shooting after breakfast, and the ladies were left to amuse themselves with a variety of diversions. Mrs Jennings and Lady Middleton sat with Marianne and her mother in the drawing room to have over the events of the previous evening. Margaret escaped as soon as she could into the gardens outside. She made her way to the yew arbour with a favourite book, although she suspected before she had even reached the seat that she would not find time for much reading. Margaret sought solitude in order to daydream and spend her time in reverie without being disturbed from her pursuit or having to answer impertinent questions. From her vantage point, on rising ground behind the house, she could see the road below, but there was nothing much to interest her there; not even a carriage rumbling by to take her notice. Opening her book, she began to read, but the printed words soon swam before her eyes in a muddle. All she could see was an image of Henry in her head. Henry's handsome face was before her, smiling with that expression, half tender, half mocking. "I wish Mrs Jennings were right for once," she thought, "how lovely it would be if Henry were to call." She twisted sideways, pulling her feet up onto the bench, and wrapped her cloak around her legs against the cold seeping up from the ground. Just as she was wishing that Henry were there by her side, her attention was caught by the sight of a horse being led by its master along the roadside. The man was talking to the horse, which appeared to be in some pain, limping along. Margaret watched with her heart in her mouth as it became apparent that the young gentleman was none other than the very person she most wished to see.

From her seat, concealed amongst the yew boughs, she was quite hidden from the road. She observed him walk the length of the thoroughfare until he came opposite her viewpoint. Margaret could sit no longer and watch. Jumping up, she ran out from her hiding place and down the slope of the lawn, past the sundial, through the yew avenue and along the narrow path, to an ivy-covered door set within the garden wall. Trying to turn the rusty key in the lock gave her difficulty and she feared she would not be able to accomplish this task before he had long passed by. At last the key turned and the door opened with a creak. She glimpsed his retreating figure and called out his name. "Mr Lawrence, Mr Lawrence, good morning!"

Margaret saw him stop and look around in surprise. "Why, good morning to you, Miss Dashwood," he answered with a bow. "What a pleasant surprise. However, I am dashed if I know how you discovered my whereabouts. If I were of a suspicious nature I might think you had been spying on me."

Margaret chose to ignore this impudence. "What has happened to your horse?"

"I am not certain except to say he appears to be lame, a stone in his hoof, I daresay. I must get him to the farrier to have him looked at."

"Pray tell, Mr Lawrence, where were you headed?" asked Margaret, knowing that his destination must be Delaford House. "You appear to be rather far from home."

"I came to call on you, Miss Dashwood, as you are well aware," he answered, and gazed so directly into her eyes that she could not look at him.

She looked back toward the house for somewhere to fix her eyes. "You could have the groomsman look at him, but I do not

JANE ODIWE

think you will be able to lead your horse through this doorway. Besides, this part of the garden has too many narrow pathways, there is not enough room for a man and his horse."

"No, but there is a post just along here where I might tie him up, so he can rest. And as you say, I could alert Jackson. I can fetch my horse in a little while, after he has been seen. In the meantime you could show me round the garden."

"Will you not come up to the house and say how d'ye do?" asked Margaret as she watched him tie up his horse. She felt rather uneasy about having stopped him now. If Marianne or, more particularly, Elinor had found out that she had behaved in such a manner, they would be shocked. Not only shocked but horrified that she had been so outspoken. And she was not sure that being alone with him in the garden would be approved of as pleasing conduct.

"I do not think that will be necessary," he smirked. "After all, I only came to see you and no one need be any the wiser. Will you not show me round? I remember an old yew arbour at the top of the lawn where I played hide and seek as a small boy with Uncle William. Is it still there?" He smiled at her so artlessly that Margaret was instantly charmed.

"Yes, I was sitting there when I saw you. There is a capital view of the road and it is the best place in the world to hide."

"Show me."

Margaret knew it was wrong but as much as she told herself that she should insist on their going up to the house, her feet immediately disobeyed her. They left their dewy prints on the rain-soaked grass and climbed the ascent to the ancient arbour, Margaret conscious that he followed closely behind with loping strides. The yew arbour loomed before them, like a giant plum pudding, its entrance almost concealed by foliage. Margaret stopped just outside.

Henry swept past and was swallowed up out of sight by the giant arms of the dark yews. Margaret looked about her. What should she do? To follow him would be most inappropriate. She heard Henry call her name. "Miss Dashwood, look here," he called.

Hesitantly, she entered the space. Henry was sat upon the seat but rose when she stepped forward. The trees dripped over their heads and a magpie chattered above, breaking the silence that ensued.

"Look here, upon the trunk," Henry said, pointing to a mark at waist height.

Margaret bent down to peer closer and saw the carving in the bark. The initials H. A. L. were hewn into the old tree. "Are they your initials?" she asked.

Henry nodded. "Uncle William gave me the knife. It was just before we left for France and I was sad to be leaving England. He said that a part of me would always remain here, not only in the hearts and minds of my family but here at Delaford, in the very soul of the place. He was very kind."

"He is one of the kindest people I know," Margaret agreed. She stood up to become conscious of their close proximity. That he was staring at her, she was acutely sensible.

"Thank you for dancing with me last night, Miss Dashwood," he said in a low voice.

"It was my pleasure, Mr Lawrence," she answered. She still could not bring herself to meet his eyes.

"Come," he entreated, taking her hand with one of his and reaching into his pocket with the other. "Make Delaford part of your history, too."

Before she had a chance to snatch back her hand, she realised she had completely misconstrued his actions. He had a small knife in his other hand, which he pressed into the one he was holding, with a plea to do as he had done in the past and carve her name. She grinned up at him before cutting into the bark, whittling away at the wood until her initials were carved next to his.

"M. E. D., Margaret Elizabeth Dashwood," Henry guessed.

"I suppose you think you are very clever," she retorted, "but you are quite wrong. I do not think you will guess my middle name in a month of Sundays. However, whilst you contemplate the possibilities, I have something to say. It is my turn to guess your name. Let me think, a letter A has many possibilities…" Margaret paused and was bold enough to look him up and down, with her head on one side and her hands on her hips.

Henry laughed.

"I do not know what you find so amusing, sir, because I am never wrong in these matters. Hmm… Alexander, I think. Yes, you look like a Henry Alexander to my mind!" she announced with a chuckle.

Henry laughed again and shook his head. "You are entirely mistaken, Miss Dashwood. I shall give you a clue. My name has a starring role in *Paradise Lost,* to name but one book in which it can be found."

"Oh, that is too easy, you must be Adam!" Margaret cried.

"Then perhaps you are my Eve. Am I not correct?"

"Nothing like, the E stands for Evelina," Margaret admitted, blushing as she spoke.

"Precisely, just as I said, you are my Eve. Have you come here to tempt me, pretty girl?"

Margaret could not hide her confusion. She was utterly aghast at his bold manner and flirtatious words. "Mr Lawrence, I think it is time for me to go back to the house. Marianne will be wondering where I am."

"I do not think your sister will mind you talking to me," he declared, taking a step nearer.

Margaret knew this was probably true, but even so she knew it was wrong to spend so much time alone with Mr Lawrence. If she were found out there would be trouble.

Henry turned toward the trunk of the tree once more to busy himself with the knife, carving fresh marks into the bark.

"I really must go, Mr Lawrence, it has been good to see you again," Margaret faltered, holding out her hand to say goodbye.

"You would not accept my heart when I offered it to you yesterday," he said. "But you see it carved here on this tree, right next to your name." He took her hand, holding it firmly within his grasp, and Margaret wondered whether he would ever let it go. She knew she must depart soon before someone came looking for her, despite the fact that she was enjoying the sensation of her hand clasped in Henry's. At last she managed to look up at him to meet his steady contemplation. His countenance bore such an expression that she could not tell whether he was laughing at her or whether he was completely serious. He raised her hand to his lips and then Margaret knew she must leave. Without a glance behind her, she snatched her hand away and ran. She ran as fast as her legs would take her and it was only when she reached the safety of her bedchamber that she dared to look out of the window. The outlook onto the garden gave a tantalising glimpse of the arbour, but she could not see nearly enough of it to be able to ascertain whether Henry was still there. She watched for half an hour and decided at last that he must have gone in search of the groom moments after she had left. She would be very careful in future, she thought, not to be left alone with him again. But, however hard Margaret tried to be cross with him, she found it to be impossible and found herself caressing the spot where his lips had brushed her skin with tender care.

Chapter 15

ON THE EVE OF the Goose Fair, Colonel Brandon returned
from an excellent morning of shooting to discover that he was
the recipient of bad news, a letter, which demanded his immediate attention. Miss Williams had written to tell him that little
Lizzy was unwell again, but assured him that it was no more than
one of the hundreds of childhood ailments that small people were
apt to contract. There were hints of fever and infections, and
though Miss Williams had stated that there was no reason for
alarm, that very insistence gave the Colonel cause for concern.
Not more than a few weeks had lapsed since little Lizzy had suffered the last bout, a sore throat and fever, which had brought
her very low indeed. She was a frail child at the best of times, and
her recovery had been slow. Brandon knew that Miss Williams
was quite capable of nursing her daughter back to health, but he
wanted to ensure Lizzy had the best care, the attention of the
apothecary from Lyme, and the most suitable medicines. There
was nothing else to do; he would make a visit and secure all
that was necessary to aid Lizzy's return to good health. Telling

Marianne of his plans, however, was a task he was not going to enjoy. His wife seemed to resent the trips away from home that he had been forced to make lately, and he was certain that this one would be no exception. But what could he do? If anything happened to Lizzy, he would never forgive himself; her welfare and that of her mother were as important to him as that of his own wife and children. It could not be helped, and Marianne would have to understand that he had no choice but to go and ensure the well-being of his dependants.

Marianne's reaction was as exactly as he had feared. "Miss Williams assures you it is no more than a common cold; how can you think of leaving us? A letter from you to the apothecary at Lyme will more than suffice; there is no need to go gallivanting across the country because Lizzy has sneezed once or twice. And what of our guests? You cannot abandon me to their sole enter-tainment. However shall I manage on my own?"

"You forget, Marianne, that I have certain obligations and duties. I cannot leave Eliza and her daughter to their fate. You cannot know the anxiety I will suffer until I have seen Lizzy with my own eyes and know that she is well."

Marianne knew this to be true. Her husband would not rest easy until he knew the truth of the situation. He had never recovered from the fact that he had been too late to save Lizzy's grandmother, and Marianne realised that to persuade him from doing other than rushing to their side was fruitless. But she was not happy and felt herself hard done by. It always seemed that William was too eager to spend time with his ward and her daughter. Marianne was jealous of every occasion, every period that was spent in the company of Miss Williams. She tried once more.

"We have our invitation from Sir Edgar to attend the fair tomorrow. Surely you have not forgotten? It will not be possible for us to attend if you do not come, and Margaret is so looking forward to spending the day with Henry."

"I do not see why you cannot honour the invitation," the Colonel replied. "Sir John will accompany you with Mrs Jennings and Lady Middleton. Margaret will not have to be disappointed. And nobody will care much whether I am there or not, I am sure."

"I will care, very much!" Marianne protested. "I will miss you so much, it is never the same when you are away. Please do not go."

"I have no choice, Marianne, you know that. But I promise that as soon as I am satisfied that my presence is no longer needed, I shall return. We have our trip to London to look forward to, and that will be upon us before we know where we are. In the meantime, do not imagine that your suffering will be your own. I will miss you too, more than I can say."

"Will you, will you miss me?" begged Marianne. Suddenly, more than anything, she did not want Brandon to go. She felt quite afraid, though of what she could not say. She clung to him and looked up beseechingly into his eyes. "I love you so much, my darling."

William Brandon looked down at his beautiful wife and not for the first time did he wonder how he had managed to engage the heart of one so utterly divine to his way of thinking. It tore his heart to see her look at him so, pleading desperately not to leave her, but his duty to all those who needed him was so strong that nothing would have diverted him from what he believed was the correct course. "I think it best if I leave immediately. As you will be engaged for Colystone tomorrow, there will be plenty to occupy you, my dear. I know how much it will amuse you to see how just you were in fancying a love match between Henry and Margaret."

"Then you think as I do!" Marianne exclaimed. "I was right, was I not? Oh, William, I am so happy for Margaret. It is early days, I know, but I have never felt more certain of anything in my life than an attraction between them. And I am sure Sir Edgar is keen on the match, too."

"Write and tell me all about it; indeed, it is my fervent wish that you will write to me every day, Marianne. I hope I shall be able to return in a few days, not more than three or four with good fortune on my side. The sooner I am gone, the quicker I will return."

Marianne knew it was useless to try to persuade her husband to anything different. "Please do not be long, William. We will all await your safe journey home."

"Come closer, my love," whispered William, pulling her with a force that took his wife almost off her feet to wrap her up in his arms. His kisses came with such passion that Marianne was left breathless and wanting more. But for all her responding affection and keen demonstration, it appeared to her that the Colonel was keen to be gone. With a final, dismissive peck on her forehead and a last goodbye, he took his leave, shouting for his servant to come quickly. "Let us make haste, Johnson, we have a road to travel and we have wasted time enough. If the carriage is ready, let us go!"

Marianne followed her husband from the room, saw him snatch up his travelling cloak, and run the length of the great hall to the waiting carriage outside. With a heavy heart she turned to make her way to the drawing room where their guests were sitting, more than likely wondering why their hosts had deserted them. She fixed her best smile on her countenance before entering the room to offer her explanations, telling them all that her husband was called away on business.

Entertaining her guests for the remainder of the day and evening was not as difficult as Marianne had contemplated, despite Mrs Jennings's constant enquiries on the habits of her husband. However, she was glad when the time came to lie down in her bed. She tried not to think about Brandon but could not help wondering what sort of a picture the Williams family made in their snug cottage. When they had first been married, the Colonel had invited Marianne to go with him on his visits, but she had declined, divided as she was by strong emotion. On the one hand, she did not want her husband to feel that she did not trust him or that she wished to interfere in his concerns in any way. After all, Eliza had been a part of his life before Marianne had even met him. She was certainly curious about Miss Williams and knew about the great love her husband had enjoyed with Eliza's mother. On the other hand, she did not wish to meet Willoughby's daughter. Marianne had feared that her own feelings would have been betrayed if she had set eyes on the baby, as she was then. Hardly had she admitted it to herself, but Marianne knew deep inside that holding his child would have stirred passions she had learned to hide and suppress. Although William never really discussed his visits in great detail and appeared to regard them as offices of duty, Marianne still speculated on his real feelings about his other family. To see him rush off to their side with such eagerness prompted deep resentment, even if she told herself that she was being silly. And when she contemplated the matter, tossing and turning until the pearly dawn light stole a pale finger through the curtains, she began to muse on the possibility that he may prefer to spend more of his time with those others that loved and depended on him.

Chapter 16

MARIANNE HAD DRIFTED INTO sleep eventually, but the hour for waking came much too soon. Sally came to announce that the sun was shining in a clear blue sky, with an early mist rising about the Park, promising a heavenly day for the Goose Fair. Marianne allowed herself to be dressed, trying to ignore Sally's probing questions about the dark circles under her eyes.

Margaret had no difficulty in rising. She had slept well and awoken to the feeling of immense well-being and happiness. Dressing with very great care, she would not admit her careful ministrations to be for any particular purpose, other than to please herself. But as she stood before the looking glass to consider her reflection, Margaret did hope that Henry would be delighted by her appearance.

After breakfast they were to set off in a great procession of carriages to meet the Lawrences on the turnpike road, at a suitable distance between Delaford and Whitwell for the journey to Colystone. James, whom his mother felt was not old enough for such frivolity, was to be tended at home by his nurse, though his protestations at being left behind were heard by everyone. Marianne kissed and petted him, drying his tears with her kerchief, promising him sugarplums and a juggler on a stick, which seemed to do the trick. When all was quiet again and her guests gathered in the hall, Marianne gave the signal to make their way out to the carriages and they were off, bowling down the driveway in a flurry of high expectation. Within the half hour they arrived at the agreed spot to find Sir Edgar and Henry Lawrence beaming from ear to ear and hallooing at the sight of the entourage, from their high perch phaeton. They both leapt down from their seats as the carriages came to a standstill. Everyone stretched their legs and reintroduced themselves with great merriment.

Margaret was relieved to see that Henry immediately singled her out. She had been rather worried that he might have been cross with her after she had abandoned him in the garden. He asked her how she did and when she held out her hand to shake his, he took it and held it, for all the world as if he would never let it go, before swiftly kissing her fingertips.

"I saw you, Miss Margaret, with your beau," said Mrs Jennings, wagging a knowing finger in Margaret's direction as they started to scramble back into the coaches with as much fervour as they had got out of them. "He can scarcely take his eyes off you! I know how it will be at the Fair, neither of you shall look nor talk to another soul, but at one another. Well, I was young once, you know, and I have not forgotten what it is to be head over heels. And he is quite worth the trouble of catching. It is as well to fall in love with a young man of wealth and good looks as any other!"

Margaret's expression left no doubt of her feelings once they set off and were out of earshot, raising her eyes heavenwards at her sister. "How long am I to endure this nonsense from Mrs Jennings?" she pleaded.

"Well, I should like to say you might be spared once you are married, my dear sister," returned Marianne, "but unfortunately you will find Mrs Jennings has only just begun. I hardly have to suppress a yawn or refuse a glass of wine to discover I am accused of being about to give birth to triplets."

Margaret laughed until her mother rebuked them both. "Marianne, you are too unkind. Mrs Jennings may be rather inquisitive but she means well, I know," interrupted her mama. "She adores you and your wonderful family and has always expressed her delight in your marriage to the Colonel." Mrs Dashwood sighed at the mention of Brandon. "What a pity it is that William could not be with us today."

Marianne nodded and as she watched the landscape flying by, the sun warming her face as she peered out of the window, she fell into a silent reverie. Had William arrived safely in Lyme? She had had no word yet but she hoped there would be a letter waiting for her when she got home. In her mind's eye she could see him setting up at the Three Cups Inn, being shown to his room where after the briefest inspection, he would be mounting his horse and riding the short distance to the village where Eliza would welcome him with open arms. She could picture the cosy, intimate family picture they would make, William rushing to Lizzy's side. Perhaps she was wrapped in blankets on a sofa by the fire. He would kneel at her side, tenderly brushing the hair from her temples, and see to every small need. Marianne wondered about the conversations they would all exchange, knew how pleased they would be to see and talk to him, from what William had divulged in the past. "It is not that I wish to be resentful but

I cannot help feeling that William has run off to see them rather more quickly than I would like. To be a man, in command of one's life, to do exactly as he pleases must be a delightful state of being. I cannot just leave whenever I wish, I would not dream of abandoning my child on a whim to go gallivanting tens of miles to see to people who are not even my blood relations." But Marianne knew in her heart that she was being peevish. What their lives must be like, she could not really imagine. To live as an outcast from true society as Eliza did would be a fate she could not endure. Although the villagers in their own community treated the little family with kindness, they were not really completely a part of it. Eliza's education placed her far above her neighbours and yet because of her circumstances, she was not considered their equal. How it must be to know that they could never be a part of the life that Marianne enjoyed, able to move freely in the best circles in the West Country and in London, received by some of the noblest families in the land was a misfortune that she knew she would never have to contemplate. Compassion she could feel, but she admitted privately that it was mixed with emotions of envy and displeasure.

The first sight of Colystone afforded as much pleasure as Marianne had anticipated. Even before they reached the village green the sounds of excited crowds chattering and hallooing, musicians strumming, beating, or blowing their instruments could be heard above the fervent din. People surged along the byway, making the carriages' progress rather slow down the narrow lane. In the distance Margaret could make out flags waving atop the bright awnings of the stalls set about the green. As soon as they could alight, the entire party eagerly stepped down and looked to Sir Edgar for direction.

"Well, my dears, my suggestion is that we roam about the place at leisure over the next few hours and that as soon as the church clock has rung its bells at three, we should all meet at the inn for dinner, if we are not all too full of sugarplums and ginger-bread by then." He laughed at his own good humour. "I should be delighted if anyone wishes to accompany me. I will be attending the auction of the geese a little later on but I think for now we should make haste to watch the procession."

Forming a little parade of their own with Sir Edgar, Marianne, and Mrs Dashwood in front, followed closely by Mrs Jennings and all of the Middletons, they progressed alongside the tumultuous swarm of bodies. As might be expected, it was not long before such a large group began to break apart and form smaller parties. Henry and Margaret soon found that due to their complete inattention to the others they swiftly became detached from the company.

"Look, here comes the pageant now," declared Henry as a vast parade of costumed minstrels, pipers, and medieval maidens marched around the green, singing and playing as they strolled. "There will be a Mummer's play this afternoon, I daresay, with Saint George and Bold Slasher battling it out, no doubt followed by death and Beelzebub to frighten all the ladies!"

"Well, I shall not be frightened," Margaret declared, "because I know it will all be fine in the end, everyone will come back to life with the aid of a magic potion. I've seen something like it before, you know; in any case, I am not of a timid or nervous nature."

"Except on occasions when you find yourself in a yew arbour with a young man," Henry retorted.

Margaret giggled. "You are such a forthright young man, Mr Lawrence, I declare my sister Elinor would be exceedingly shocked if she could hear you run on so."

"But I think Mrs Brandon might not share her point of view," he answered immediately, "I am clearly a favourite with my pretty aunt."

"Are you always so outspoken and thoroughly outrageous? I cannot think that I ever met such a young man in my life. If Elinor were here she would extract me from your side at a moment's notice!"

"But she is not here and I have the perfect delight of sharing your company all day. At least, I hope you wish to accompany me around Colystone and its environs for the rest of the time we are in this delightful village. Will you do me the honour, Miss Dashwood?"

"It would be my pleasure," Margaret exclaimed as she fairly skipped along at his side.

There was so much to see and do. Mr Lawrence led her along to peruse the stalls set up around the edge of the green. Tables were laden with all manner of fairings, from trays of twisted barley sticks and spiced gingerbread gilded with candied peel, to the neat rows of mutton pies and fat, round butter pats, garlanded with green leaves. Pails of golden walnuts, rosy apples, and yellow pears adorned with dollies of corn looked as tempting as any of the sweeter fayre. Bottles of spruce beer, orange wine, and ladlefuls of heated negus warmed the constitutions of the passing patrons and relaxed the hold on their pennies, which they gladly exchanged for enticing treats.

"What may I tempt you to, Miss Dashwood?" asked Henry, showing her a basket of heart-shaped peppermint creams. He took one and instead of merely offering it up there and then, bowed with a great flourish before bending down on one knee.

With an expression of solemn sobriety he begged her to consider his plea in loud enough tones for the whole village to hear. "Please, Miss Dashwood, you have rejected my heart twice before. I beg you, take this or else I am undone!"

Such a little crowd gathered around them at the spectacle, now urging her to do exactly as he commanded, that Margaret felt unable to do otherwise. To a resounding cheer she accepted his heart with good grace and even bit into the soft confection, flouring her lips with icing sugar as she nibbled.

Mr Lawrence rose to his feet. "There is no going back now, we have witnesses to our pact, Miss Dashwood, and you cannot give back what you have taken. You have my heart and what is more, you have sunk your teeth into the flesh!" He staggered about as if he might drop dead at any moment to yet more laughing from their audience.

Margaret could not help but laugh at him, though she could not decide how much of what he said was merely in jest. Sometimes he looked as if he believed every word he said, his expression was so sincere, but then in the next breath his teasing was of such a merciless nature that she felt more confused than ever by his behaviour.

They walked towards the swing boats where two children whooped and laughed as they pulled on a rope to make their vessel move. Margaret watched them with amusement and did not immediately notice that Mr Lawrence had suddenly left her side to stride in the direction of the dobby horses just a few yards away. Her stomach knotted with nerves when she saw whom Henry addressed.

"Willoughby, how glad I am to see that you could come after all. Is your business finished to your satisfaction?"

"It is all done, and on such a fine day I thought I should take you up on your invitation. A fine goose is on the top of my list and then a visit to the horse dealer; a chestnut gelding is my fancy."

The men turned and walked towards Margaret, who at this moment was feeling most disconcerted. She wondered where Marianne could be and if she knew of Willoughby's proximity.

"I believe you are a little acquainted with Miss Margaret Dashwood of Barton Cottage, are you not, Mr Willoughby?"

"We have met before," Willoughby answered with a bow toward the young lady, "though it is a few years now since we have spent much time in one another's company. Forgive me for saying so, Miss Margaret, when we met at Barton the other day I would not have known you but for the fact that you are growing to be very like your sister. You have altered so much that I can quite understand why Mr Lawrence cannot talk of anyone else when I am in his company."

Margaret blushed and looked toward Henry, who had started with some animation.

"Then you know my aunt, Mrs Brandon?" cried Mr Lawrence in surprise. "Why, I had no idea you were so well acquainted with the family."

"I know them a little, but I expect that the family did not realise that I had returned into Devonshire to make it worth mentioning," answered Mr Willoughby, fixing his dark eyes upon Margaret's face and holding her gaze with steady scrutiny.

Margaret looked down at the floor. What could she say? It was better surely to pretend that the past had not happened and that the acquaintance had been of the briefest sort.

"Sophia and I have spent our time largely in Somersetshire for some considerable time, with the occasional visit to town," added Willoughby. "In any case, I expect the Brandons and the Dashwoods have long since forgotten me."

Margaret raised her eyes to see something flicker past Willoughby's countenance, the merest hint of his discomposure that to her alone was easily construed. He had never recovered from his love for Marianne, she was sure.

"Oh, look over there," she exclaimed, pointing to the wooden staging where the Mummers were gathering, "I think the play is about to start!"

On the other side of the green, Marianne, who had become separated from Mrs Dashwood, Sir Edgar, and the Middleton party, was pleased to have found solitude and dawdled along in her quest to find a treat to take home for James.

A toyman with a tray laden with all manner of trinkets and gewgaws strolled past. He made a curious picture. From his shabby tricorne hat were suspended a variety of goods on strings: lace bobbins, wooden spoons, buckles for shoes, and bunches of ribbons. Snuff boxes, skeins of silk, candles and kerchiefs, dolls and toy soldiers were all neatly arranged on his tray, suspended by straps around the pedlar's neck. A tumbler on a stick was lying next to a red-cheeked wooden doll that was beautifully dressed in a piece of worked Indian muslin with real black hair jutting out under a satin hat. Marianne paid the pedlar for the toys, which she knew would make both James and Anna very happy. As she turned to make her way back in order to find the others, she was stopped in her tracks. Her reddened face showed her discomposure as she stared at something or someone in the distance.

Chapter 17

MARIANNE COULD NOT BELIEVE her eyes. Margaret, Mr Lawrence, and a man who could not be mistaken for any other but Mr Willoughby were engaged in animated conversation. They were walking toward her but as yet she was sure they had not seen her. Like a captive bird whose wings are clipped, she felt powerless to move. Mr Willoughby, she could see, was dressed for the country in a chocolate brown coat, with buckskin breeches moulded to his legs, encased in expensive tan boots to match his gloves and his waistcoat. His air of confidence and self-assurance struck Marianne once more. Fortunately, he was so engaged with her sister that she was certain she had not been spotted by any of them.

"Is anything amiss, madam? You look quite affrighted," the old pedlar asked.

Marianne recovered herself enough to speak. "I am well, thank you," she responded.

Turning on her heel and heading off in the opposite direction, Marianne decided it was time to see if she could latch onto the safety of a larger party. Seeing Mr Willoughby again had been a shock, but she was sure she would feel better if her own mother were at hand. The play started in earnest. Huge numbers flocked toward the makeshift stage, which made it doubly difficult to forge ahead. Looking into every face and turning at the sight of a bonnet or cloak of the same hue as that belonging to Mrs Dashwood, Marianne began to despair that she would ever meet up with her mama again. But just as she thought she would have no choice but to turn again, she caught sight of Sir Edgar, Mrs Dashwood, and Mrs Jennings coming out of the refreshment tent.

"We are all going to see the play," said Mrs Jennings as Marianne approached. "I daresay we shall catch up with the others. The Middletons were here just a moment ago; I do not know where they have gone now. It is so easy to lose one another in this sort of crush. Where are Miss Margaret and her beau? Have you seen them, Mrs Brandon?"

"No, I have not," Marianne quickly lied.

"I expect we will see them, by and bye," chuckled Sir Edgar.

"I should not count on it, if I were you," Mrs Jennings smirked, "I do not think our pretty pair will be so interested in a village play as the rest of us."

Marianne bit her tongue, though she would have liked to tell Mrs Jennings that she was being a little too easy with her imagination. It was fairly certain that Margaret and Henry liked one another, but she alone knew what sort of damage idle gossip could do. She did not want Margaret to be subject to the sort of speculation that she herself had been all those years ago when Willoughby had courted her. Perhaps she ought to warn her sister. Had she been wrong to encourage Margaret to spend time unchaperoned with Mr Lawrence? What would Elinor do if she were here?

Mrs Dashwood, who was listening to this exchange, expressed her concern to Marianne in a low voice as Mrs Jennings continued to spout forth on the subject of courting lovers. "Will you go and look for her, Marianne? I think I have been unwise to let her out of my sight for so long."

Marianne hesitated. The last thing she wanted was to have a conversation with Mr Willoughby.

"Please hurry, Marianne," her mother entreated, "I will feel much better if she is here with us. I have given her too much of a free rein, I think."

Smiling reassuringly at her mother, but with a sinking heart, Mrs Brandon sallied forth, determining to find levels of courage she felt she did not possess. Heading in the direction where she recalled seeing Margaret last, Marianne did not know whether to feel relief or alarm when it was clear that her sister was not in the immediate vicinity. Easing her way through the rapt audience, who were cheering and booing by turns at a figure with a painted red face, she could see nothing of Margaret's blue bonnet or Henry's tall black hat. Working back toward Mrs Dashwood, Marianne realised it was a fruitless task; they could be anywhere, the assembled throng was larger than ever. Reluctant to return without her sister, she decided to circumnavigate the outer boundary of spectators, tiptoeing as she went, looking high over their heads. And then she saw them. Margaret and Henry were together and alone, she observed with some relief. However, this feeling soon gave way to one of apprehension. The pair appeared to be in a hurry, fairly running along away from the crowds across the green in the opposite direction. Marianne made up her mind to follow them, or at least be certain of where they were going. They moved with such urgent intent it was clear they had some purpose. She was almost running to keep them in view, but stopped suddenly with a sense of defeat, when she saw exactly where they were headed. Sighing with frustration, she saw Mr Lawrence hand Margaret into his father's phaeton, before seating himself beside her on the seat. He took up the reins and with a crack of the whip, she saw the carriage lurch into motion and set off at speed.

What would her mother say, and even worse, what would Mrs Jennings have to say on the matter? Marianne shook her head and emitted a long sigh.

"Let them be, Mrs Brandon, I beg you."

Marianne had no need to turn in order to identify the voice that nonetheless had her reeling round with a look of astonishment. "I beg your pardon, Mr Willoughby." It was a rebuke, not an apology.

He bowed. "Please do not be severe upon them. They are young and Henry is a good fellow."

Marianne lifted her chin and found her strength. "I do not know how or why this should concern you, Mr Willoughby. I will decide what is to be done and I should be very glad if you would now excuse me."

Turning abruptly from him, she started to walk away, but an arresting hand on her arm prevented her progress.

"Wait, please, I beg you, Mrs Brandon… Marianne," he continued. "Forgive me, but I entreat you to allow me to speak."

Marianne could not move nor utter a word. His manner was calm, very gentleman-like, and though she wished to be on the other side of the country at this moment, she knew she ought to hear what he had to say. Indeed, a part of her could not deny that she wished very much to hear him out.

"Now that I have your attention and the power to talk to you at last, I find it difficult to express my most sincere feelings," said Mr Willoughby, looking into her eyes, with his own dark pupils like pools of black ink fixed on hers. "But I will come to the point, Mrs Brandon." He paused and Marianne saw him swallow hard. "I have never had the opportunity to offer my most heartfelt apology to you for my past conduct and…"

Marianne could not bear for him to go on. "Mr Willoughby, this is neither the time nor the place. There is nothing to be gained by bringing back the past and I, for one, would prefer that it remains that way. Please forgive me, but I must return to my mother, who will be worrying about what has happened to Margaret and me."

All his quiet reserve slipped away. He snatched her hand, pleading with her to listen a moment longer. "I cannot live in this world knowing that you despise me. All I ask is your forgiveness; I want nothing else and I promise I will never bother you again. Only, please tell me there is a chance that you might in your heart acquit me of my crimes, my follies, the greatest mistake I ever made!"

Marianne could not listen without compassion. His expressions, his sentiments seemed sincere. All that he had ever been to her and all the feelings she had ever possessed in his favour came rushing forth in a wave of nostalgia. He had meant the sun and the moon to her, he had been her reason for being, and though such feelings had been replaced with something deeper, the great love she bore for her husband, she could not deny all that he had once been.

"Mr Willoughby, please do not worry that I feel injured or have been made unhappy enough by you to bear a grudge." Marianne returned his beseeching expression with a weak smile. "I am very happy with my husband and my child who love me. My life is complete. You have had my forgiveness since the night you saw my sister Elinor and there is an end on it. I thank you for your apology, I mean that most sincerely, but I must go now. Excuse me, sir."

Marianne curtseyed and left before he had a chance to stop her again, hoping that perhaps finally, this nonsense, the unfinished business with Mr Willoughby was over for good. Her spirits felt crushed, her nerves brittle as broken glass, but she forced herself to rally. Elinor would have been proud of her.

Joining the rest of the party, she managed to communicate to her mother that she had seen both Henry and Margaret, and that they were quite well, assuring her that they would be joining them in a little while. Marianne did not want to acknowledge the reason why she told such a lie, though in her heart she recognised the truth, recalling past memories and those precious, snatched moments between lovers who are otherwise closely chaperoned.

Thankfully, within the half hour Margaret and Henry were returned and reunited with the party. Although they had managed to escape being found out, they did not manage to evade Mrs Jennings's tongue. She teased and taunted till Margaret thought she might lose all her resolve by being downright rude to the old lady.

Marianne took her to one side. "I see what you are thinking, Margaret, but you will suffer your punishment unless you want me to tell her what you have been up to with Mr Lawrence. I saw you."

Margaret's eyes were round. "I did not think anyone had seen us and we were only gone for a few minutes. It was such fun, though Henry drives like a madman, but perhaps I should not be telling you that! Do not look like that at me, Marianne, I remember when you were considerably younger than I am now how you liked nothing better than riding about the countryside for hours on end with a certain beau!"

Off she flounced before Marianne had chance to utter another word. "But in any case," she pondered, "what on earth could I have said?"

Chapter 18

MARGARET DID NOT HAVE to suffer Mrs Jennings's teasing for much longer, however. By the Friday of the following week both that lady and the Middletons had returned to Barton, Mrs Jennings bent on making preparations to make a long visit to her London home. Marianne and Margaret both felt immense relief in equal measures.

The Colonel's expected letter to tell Marianne of his safe arrival in Lyme had been there on her return from the Goose Fair, but Mrs Brandon had felt it sorely wanting. It was a mere scribble, clearly written in haste, and since then there had been no other. Several times Marianne had sat down to compose a letter and abandoned it, feeling the impossibility of writing about their day out without revealing the presence of Mr Willoughby. William would not approve of his being in company with Henry or Margaret, and she felt it might be prudent to tell him when she could see him face to face. At least, that was what she told herself. "In any case," she thought, "I am sure of William's return home soon. After all, didn't he say he would not be away for long?"

However, Marianne started to feel more anxious when she had received no further communication by Wednesday. An express letter would do the trick she felt certain, so she wrote immediately begging for an answer. At last the letter came.

Three Cups Inn
Friday, October 29th
My dear Marianne,

Please forgive me for not writing sooner but we have all had a great deal of worry here these last few days. Indeed, I wish it were in my power to send you good news but sadly the situation is grave and little Lizzy's health is not safe. She is not yet over the worst, though I hope and pray that all our efforts are not in vain. Eliza is worn out with caring for her daughter, and I know you will understand when I tell you that I think it best if I stay with them to help as much as I can. I have returned briefly to the inn to collect my belongings but will remain at Wolfeton for the time being. Keeping a vigil at Lizzy's bedside is all I can do now, and with the help of Mrs Eldon from the village who has been kindness itself, I hope I shall soon be able to send more fortuitous tidings. I have the best help and medicine; please ask God in your prayers to supply the rest.

I know that our separation is hard to bear but I also am assured, my dearest Marianne, that you have the strength and fortitude to endure all that life throws in our path. Until we can be together again, I remain,

Your affectionate husband,
William Brandon.

Marianne received this missive with mixed feelings. On the one hand she was genuinely sorry to hear about the child, empathising completely with the anxiety of her mother and that of William also. On the other, she did not like to think of her husband taking what she considered to be such an unnecessary step. She felt there were already enough people in the vicinity that would only be too glad to help the family and she wanted her husband home.

"I cannot bear to think of Brandon and Eliza spending so much time together, of sitting alone with one another," thought she. "I know Lizzy is ill and I can imagine how concerned everyone must be, but William does not need to be there in the same house all day and all night. I need him to be here with me, and James misses him, too. And as much as he expresses his affection for me on paper, it is not the same as having him here, loving me in the way I need and want to be loved. Does he not ache for me in the same way as I do for him? He cannot or he would be here."

Once again an image of the first Eliza, William's first love, rose up like a spectre, separating her from Brandon, keeping them apart. But in truth, her fear had little to do with a ghost; this apparition in her head was all flesh, young and beautiful, a girl who was a desirable creature. "Surely Brandon cannot look upon Eliza Williams without seeing her mother and the idea that they are moving to an understanding of another kind looms with intensity. Although I try to tell myself that my fears are unfounded, I am unable to extinguish the visions that creep stealthily into my imagination. There is more at stake here than the frail child who lies ill. How I will cope until he returns to tell me that he loves me alone, I cannot think. I feel my sympathy for the Williams's predicament slowly turning to resentment however much I tell myself that I am being merciless. Brandon has chosen his other family over ours—it angers me. But there is nothing I can do; I am powerless to change the actions of my husband. My only option is to wait for him to come home and in the meantime I must send messages of comfort and condolence to Eliza and her child."

November brought sparkling frosts and freezing rain but as the cold weather hardened so did Marianne's heart, even if her husband's letters were as affectionate as ever with promises to return as soon as Lizzy showed signs of real improvement. As she recalled that the child's birthday was at the end of the month, she suspected that Brandon would not yet return even if the child were recalled to full health. At least she had Margaret, her mother, and little James for company. They were a sombre party enlivened only by visits from the parsonage.

Margaret despaired at the weather, which prevented little society from attending them. When she would see Henry again she could not imagine, so she was delighted when an invitation came for them all to dine at Whitwell. Sir Edgar hoped very much that they would join them for a small family dinner. Marianne was pleased to have the opportunity to get out of the house; she was in poor spirits. As each day passed her anxiety increased. An evening out would do her good, even if she had to suffer Hannah's company. At least Margaret would be able to see Henry and with luck, her mother might be prevailed upon to entertain Lady Lawrence. A quiet dinner would be perfect, Sir Edgar always cheered her up, and what was more, he also seemed as keen as she to promote his offspring's growing attachment to her sister.

On arriving at Whitwell, the news that Henry met them with gave rise to sudden feelings of trepidation and alarm. He bounded down the front steps like an exuberant puppy with warmth and affection, greeting them all with great affability.

"Welcome once more to Whitwell," he declared with a flourish and a scraping bow. "I could not wait for you to come; we have been so dull here since the Goose Fair. Come in, Mother and Father are waiting within and relying on you all to enliven the party and amuse our guest."

"But I thought it was only to be a quiet, family dinner," said Marianne, who did not think she could cope with any well-meaning neighbour to talk to and entertain at present.

"Oh, it is only Willoughby," Henry cried, "his wife has left him to visit friends, so I took pity on him." He took Margaret's arm and marched her up the steps at speed, disappearing through the great front doors. He suddenly reappeared to shout and wave his arms at Marianne and Mrs Dashwood, who were exchanging looks of great misgiving. "Come along, Aunt Brandon, I know you will be able to divert my friend and stop him yawning. Poor thing, he has spent too much time in the company of my mother!"

Marianne could not have been met with worse news than if she had learned that there were to be an entire neighbourhood present. Her only desire was to turn tail and run home with or without the carriage that had conveyed them.

"My love, it will not be so very bad," whispered Mrs Dashwood. "And we do not have to stay long; I will complain of a headache after dinner and we may go home."

"Oh, Mama, this day will finish me off, I am sure. If only William would come home. What can he be doing to leave me for so long, completely at the mercy of his relatives?"

There was no more time for Mrs Dashwood to answer. Henry escorted them all to the drawing room, where Marianne soon perceived that after her mother was seated beside Sir Edgar with her sister on the other side of Henry and his mother, that the only empty seat in the room was next to the one occupied by Mr John Willoughby.

Thankfully, there was no immediate need for conversation as Lady Lawrence held sway for the first ten minutes. She barely acknowledged Marianne, completely ignoring her attempts to enquire after her health. Hannah Lawrence was too busy launching into an impassioned speech on the folly of marrying too soon and the benefits of a gentleman's education, assuming that the whole room was rapt by her discourse.

"Of course it was another matter in my day, especially if a suitable alliance had been made. But I am apt to think quite differently on the subject nowadays. Our young men must see something of the world before embarking on matrimony, I feel. I do not consider a gentleman ready for wedlock until he is at least thirty years old. His education is paramount. Do you not agree, Mrs Dashwood?"

"I do believe that a good education is desirable," answered Mrs Dashwood, pausing to smooth her gown, "but I think it might take many forms. Marriage can be an education in itself; I believe I learned far more in my marriage about the world and life in general than I ever did before it."

"For the weaker sex, I think you are quite correct, Mrs Dashwood, but a young man needs so much more in order to become fully informed, enlightened, and polished." Lady Lawrence put her hand out to rest her long jewelled fingers on Henry's arm.

"I am sure there is no other young man so informed or culti-
vated as Henry," Marianne interjected. She was certain Lady
Lawrence was trying to make the point that he was not ready to
marry Margaret.

"Forgive me," interrupted Mr Willoughby, "but I am inclined
to agree with Lady Lawrence. A man should school his mind
thoroughly before he marries; one is a very long time married.
If I had a son I should encourage him to see a little of life first,
whatever his opinions on love."

Marianne stared at him in contempt. How dare he agree
with that old dragon of a woman?

"Not all men make correct decisions at a tender age, Mrs
Brandon," Willoughby added, looking directly into her eyes.
"An older, wiser gentleman with more qualification to under-
stand the world might make more informed decisions."

Picking up her fan in an attempt to cool her pink cheeks,
she felt more agitated than ever, yet she believed that he had
meant her to understand that he wished his circumstances
had been different before he had married, she was sure of that.
Mrs Dashwood's eyes were upon her. Marianne blushed deeper
than ever.

"A Grand Tour," declared Lady Lawrence with a huge smile.
"A few years visiting the spectacular sights of Europe are the
ideal finale to an Englishman's education, and now we have
peace again it is possible once more. What do you say, Henry?"

Henry looked as if he would be very pleased to be anywhere
else at this moment as he gazed through the long windows
into a distant vista. Was he imagining himself floating down a
Venetian lagoon, Margaret wondered, with titian-haired hand-
maidens calling to him from their Byzantine towers? But he

turned from the view to catch Margaret's eye, merely laughed and looked to his father as if in quest for help.

"Grand Tours and education are all very well in themselves, but I fancy that if a young couple know their own mind then they should be allowed to get on with it," Sir Edgar smirked, with a nod and a wink in Margaret's direction.

The latter was mortified, and determining to change the subject, endeavoured to introduce any topic that came into her head. "Shall you all be going to London for the season, Lady Lawrence?"

"Yes, indeed, we are travelling the week after Christmas as a matter of fact," Sir Edgar butted in. "I hope we shall be seeing you there too, Miss Margaret."

"Colonel Brandon has promised to take me with Marianne," Margaret pronounced, her joyful exuberance betraying her enthusiasm for the scheme.

"Then we shall all meet by and bye," chuckled Sir Edgar.

"When is Brandon to return?" his sister enquired. "He is there on business did you say, Mrs Brandon? Has he been gone long?"

Marianne felt everyone must be aware of her perturbation so she spoke quickly to cover her discomfort. "He is to return on the morrow," she said, not really knowing whether this was true or not. She fiddled with the tassel on her fan, knowing that Mr Willoughby was staring at her countenance. Indeed, he had not taken his eyes off her since she had entered the room and this was only adding to her sense of unease.

"Well now," proclaimed Sir Edgar, "it must be time for dinner!"

He rose, proffering an arm each to Mrs Dashwood and his wife respectively. Marianne could see Henry making a beeline for her sister, which meant there was only one person who could accompany her into dinner. Mr Willoughby was at her side in a moment. Though Marianne hesitated, she knew she had no option. Slipping her hand through his arm, she allowed herself to be escorted, though she felt the impropriety very much. It felt very strange to feel the expensive cloth of his coat underneath her fingers and impossible not to feel the strength of his arm however lightly she took it. Despite purposefully leaning as far away from him as she was able, she could not help but be aware of his nearness, and of his smell, emanating like an elixir from a bygone age, mingled into a potpourri of fragrant images from the past. Taking her seat at the dining table between him and Sir Edgar at the head, she knew that it would be impossible to completely ignore him. With her host completely engaged with her mother on the other side and with everyone else talking nineteen to the dozen, she could only turn her attention to Mr Willoughby when he spoke.

Chapter 19

"FORGIVE ME, MRS BRANDON," he started in a quiet voice, "I know this situation must be one of great difficulty for you, but if I had known that you were to be invited today, I should never have come. Please believe me when I say I have no wish to distress you; Sir Edgar informed me that it was to be a quiet family dinner."

Marianne had to smile. "We were all misinformed, Mr Willoughby."

"But I must say that I am glad to have been given another opportunity to speak with you," he began again, "though I assure you that the subject on which we last spoke is closed forever. I wonder if I might ask you about another matter altogether, though in its own way it is one of a most delicate nature."

Marianne looked up at him enquiringly, with a suspicion that she might have an idea at what he hinted.

"What are you whispering in my aunt's ear, Willoughby?" shouted Henry from across the table. "Let us all have a share in the conversation. Do be careful, Aunt Brandon, Mr Willoughby can never resist telling tales if he thinks he has the attention of a beautiful woman."

The entire table stopped to stare until Marianne spoke with a levity she did not truly feel. "Mr Willoughby was telling me of the plans for Allenham Court, and I must say Mrs Willoughby's schemes for new decoration sound admirable. How delightful it must be to newly furnish a home."

"There is nothing finer to my mind," joined Lady Lawrence. "It is a pity that dear Mrs Willoughby is away visiting friends at present. I should so much like to have heard all about it—a lady with such similar tastes as my own. I have enjoyed giving her the benefit of my own knowledge, which she was most thankful to accept. I was lucky, of course, to have had the advantage of being schooled by the French, who are unsurpassed decorators of elegance. Mrs Dashwood, you must come and see my new scenic wallpaper. You shall be transported to a tropical isle if you will just sit in my petit salon for five minutes!"

Marianne and Margaret caught the other's eye and for a moment it was all they could do to stop from bursting out laughing. Henry did not help matters.

"'Tis too true, ma'am," he enthused, simultaneously mopping his brow with a kerchief and slapping his arms at imaginary insects, "I swear you'll come over in a heat rash and find yourself swatting poisonous flies after a mere five minutes!"

"Oh, Henry," his mother laughed, "you are such a tease."

Marianne was pleased that her companion did not attempt to speak on any other subject for the rest of the dinner. The magnificent spread of white soup, roasted goose with prunes, salmon pie, and apple puffs was attacked with abandon by the rest but wasted on Mrs Brandon, who picked at her food. Her nerves had the better of her and she was unable to do her meal true justice.

She was relieved when they retired to the "petit salon" to imagine themselves in foreign climes. A wallpaper frieze adorned with palm trees dripping with coconuts, and a landscape peopled with exotically robed figures, ran round the length and breadth of the room. Coupled with a hand painted ceiling of a blue sky, with scattered clouds edged in sunset pink, Marianne was inclined to think it all rather too fanciful for her taste, so she was pleased when her mother made all the right noises.

"Lady Lawrence, I declare I have never seen anything quite like it," Mrs Dashwood assured her hostess.

Marianne was quite certain her mother never had and made a long perusal of a tropical plant as another fit of mirth threatened to overcome her.

"No, indeed," Hannah Lawrence prattled on, "I am happy to tell you that I am the very first, proud owner of such a device in all the West Country."

"As you may imagine," Marianne heard Henry whisper to Margaret, "we are hated by our neighbours, who are consumed with envy."

Margaret stifled a giggle but it was too late. Not for the first time did Marianne see Lady Lawrence look at her sister disapprovingly.

Sir Edgar, who was keen to have Margaret shown off to her best advantage, immediately diverted the conversation by inviting her to play for them. Everyone took their seats; Marianne was relieved to be at a distant and quite opposite seat from Mr Willoughby. A lover of any romantic song, Margaret sat at the pianoforte in the corner and with the help of Henry chose a song. They sang together, an Irish melody of sweet remembrances that was not only familiar to Marianne but had once been dear to her heart.

> *"Other arms may press thee,*
> *Dearer friends caress thee,*
> *All the joys that bless thee,*
> *Sweeter far may be;*
> *But when friends are nearest,*
> *And when joys are dearest,*
> *Oh! Then remember me!"*

Glancing across at Willoughby, Marianne was unable to resist seeing if any recognition of a song they had sung so often together was detectable in his countenance.

> *"When around thee dying,*
> *Autumn leaves are lying,*
> *Oh! Then remember me."*

As their eyes met across the room, Marianne scolded herself for her stupidity. The last thing she wished was for Willoughby to think that she still had any attachment to either the libretto or the tune. She turned to stare into the fire, with the instant realisation that she had made yet another mistake.

> *"And, at night, when gazing*
> *On the gay hearth blazing,*
> *Oh! Still remember me."*

Turning her eyes from the fire, Marianne studied the performers with unvarying scrutiny. The fact that Mr Willoughby was still staring unnerved her more than she would admit, but she was determined not to show her feelings.

Marianne led the applause as soon as the song was finished, clapping with great enthusiasm, but she could not resist saying above the general noise, "I am surprised you should sing such an old song whose sentiments are bordering on the ridiculous, Margaret. Henry, help her to find something more modern, those old Irish airs are not only antiquated but rather pathetic."

"Oh, Marianne, how can you say so? That song has such romance. And I am sure I have heard you sing it often!" Margaret declared, shuffling the pile of music in search of something else. To sing with Henry was a delight and she could not wait to do so again.

"It is a favourite song of mine, though I seldom hear it sung nowadays," spoke up Mr Willoughby, whose eyes did not leave Marianne's.

"I daresay it has resonances for most of us," Sir Edgar added with a wistful expression, and though his wife insisted that it had been a special song for her also, Marianne could not help feeling that her spouse's fondness for the air was due to the memory of someone else from his youth. Willoughby's words would not leave her; and now Margaret and her mother were staring in her direction, surely with the remembrance of times past.

Although Marianne was delighted to see how much Henry and Margaret were enjoying one another's company, the conclusion of the evening could not come soon enough. Listening to her sister and her beau, their voices twinned in song, brought forth more disturbing emotions than she was prepared to admit, and when finally Mrs Dashwood made their excuses, she was very relieved to say goodbye. Fortunately, Mr Willoughby made no further attempt to talk to her on any subject. It was only when they were safely settled in the carriage to make the journey home to Delaford that she recalled his entreaties to speak to her on a subject of a delicate nature. Although she could not be sure, she had a feeling that his appeal had something to do with someone else from his past, a lady that occupied a presence in each of their minds and concerns.

Much to Marianne's surprise and great joy, Colonel Brandon did return on the following evening. He entered the house with the same bluster as he had left it, but his wife could immediately sense and observe the change in him. He looked older and weighed down by his worries; she was shocked to see the extra grey hair at his temples and his pale complexion. Marianne was sure he had lost weight, too; had Eliza not been feeding him properly? Unable to bring herself to ask too many questions, she felt duty bound to enquire after the child.

"Lizzy was stable when I left," sighed Brandon, removing his cloak and hat, "but I do not think we have seen the last of her illness, however reassuring the apothecary meant to be. Mr Oliver has my complete faith in his ability, he is the best man for the job, but Lizzy has succumbed to such putrid infections before and with each one she is left weaker than the last."

"The child is in good hands, William," Marianne answered. "It was right that you should come home. I am sure Eliza was very grateful to you for your assistance but she is more than capable of nursing Lizzy back to health."

"Eliza is a wonderful nurse," he agreed and paused as though conjuring a picture of her in his mind. "Her sweetness of temper and patient disposition are qualities rarely seen in human beings, I think. It is very touching to see the care she lavishes on her daughter with not a thought for herself. Many a time, trying to persuade her in the early hours that she should go to her bed was an impossible task. We kept vigil together, more often than not…"

Brandon trailed off at this point; Marianne watching him closely became aware that he was lost in thought.

"I am very tired, Marianne," he said at last, raking his fingers through his dark, untidy mane. "If you do not mind, I will retire to catch up on my sleep." He dropped a kiss absently on the top of her head, before turning wearily, his shoulders hunched and his gait ponderous.

Marianne watched him slowly climb the stairs. "My fears are not allayed," she said to herself. "The disappointment and frustration I feel threaten to spill out in a torrent of fury. I want to shout at him, demand that he show some interest in James or myself. He has not asked one word about how we have fared in his absence; his only conversation involved those others of whom I have little care!" Sitting up until the early hours made her feel no better. It was only when Thompkins disturbed her as she slumbered in a chair that she forced herself to bed. As she moved quietly about the bedchamber, being careful not to wake her husband, she was momentarily moved by the expression on his face, soft in the glow of candlelight. He looked like a small boy; the cares of the day seemed to have left his countenance as he smiled in his sleep. Marianne smiled too, until she began to question the subject of his dreams. Who was it that made him smile spontaneously in his sleep like that? Climbing into bed, she nestled down into the cold sheets until she found the warmth of her husband's body. Wrapping herself around him, she only felt comforted when he turned in his sleep, responding to her touch by taking her in his arms.

Chapter 20

MARGARET TOOK THE SHORTCUT through the park to the rectory. Deep in thought, she felt in raptures at all that she saw about her. Every tree, every leafless twig seemed to possess magical properties that she had not noticed before. The sun shone like spun gold in a heavenly sky, the air was never so sweet, and the entire world seemed an enchanted haven on this mellow December morning. Her thoughts were occupied not only with a young man who was becoming very dear to her heart but also with the fact that she would be leaving for London within a couple of weeks. Unable to settle to anything at Delaford, she had decided to visit her eldest sister and cousins to bid them a fond farewell. Elinor would, no doubt, have something to say on matters of the heart before she left, but today she felt she could endure anything.

"I am in love with Henry," she told herself and said it out loud to the horses in the fields as she walked. Her excitement at the trip to London was boundless; after all, she imagined that they would be able to meet frequently. On his marriage

Colonel Brandon had swiftly left his bachelor lodgings in St James's Street and found him and his new wife a fine house in Manchester Square. As the Lawrences had their own establishment in Portman Square, Margaret was certain there would not only be frequent calls, parties, and the like but also every chance of bumping into Henry in the street and round the town. Lower Berkeley Street was all that would separate them. Margaret's heart leapt at the thought.

Anna greeted Margaret with great excitement and hugs of affection. Elinor bade her sister sit by the fire whilst she poured fragrant tea and proffered a dish of buttered muffins.

"How is everyone at Delaford?" she asked. "I expect you are all in a state of high expectation and nervous tension. Have you packed every last gown that you own?"

"I have been packed for a week, Elinor, and I confess, I cannot wait to be gone to town. I am almost giddy at the thought of all the balls and dances. I only wish everyone were so keen. Perhaps I should not say so, but some people do not seem to share my enthusiasm. My sister, for one, is so bad tempered lately and as for my brother Brandon, I have never seen him so ill-disposed."

"Oh, Margaret, they will have a lot to organise. It is no mean feat removing an entire household to another part of the country," urged Elinor. "Do not be too hard on them. Perhaps you should be helping out a little more."

Margaret hesitated. She didn't like to tell tales but despite her happiness at the prospect of the London venture, she was more than a little disturbed by the present atmosphere at Delaford Park. "Well, Mama is doing all she can, of course," she started, taking a moment to sip her hot tea and reflect on her concerns. When at last she spoke, her words rushed along like the brook at Barton, tumbling and gathering pace with every breath. "Elinor, I think Marianne and William have fallen out with one another. I do not want to tittle-tattle but they seem so at odds with one another just now. It is not right. Marianne is silent and grave; she hardly utters a word or even looks at her husband. William has been out on business every day since he came back from Lyme and spends all his time writing long letters when he is not spending it with little James."

Elinor looked thoughtful. She knew if anything were to discompose Marianne more and upset her temper, it was her husband's visits to Lyme. Marianne's irrational jealousy of Brandon's ward and child, which Elinor knew her sister found hard to curb, must be at the root of this present situation. However, she knew Marianne would be most upset to have it talked of and discussed, even if with another sister. Elinor chose her words carefully.

"I am sure it is nothing which won't blow over eventually, Margaret," she assured her sister. "I daresay the trip to town with all its last-minute arrangements is taking its toll. You'll see, everything will be fine when you get to London."

"But it is the one thing that is spoiling everything," cried Margaret, putting her plate down with a petulant sigh. "We were to have such fun, but we won't have any with such disagreeableness. Mama has noticed it, too. She said William is too occupied with other concerns and should look to his own home." Margaret stole a glance at Elinor, who wore a most concerned expression.

"I hope it was only to you that she voiced these fears," she said at last.

"Yes, well, not strictly speaking. I was passing Marianne's dressing room and I heard her and Mama talking. I heard other things, too."

"Margaret, no good ever comes of eavesdropping, you should know better," scolded Elinor. "I do not wish to hear any more. Now, tell me, how is young Mr Lawrence? I am well aware that he has been to Delaford several times lately to call on you, but I have never had a chance to quiz you about the evening you spent at Whitwell. Indeed, I have almost thought you all avoiding my enquiries, so many times you and Marianne have omitted to furnish me with the events of that meal."

Being very careful to stick to her subject, Margaret informed her sister of the pleasant evening she had spent in the company of Henry at Whitwell. Elinor's interest in the conduct of that young man and her questions about the songs they had sung together exhausted the topic of Whitwell quite enough, Margaret thought. Would it really matter if she did not mention Willoughby's presence to Elinor? Margaret was undecided and indecisive, not wanting to ask herself why she kept back the information. But she knew that once out, it would prompt many more questions, which she would find tiresome and troubling to answer. Apart from the memory of a wonderful evening spent with Henry, the one other recollection that stayed so prominently in her mind was that of Marianne and Willoughby, arm in arm, walking into dinner. So it was with a glad heart and a clear conscience that she listened to Elinor's following entreaties to enjoy herself in London, remembering to act thoughtfully and prudently on all occasions.

Margaret took her leave soon after. "I wish you would come, too," she begged Elinor. "You never go to town and I am sure you would love to go shopping and see the sights."

"Oh, Margaret," Elinor cried, "believe me, I have all the sights I could wish to see here at Delaford. Why should I wish to go to London with all its noise and dirty streets? I have only to look out of the window to satisfy any longing for variety. Besides, Edward prefers to stay here and where he is happy, so am I."

Margaret looked back with envy at her sister as she set off down the lane, waving until the house and the sight of Elinor standing at the gate was out of view. Elinor and Edward had the perfect marriage to her mind. "And that is just how it shall be for Henry and I," thought she.

Elinor tied on her apron and walked out into the herb garden. So that was why Marianne had not called. Something must be quite wrong. If either sister were to go away, they never left without first saying goodbye. "And if I know my sister," Elinor thought to herself, "the fact that she has not been to see me for three days must mean that there is something she feels uncomfortable discussing with me. She knows I will see through her straight away; even when she was a little girl she could never hide her feelings from me."

Cutting sprigs of thyme from the herb garden for a tisane, Elinor gathered the leaves into her large apron pocket before heading for the kitchen door where she was sure of a warm welcome from the cook and the kitchen maid. Standing on the threshold, she paused to look back at the vista. From here, she could see the mellow brick and the smoking chimneys of Delaford House itself. "Perhaps Marianne will come this evening," Elinor thought with the hopeless certainty that she wished in vain.

Chapter 21

AFTER TRAVELLING FOR THREE days with two nights spent in comfortable inns, Margaret felt tired but elated to find that they were entering London and being driven down Oxford Street at last, moments from their destination. Fascinated by everything she saw, marvelling at the shops on every side, Margaret exclaimed at all she witnessed. Watchmakers, silk stores, and silversmiths displayed their wares behind sparkling glass, illuminated by the amber glow of oil lamps. Exotic fruit and towering desserts in the fruiterers and confectioners formed a dazzling spectacle; pyramids of pineapples, figs, and grapes cascaded from porcelain epergne. Marchpane castles, rosewater creams, and fruited cake vied for attention on platters of every shape and size. And the crowds of people stretching across the wide pavements, the ladies gathered outside in admiration of the linen shops, draped with silks, chintzes, and muslins were a sight to behold; such fashionably dressed gentility as Margaret had never seen before. Turning onto the relative quiet of Duke Street after the busy thoroughfare, they pulled up at last outside a substantial house where an army of staff awaited their master and mistress. Sharing a carriage with her sister and brother had not turned out to be the daunting task she had feared. Much to her relief, she was pleased to find that Elinor had been correct. William and Marianne were restored to their former good humour, the latter appearing to be almost girlish and flirtatious with her husband.

"Perhaps coming away with an opportunity to leave all their responsibilities behind will give them a chance to spend more time with one another," Margaret decided, stepping down from the carriage. "With only themselves to think about, surely any rift will be healed quickly."

"Margaret, how do you like your new home?" Marianne asked, taking her sister's arm and leading her under the fanlight into the house. "I will show you to your room and you can settle in. Dinner will be at five, so take your time."

"Marianne, I love it!" Margaret declared, her eyes everywhere at once. "Thank you so much for bringing me. I am sorry to leave Mama behind, but I am so happy to be here."

"Do not worry about Mama, I know she is delighted to be staying behind to help look after James. And he will have Elinor, Edward, and his cousins to spoil him. Mama could not wait for us to be gone!" cried Marianne.

"I wonder if Henry has arrived in town yet and when he will call. Oh, Marianne, to think he is just around the corner. I hope we will meet very soon."

"I think you may depend on that," smiled Marianne, "and I declare you shall be quite sick to death of one another's company before the month is out."

"I'm not sure that will be possible. I could never tire of Henry's company. Do you really think we shall see much of the Lawrences? I will just die if we do not meet soon."

"No one ever really died of longing, you know, Margaret. And I am certain that we shall see quite enough of the Lawrences. I wonder that you are so keen to see his mother as you surely will if you insist on seeing Henry."

"I can endure anything, so long as I can spend a whole month with Henry," Margaret laughed.

Margaret was delighted with her room. Wall hangings of violet silk, capped with a buff pelmet edged in gold, swathed the room, giving her the impression of being wrapped in spring blooms. An elaborate day bed adorned with garlands and veiled by a coverlet of fine gauze over painted satin was set against one wall, draped in spangled muslin curtains that hung from gold chains from the ceiling. Empire style was in profusion. There were candle stands of marble, cameo medallions, and an ornate pier was hung between the windows, which to Margaret's mind were the best features of the room, giving splendid views across and down onto the square. She stood at the window and was just admiring a very smart curricle just pulling up outside when she recognised its owner with a quickening of her heart. Down jumped Henry, dressed for town in a navy blue coat and looking smarter than Margaret had ever seen him. It was all she could do to stop from running downstairs to open the door herself. Telling her heart to stop beating so wildly, she took a deep breath and walked out of her chamber as calmly as she could. She found Marianne in the drawing room.

"He is come, Marianne. He is come!" Margaret shouted with excitement, unable to contain her emotions any longer.

Marianne could not fail to catch her sister's enthusiasm. "Oh, Margaret, you remind me so much of myself at your age. You are in love, that is clear, and Henry is as keen as I think a young man ever can be when besotted by another. I am so pleased for you, Margaret. To find someone who returns your affection is truly all I could wish for you. Will you say yes when he asks you?"

"Marianne, I dare not think that he should ask me to marry him but I think we both know what my answer would be if he ever should."

They were interrupted by Henry's arrival. He greeted them both with great cordiality and immediately applied to Marianne for permission to take Margaret out in his curricle.

"I hope you will grant this small wish, my dear Aunt Brandon," he beseeched her, "We have a little time before the dinner hour and I promised Margaret I would take her to Gunter's on our very first afternoon. There may not be another chance. My mother has gone to see her dressmaker and my father set off for his club as soon as he arrived, so you see, I would be left all alone and feeling very miserable if not for this opportunity to sample London's supreme ices and your sister's finest company."

Marianne recognised the look in Margaret's eyes, which begged her agreement to the scheme. Nodding her approval, she was amused to see them hasten out of the room with hardly a nod or a backward glance. As Margaret wrested her pelisse and bonnet from the arms of the waiting servant, giving no time to fastenings or ribbons, the front door opened as if conspiring to let them out as quickly as possible.

"Good day, Uncle Brandon," shouted Henry, taking Margaret's arm with a movement toward the iron railings and white steps as the Colonel passed through into the hallway. "Please forgive me for not stopping, but Miss Margaret and I have an appointment to keep."

With barely a nod of his head or a curtsey from his friend, the pair escaped as Colonel Brandon started to open his mouth to acknowledge them. With a bemused expression he watched them mount Henry's vehicle and drive away at a trot.

Henry's route was not the most direct but all the more colourful for riding down New Bond Street so that Margaret should be able to see the very best of the shops from her wonderful vantage point. After the relative quiet of life in Devon and Dorset, she could not believe how noisy London was to her ears; not only the sound of rumbling carriages and carts, but the clatter of pattens on pavements and the distinctive cries of street sellers rang everywhere about. Henry pointed out the landmarks and shops, not failing to direct Margaret's attention to any sight, which he thought might amuse or entertain. They were in high spirits as they trotted into Bruton Street.

"I'll take you to Piccadilly and Hyde Park next time," Henry announced, reining in his horse as they rapidly approached their destination. "Here we are arrived at Berkeley Square for your pleasure and there under the sign of the pineapple is Mr Gunter's celebrated tea shop. Now, which is your favourite ice?"

"I have no idea," Margaret admitted, "I really have little experience of exotic flavours such as I have heard Marianne describe."

Helping her down from his equipage and taking her across the road to see the window of the shop with every variety of ice imaginable, Margaret was stunned into silence by the display. Glasses of fruit ice decorated with crystallised rose and violet petals, sugar baskets filled with painted paste flowers and artificial gardens with parterres of mousseline and gravel walks of sugar sand occupied every tier in the window. Pastilles de chocolat, curled wafers, and candied jonquils overflowed from bonbonnieres onto snowy cloths. But the centrepiece, a sugar turban on a tasselled cushion complete with flowers, crescents, and a tall, waving feather, made Margaret catch her breath with pleasure.

"My particular favourite ice is muscadine, with the flavour of elderflower, but rissolis and burnt filbert are excellent, too. As you see, there are endless varieties," said Henry.

"Oh, a muscadine ice sounds perfect," Margaret answered, scarcely able to tear her eyes away from such a mouth-watering exhibition.

Before long a waiter directed them to a corner table. Margaret felt they were hardly noticed, such was the hubbub of chatter and laughter, the clink of china and spoons upon glass. After the chill of the outdoors, the interior steamed with warmth. Margaret unbuttoned her pelisse and removed her gloves. Their order was taken, the waiter slightly bemused that he could not tempt them to some warming turtle soup. He then quickly returned with glasses of ice topped with crystallised fruits.

"Thank you, Henry, this is such a treat," Margaret said, taking a spoonful of fragrant ice and licking her lips.

"Hopefully, it is the first of many. I could not miss seeing your first impressions of London, nor would I have overlooked observing the way you have attacked that confection for the world," he smirked before he paused, staring at her mouth. "To be an ice would be very nice on Miss Dashwood's lips."

"Henry Lawrence!" Margaret cried, pretending to be outraged but secretly thrilled and blushing with delight at his words. "Someone will hear you and I would imagine in a place like this there are spies all around. We will never be let out alone again."

"I do not care," he retorted. "There is certainly no one here that I know and in any case why should I care what others think of me? I always speak the truth. And the truth is, Miss Margaret, that I hope we will find somewhere to go on our own every day. Why should we not?"

"Some might consider it improper." Margaret paused as she considered how she might broach the subject uppermost in her mind. "Your Mama, for one." Margaret put her spoon down in the saucer for a moment and returned Henry's steady gaze. "I will speak the truth. I do not think your Mama likes me, Mr Lawrence."

Margaret did not fail to notice that Henry was suddenly absorbed in his glass of ice, scraping the last of the sorbet from its depths with determination. Looking up, he spoke carefully.

"My mother is a difficult woman, but what you imagine to be a dislike of yourself is to make too personal a judgement. The truth is that my mother has no time for anyone, except perhaps for my father and Uncle Brandon, and to the former her behaviour may be described as equivocal. That is her way and I am sure she does not disregard you any more than she does anyone else."

Margaret felt dissatisfied with his answer. Why did he defend his mother like that? Although with reflection she thought she recognised that what he said was perfectly correct. Hadn't Marianne complained about Hannah Lawrence from the moment they had met? Theirs was an uneasy relationship, complicated by the fact that the latter did not wish to share her brother with Marianne, Margaret felt sure. Lady Lawrence scarcely acknowledged her sister. What hope was there of the lady embracing Margaret with open arms?

"That is not to say that I think her behaviour acceptable," Henry added. "I hope in time that she will come to regard you as I do. I wish you to become very much more acquainted with my family. Indeed, it is my greatest hope..."

"Halloo! Halloo!" A voice called out, interrupting Henry and alerting the couple to a figure they both recognised very well. Mrs Jennings was almost doubled up in her efforts to attract their attention from the door several feet away and even when they acknowledged the lady, her waving arm would not be still.

They both immediately laughed out loud. "Now we've done it!" cried Henry. "We shall never hear the end of it. Mrs Jennings will make jokes and hints until she has raised the curiosity of everyone."

"Oh, goodness!" Margaret cried, unable to stop laughing, "However shall we bear it?"

"Well, we've managed thus far and I'm sure we shall again. I do not think she will give us away completely, her cruelty will be for our benefit alone," smiled Henry, shaking his head at the thought.

Mrs Jennings was at their table in a moment. "I have just come to decide on a few treats to take home. My friend Mrs Clarke is with me so I cannot stop to talk to you, more's the pity. Well, I expect you've got quite enough to say to one another without an old lady like me butting in," she chuckled. "I'm sure we shall meet soon. Send my best compliments to your families. Goodbye!"

With a last wave she was gone and Margaret was able to breathe again, though so embarrassed by what she felt must seem rather underhand behaviour. To be sat eating ices with a young man in a London shop. Goodness, whatever would Elinor say? But she did not dwell on these remonstrations for long. Henry was so charming and so easy to be with that she soon forgot her feelings of unease.

"Did you enjoy your ice, Miss Dashwood?" Henry enquired.

"Mr Lawrence, I shall never forget my first taste of muscadine ice in Berkeley Square," Margaret declared with enthusiasm. "I hope it shall not be the last."

"I promise we will come again, and it is true that this establishment is unrivalled. Could you imagine what it might be to sample the delights of such desserts in the land of their origin? I dream, I confess, of visiting Italy again and tasting a granita made by the master confectioners. I can picture myself in a Florentine square in the sunshine, or perhaps in St Mark's in Venice."

"I should like to travel the world too, though I fear it is an ambition I will never fully realise," Margaret said with a sigh.

"To explore Italy, Switzerland, and to see France again would be my delight," Henry enthused.

"I'm sure now we have peace again, it will be a matter of time for you. Thousands are flocking over to the continent, you would never think we had been at war five minutes ago," answered Margaret, noting how excited Henry had become at the mention of adventure overseas.

"Well, ordinarily perhaps, I might be keen to be away seeing the world but I have enough to do at home for the present," Henry admitted. "If all goes to plan, my new house and estate will take up all my time, and travels abroad will have to be delayed until much later. Besides, there are other reasons why I wish to stay on home ground." He raised his eyes to hers with a look so intense Margaret felt they were the only two people in the square. Everything and everyone else faded away as she gazed at him, lost in the moment.

"I have not yet come into my money, nor could offer any young woman a furnished home, but I hope that day will soon be at hand," Henry said at last, never once taking his eyes from hers. He paused, a frown furrowing his brow as he looked away into the distance. Margaret noted his troubled expression, wanting to smooth away the creases and make him smile again, or at the very least have him stare into the depths of her being once more. "However," he continued, "such dreams are not always within our imminent grasp."

"I am sure you are capable of making any dream come true, Mr Lawrence," Margaret declared, unable to stop herself. She sat forward in her seat, her hand reaching out to touch Henry's arm in reassurance.

"I truly hope so, Margaret," Henry said softly, covering her hand with his own.

Margaret looked down as they both observed the spontaneous gesture for a moment, only to break apart just as quickly. The touch of Henry's strong fingers clasped over her own had been enough to send a thrill of pleasure through every nerve in her body. There was that feeling again, of time standing still, the noise and bustle of city life seeming to be distant. However, somewhere, not far away, church bells were striking the hour. Five chimes, five o'clock, the dinner hour was striking, telling them they were late.

"Goodness," shouted Henry, "I hope your sister won't be too cross with me for not having got you home sooner. The time has run away with us."

All Margaret could do was laugh as they hurriedly left Gunter's, Henry helping her up before leaping onto his phaeton to crack the whip and frighten the horses into a gallop as they careered round the square and headed home.

Chapter 22

GIVING HER EXCUSES AS she sat down to dinner, Margaret was well aware that she must look a fright, having had no time to change, dress her hair, or even run a comb through it. Still, neither William nor her sister seemed to mind; they didn't even scold her for being late. Marianne was in good spirits, asking Margaret to tell her all about her expedition around London. Margaret soon learned that Marianne had received a visitor that afternoon and could guess why the caller had presented herself so quickly.

"Mrs Jennings came whilst you were out," Marianne informed her sister with a smile and then paused as she witnessed Margaret's expression, a mixture of resignation and good humour. "Yes," she added, "she informed us that she had seen you and Henry in Berkeley Square. I hope you and he are of a strong constitution, for she has invited us all to an evening party tomorrow. I think the lady is expecting an announcement any day."

"Oh, Marianne, must we go? I know she will never leave us alone if we so much as look at one another."

"If we do not go, you will not see Henry," Marianne informed her. "The Lawrences are invited and I am sure as it will be their first diversion in London that they will attend." Marianne nodded in William's direction, adding, "Besides, Lady Lawrence has not seen her brother for a while and I am certain she will not pass up on an occasion to see him."

Margaret longed to confide in Marianne, but it was impossible with Brandon looking on. He adored his sister and eagerly dismissed any suggestion that she was less than amenable by excusing her irritability as poor health. Marianne would understand Margaret's fears about Henry's mother, she was sure. Besides, she wished to tell her sister about the hints he had made about offering a young woman a home. Waiting would not be easy, but she would just have to speak to Marianne later. At least Henry would be there tomorrow and they would be able to spend some time together. Hadn't he promised they might have an outing also?

Marianne looked on Margaret's countenance with satisfaction. "My sister has a glow about her," she thought, "a radiance that seems to effuse from every pore. Despite her untidy appearance, her skin is flushed to a rosy luminosity, her lustrous curls tumbling and escaping in gleaming profusion from the ribbons in her hair. There is a girl in love."

Marianne had spent a quiet afternoon pottering about as she saw to all the arrangements necessary to their arrival in town. Meetings with the household staff, the discussion of menus with the cook, and the particulars of the daily routine with the house-keeper had taken up much of her time. Mrs Jennings had called, staying far longer than was the usual calling time. Brandon had gone out again all afternoon, and so they had not had the opportunity of speaking more than two words together.

Although to any casual observer Marianne was convinced that as a pair they appeared to be perfectly amicable, she recognised that this was not an entirely true reflection of reality. Even if there had been an opportunity to share more time together, she was sure they would not have spent it in conversation. Brandon had withdrawn from her, she felt, and, though as civil and polite as ever in company, when on their own they were not truly communicating with ease. It had not escaped her notice that William's valet had organised her husband's belongings, directing them to be placed in the rooms adjacent to her own. Ordinarily, that might have been completely acceptable behaviour for most husbands and wives, but not for them. William always slept in Marianne's room, they always shared her bed, a vast canopied Queen Anne four-poster that Marianne had had transported from Delaford on their marriage, to remind them both of their home. Knowing that William's valet would not have acted without his instruction, she could not help but feel alarm and worry at his actions. The time to question him had not arisen. Brandon was stiff and awkward in her company, answering any enquiry with words of one syllable. Trying to be light-hearted and jovial had given way to a certain gravity in her own manner, relieved only by the timely arrival of her sister to force them into conversation once more.

After dinner, Marianne was feeling tired by the journey, brought on by the fretful anticipation of being in town and worn down by her general feelings of anxiety. Margaret chattered away animatedly enough about her hopes for a tour of all the sights during the coming week and Marianne was happy to sit back, letting her make all the conversation.

Colonel Brandon was sitting at a desk with a sheet of paper before him, dipping his pen into the ink and staring thoughtfully into the distance before committing it to his letter. He wrote rapidly, filling two sides in as many minutes, before taking another sheet and beginning again. Marianne did not ask about the recipient of his letter, as she was certain she knew to whom he was writing. That Eliza and Lizzy Williams filled his every waking thought, she was certain.

He soon finished, sprinkling the wet ink with sand before folding the letter with precision and sealing it with red wax. Marianne observed his profile, the candlelight illuminating his furrowed brow and highlighting his dark waves of hair with glints of gold. "He looks so worried, his mind full of concerns and yet I cannot speak with him. I wish I could run to his side to caress his hair and drop a playful kiss upon his lips, but I am convinced that my desires would be unwelcome to him. Everything about his posture suggests a man feeling ill at ease. He looks lost in thought, yet his agitation bristles in waves of tense brooding."

Sitting in silence, the stillness was broken only by the soft, repetitive tapping of the letter upon the table, a sound that further alerted Marianne to the impression that her husband had something on his mind.

"I saw Sir Edgar at my club this afternoon," he remarked, turning in his chair to face them, his expression impassive. "He complimented me on my charming wife, as he always does, but there was an enthusiasm and eager passion in his tones that I must confess excited my interest. He was kind enough to elaborate on his reasons for his present fervour, saying how delightfully you entertained Mr Willoughby in my absence at their family dinner at Whitwell."

Marianne experienced the sensations of extreme heat and cold in one, feeling instantly nauseous as she realised how it was that Brandon's irritability could be explained.

"I did not embarrass my brother by revealing my ignorance of the event but returned his compliments, assuring him that you had been delighted to have been of assistance in diverting his guest. I told him that I could quite imagine that you were as attentive as he proclaimed. Indeed, he remarked that if he hadn't known better he might have imagined you both to be long acquainted from the way 'you did rattle on together.' I do not know why you felt it necessary to neglect to mention these details, Marianne, but I hope, in future, you will consider my feelings and keep me better informed."

Picking up his letter, he bowed in their direction and without uttering another word, left the room.

Marianne sat stunned and unable to move. Her mind was racing with all the possible intelligence that Sir Edgar might have revealed and how such a description of the events of that evening might have been painted. But no sooner was this done than she began to feel angry. Perhaps she had been wrong not to tell Brandon about the dinner in any detail, but she had been thinking of her husband, trying to protect him. Marianne had known how he would have disapproved of it all; her only hope was that Sir Edgar had spared William details of their walking in to dine together. But what could she do now? What should she do for the best? Her first instinct was to run after him, but reason told her that by doing so her guilt might be implied. As far as she was concerned, there was nothing to feel guilty about. The circumstances had been most unfortunate, but she had borne it for Henry and Margaret's sake. Not once did she remind herself of the disturbing effect the whole episode had made upon her mind. Those emotions Marianne had buried almost as soon as they had left Whitwell.

"Oh, Marianne," Margaret started, "I've never seen William so cross. I must confess I am not surprised that you chose to keep your silence, but he was bound to have found out sooner or later. Why ever did you not tell him?"

"William has no cause to be so upset. His behaviour is little better than a small child who cannot have his own way. Surely he must see that there was nothing we could do about the situation. Storming off in such a fashion is ridiculous, and if he thinks I am going to rush after him, he can think again." Marianne rose, smoothing her silk gown with her slender fingers before announcing, "I have a headache, Margaret. If you will excuse me, I will go and lie down."

Margaret was left alone with her thoughts and fears. Her hopes for reconciliation between her sister and brother had been dashed for the time being. Even so, her present mood could not be entirely deflated. An evening party with Henry in attendance promised to be an excellent diversion. How she could wait until tomorrow, she hardly knew.

Alone in her room, Marianne lay on her bed but she could not rest. Hot tears stung in her eyes, spilling over her cheeks. Giving in fully to her emotions, she sobbed until there were no tears left, feeling herself injured and indignant. Gradually the sounds of the city subsided, darkness descended, and beams of moonlight crept stealthily through a chink in the blind, sending a shaft of silver to illuminate her ghostly reflection in the glass on her dressing table. Never had she felt so alone. As she lay half hoping that the Colonel would come to her and all would be well, there came a soft knocking at the door. William's voice called her name beseechingly and though she wanted to call to him, something inside prevented her from doing so.

"I will not be so easily persuaded," she railed. "If he thinks I will forgive him so quickly for making me feel so wretched, he can think again. He can apologise to me tomorrow if he wishes, and perhaps he will act with more forethought in future than to make me feel as if I have wronged him. How dare he!" Brushing her damp cheeks with the back of her hand, she blew her nose once more and snuffed out the last whisper of light from the candle by her bed.

Chapter 23

MARIANNE'S TEMPER WAS NOT improved when Margaret suggested over breakfast that she should have made her peace with her husband, forgiving William for his brusque manner, which surely had resulted from a natural jealousy.

"Mama always used to say that you should never go to bed with an argument unresolved. Besides, Marianne, you look awful. You have dark circles under your eyes. Did you sleep at all?"

"I confess I did not sleep at all well, but it is not my fault. And now it appears that William could not have really been serious about wanting to ask my forgiveness, because he has left the house already. I expect he has gone to be with his cronies at the club. Well, we too shall go out, Margaret. You and I are going shopping."

Whilst Margaret would typically be very happy to accompany her sister on a shopping trip, she did not want to miss Henry and she believed he would call during the morning to take her out. A trip to Hyde Park was a most enticing prospect and Margaret longed to see the spectacle that such an outing would afford. However, Marianne seemed very upset and in any case she was to see Henry later.

"I would love to go shopping, Marianne," Margaret managed to answer, taking in her sister's stern expression, with her cheeks flaming as they always did when she was upset. "Some air will do you good, and I confess I am looking forward to seeing the delights of London shop windows at closer quarters. I have a little money, which I intend to use. If I can find a treat for Mama too, then I shall be very happy."

After this exchange, a rapid excursion to the shops was made. A tour of Bond Street was their first port of call and before long the ladies found themselves in Sackville Street, outside Gray's the jeweller. Just as they were on the point of entering the shop, they were surprised to bump into Edward Ferrars's brother Robert, and his wife Lucy.

"Mrs Brandon, I declare, I have not seen you for an age," Lucy pronounced. "And Miss Dashwood, this is so exciting, for we were just talking of you, were we not, my dear?" she addressed Mr Ferrars, who yawned and managed a nod in their direction before paying his fullest attention to an arrangement of fobs in the window.

"I was just saying we were to have the pleasure of seeing you this evening at my dear cousin, Mrs Jennings's house," Lucy continued. "We were to call later but now we are saved the bother. There are always so many people to call on. That is just the trouble of having such a large acquaintance and Mr Ferrars is never so happy as when we are in the company of old friends such as yourselves."

Marianne glanced over to Robert Ferrars, who had moved as far away from them as was possible and was totally ignoring them. His perusal of the jeweller's window was performed with such studied concentration as to entirely negate any idea that he could be interested in their association on any level. "He always was an utter coxcomb," thought Marianne.

"It will be quite a little party," Lucy went on, hardly drawing breath. "Mrs Jennings has told me that Mr Lawrence is to attend, Miss Dashwood. Is he as good looking as they say? I daresay you have an opinion on that!" She gave a knowing nod in Marianne's direction and winked at Margaret.

"Henry Lawrence is a very pleasant young man," remarked Marianne. "We are pleased to have made his acquaintance at last."

"He is a very rich man, or will be when he comes into his money, I hear," added Lucy. "And you know, Miss Dashwood, both your sister and I have proved beyond question that it is not necessary to have a fortune of one's own to marry well. Our charms were quite enough, were they not, Mrs Brandon. I daresay, Miss Dashwood, you will be engaged before Easter is upon us!"

Margaret was incensed. Trust Lucy Ferrars to be so tactless.

"Do you remember Charles Carey, Mrs Brandon?" Lucy rattled on. "My sister Anne and I met him at the Middletons' several years ago, you know, when you first came into Devonshire... Well, perhaps the less said about those days the better. He was just a boy then and went away to sea we heard. Now he is grown to a man, he is raised to a Captain and returned from the wars. My sister Anne is on the lookout for a new beau and she is in high hopes that he will be the man! A woman of more mature years is never a real impediment to true love, and I feel sure she must meet the right man sooner or later."

Instantly recognising the name of her old friend, Margaret was intrigued. "Is Mr Carey paying his addresses to your sister?"

"They have never met, I confess, but Anne is ever hopeful. No, he is to attend Mrs Jennings's party with his friend, another sailor, I believe. My cousin mentioned some French émigrés also, a particular friend of Henry Lawrence, at least that is how Lady Lawrence described the young lady. Such an exotic name, Antoinette de Fontenay, don't you think? Mrs Jennings said that Lady Lawrence told her how she and her mother escaped during the terror, just missing having their heads chopped off by a mere hair. How droll!"

Margaret looked enquiringly at her sister. "Do you know anything of these people, Marianne?"

"I confess I cannot tell you anything other than that information which Mrs Ferrars has so obligingly conveyed. I do remember having heard their name and something of their plight. I believe they are settled in London and have been for some years."

"We shall be a merry party," Lucy enthused. "I am dying to see Mademoiselle de Fontenay; the French are so sophisticated and I am longing to see her style and how she dresses her hair. I wonder if our French friends will be travelling back home now we have peace again."

"I shouldn't think anyone who has endured what they must will be in any hurry to go back to a land where their own countrymen saw fit to put their fellows to the guillotine," Marianne instantly retorted, looking aghast at Lucy, whom she had always considered to be more than a little silly. "Besides, that is precisely how the Comte de Fontenay lost his life."

"How terrible!" Lucy exclaimed with a look of genuine horror on her countenance. For the first time she was considering why it had been really necessary for the family to flee from France.

Margaret was only half listening to the exchange. She was contemplating the fact that she had heard Lucy declare that this mademoiselle was a particular friend of Henry. This idea was not one Margaret was keen to acknowledge. The thought of Henry paying attention to anyone other than herself gave rise to feelings so strong that she could think of nothing else. When Lucy spoke to her again, she was so lost in contemplation on the matter that she had to pretend she hadn't heard because of a passing carriage. At length, Lucy gave her adieus with many exclamations on the prospect of the pleasure it was to give her husband to see them later. Robert Ferrars paid no heed to his wife, nor to the sisters, turning after the slightest hint of a bow and marching off down the street as his wife tripped after him.

"What did she mean about Mademoiselle What's-her-name being a particular friend of Henry's?" asked Margaret as soon as Lucy was out of earshot.

"Oh, you know Lucy, she can't resist an intrigue. It's probably nothing at all. I expect Lady Lawrence is trying to create mischief and spreading this gossip about because she knows how 'particular' Henry is about someone else. Don't worry, Margaret," soothed Marianne, taking her sister's arm in hers to lead her into the shop, "I certainly have never heard anything. And, in any case, you only have to see the way that Henry looks at you to see how much he admires you. Now, let us see if we can find a trinket for you to wear this evening. If Henry does not give you some sign of an understanding tonight, then my name is not Mrs Brandon."

Margaret could not resist telling Marianne about the conversation that had been interrupted as she and Henry ate ices in

Berkeley Square and felt quite mollified again, when Marianne's reaction was everything she had hoped it would be.

The entire morning was taken up with purchases of jewellery, hair ornaments, shoe roses, and ribbons, besides considerations of new muslins and lace. Margaret was thrilled with her purchases, secretly deciding that she could not be better prepared to do battle with a French miss, if that was required. After all, she had the advantage of knowing that Henry was to call on her later and surely after their time together he would be keener than ever to keep her company this evening.

Marianne had not mentioned Colonel Brandon all morning, despite Margaret's efforts to persuade her to talk. However, as they had gone about their business Mrs Brandon's thoughts had never been far away from the situation. Now she was beginning to think that she had been in the wrong despite what she deemed as her honourable motives, and she was determined to set things right. They had never quarrelled like this before, and she recognised it was her own fault that they were at odds with one another now. As soon as they reached home she would do all she could to make amends.

On their return, Marianne hurried away to find the Colonel, whilst Margaret made enquiries of the servants as to whether they had received any calls during the course of the morning. Relieved to discover that she had not missed Henry, she went off to her room, to occupy herself happily with decisions about what to wear and how to dress her hair for the evening. It was impossible, however, not to be diverted from her activities by every carriage that rolled around the square and stopped outside. Margaret could not help looking out of the window anxiously to see if Henry might be down below, but was disappointed every time. Once or twice, there was a knock on the front door, but it turned out only to be old army friends of the Colonel, calling to see the Brandons, now news was spread abroad of their being in town.

Once more, Marianne found little opportunity to actually speak to her husband. He was a very popular man, and those that had missed him at his club were now calling on him. To her great comfort, however, William caught her eye several times during the afternoon, even in the midst of conversation with others. His eyes held her gaze and he smiled warmly. Returning his looks of love, Marianne felt quite reassured that all would be well with the world again. When everyone had gone, they sat together by the fire in the stillness and quiet of the darkening afternoon. William put out his hand to cover Marianne's, neither of them wanting to return to the subject of their quarrel. She spoke first.

"William, I cannot decide what I am to wear this evening." Inclining her head to give him the benefit of an expression, which only he could understand fully, she added, "We have a couple of hours before we go out. Sally has her afternoon off, so I wondered if you could assist me."

"Nothing would give me greater pleasure," answered Colonel Brandon and without uttering another word he escorted his wife as swiftly as was seemly to her chamber.

Chapter 24

THE PARTY THAT SET out from Manchester Square were in high spirits. Marianne and William had resolved their differences without a word having been said. Love bound them with sweet reconciliation meted out in an afternoon's blissful reunion. Margaret, having been starved of Henry's company all day, knew that she was going to spend all evening with her love and could not wait to see him.

Mrs Jennings greeted them with her usual affability. The majority of her guests were already arrived. Margaret scanned the room on entering for any sign of Henry. She could see Lady Lawrence and Sir Edgar busily engaged in conversation with a rather grand-looking lady, whom Margaret quickly surmised must be the Comtesse. An air of elegance exuded from her thin frame, her bearing and dress displayed signs of wealth and fashion. Before Margaret had a chance to take in anything or anyone else, all eyes had turned toward the party who had just entered. Lady Lawrence immediately stretched out a bejewelled hand towards her brother, simultaneously managing to greet and cut Marianne and Margaret at the same time.

Standing to meet her was Margaret's old friend Charles Carey, but before she could cross the room to say how do you do, Lucy and her sister, Anne, were upon her.

"Miss Dashwood, here is my sister, who is longing to see you again," cried Lucy, thrusting Anne in her path.

Miss Steele held out her hand and shook Margaret's vigorously. "I've heard so much of you and your beau, Miss Dashwood, though I've not clapped eyes on him yet. Lucy says Mr Lawrence is prodigiously handsome by all accounts and is the finest beau in London!"

"I think you are misinformed, Miss Steele," Margaret answered as quietly as she was able. "Mr Lawrence is, I would like to believe, a very good friend of mine and, of course, related to me by marriage, but could hardly be described as my beau."

"Mrs Jennings has told us all about it; you needn't worry, she is the soul of discretion."

"I see. Well, Mrs Jennings does not know anything of the matter, I assure you. In any case, I was not aware that you were acquainted with Mr Lawrence, Mrs Ferrars, to know anything about him, let alone whether he is handsome or not."

"Oh, no, she's never met him," cut in Anne, "and between you and me, we are wondering if we ever shall, because Mrs Jennings said he's been out all day with Mademoiselle de Fontenay. They were with her mother, but as you see, that lady is sitting over in the corner. Where do you think they can have got to, Miss Dashwood?"

"I'm sure I have no idea." Margaret felt both sisters staring at her with great scrutiny. "Is that Charles Carey over there?" she said, knowing perfectly well that it was he. "Excuse me, I have not seen my old friend for sometime."

Miss Steele put out her arm to arrest Margaret's progress across the room. "Was not Charles Carey a particular friend of yours at one time, Miss Dashwood? Mrs Jennings said he only went to sea so he could forget you. He reminds me very much of the doctor who came to court, but he was so much teased about me, it quite put him out of countenance. I've always liked a uniform and the Navy men look so dapper, very clean cut. He'd make a lovely beau. Perhaps you'll regret giving him a wide berth when you see him again now. If he should ask about me, you will tell him I am your oldest unmarried friend, now won't you? Oh no, that does not sound quite right—I only meant that we have been acquainted for such a long time, not that I am aged in any way. He does keep looking over here but I think he must be afraid to start up a conversation. I did try to engage him in some talk earlier. Would you say he is shy?"

Margaret excused herself again and made her way over to Charles, who was standing with his friend. Thoughts of Henry and his present conduct were gone for the moment, as Mr Carey stepped up to introduce his friend and take her hand.

"Miss Dashwood, it has been too long," he smiled with a short bow. "May I present my friend, Mr James Mortimer."

Margaret thought how dashing Charles looked, his black hair still as wavy and his dark eyes twinkling with merriment in a tanned skin, weathered by the elements and exposure to the sun in foreign climes, no doubt. His profession certainly seemed to be suiting him. James was of a similar age and appeared to be just as cordial. He had an open face, with light brown hair and eyes to match the October sky outside.

"I'm very pleased to meet you," Margaret began, holding out her hand before turning to address Charles. "It is lovely to see you again, Mr Carey. What are you doing in London?"

"I am staying with James's family in Wimpole Street and making the most of peaceful times, though how long it will remain so is anyone's guess. We are enjoying seeing the sights of London, but I will be going back to Devonshire for a while, to see them all at home."

"If I know Charles Carey, he won't be content to sit about in the Devonshire countryside for long," interrupted James. "He'll be moping about until he gets back on board ship, won't you, my friend. Miss Dashwood, he may talk of enjoying peace, but between you and me, he is as anxious as I am to be back in the thick of it."

"I like to be occupied, that's all, can't bear to be idle," interrupted Charles. "Give me a ship and men to command, that's all I ask. What can a naval man do at home but think of the day when he can be afloat again, sailing the rolling waves? I was born to be a sailor, that is all there is to say."

Margaret could only admire this fine speech. As she listened to their exploits in the war, she was struck by the fact that these brave men had only been too willing, not only to fight for their country but also prepared to die in battle. They were eager to be of service again and she felt quite humbled in their presence. How wonderful it would have been to join them and see the world.

"I have to admit there are times I wish I had been born a boy. To be a sailor, a Captain in the Navy, is the most noble of professions. I envy your lot."

Mrs Jennings appeared at that moment to whisk James away in order to encourage him to make up a table at whist. Charles and Margaret were left alone.

"I, for one, am most grateful that you were not born to be a man, Miss Dashwood," Charles spoke softly. "It is so good to see you again. You look very well."

"I am very well, thank you." Margaret did not know what else to say. Charles was looking at her with the same intensity he had always shown, an expression of adoration that was so difficult to bear. Charles Carey had always been a good friend and she loved him like a brother, but that was all. All the old feelings came flooding back, she felt as trapped as if she were a small caged animal. It was time to join one of the other parties that were forming, she felt. Where was Henry? Why was he not here to rescue her?

Just at that moment, the drawing room doors were flung open to admit Mr Lawrence and a young girl, who appeared to be about Margaret's age. Possessing all the gentility and elegance of her mother, she was blessed with good looks also. Mademoiselle de Fontenay was petite, immaculately dressed in the softest, sheerest muslin that Margaret had ever seen. Her strongest features were her ebony eyes, like polished black orbs of onyx, framed by dark lashes, fluttering against olive skin. Everyone in the room turned to marvel at the beauty before them. Indeed, she was the sort of girl who commanded attention; that everybody felt attracted to and wanted to know. Her natural grace and elegance made Margaret instantly decide that the battle was already lost. How on earth could she possibly compete for Henry's heart with such a stunning opponent? It was obvious that Henry was as drawn to her as she was to him; Margaret observed the way their eyes locked in mutual admiration. "I must not show them that I care," she thought. "Henry must not see the despair on my countenance. Even now, Mrs Ferrars and Miss Steele are watching me; I must be strong!"

The introductions were performed all round. Henry apologised for their lateness, blaming the extraordinary number of carriages on Oxford Street that had impeded their progress, before promptly seating himself next to Mademoiselle de Fontenay on a velvet sofa, on which there were so many pads and bolsters, that it would not admit more than two.

Margaret looked across at Henry, who seemed to be unaware of her existence at first.

"Are you very much acquainted with Mr Lawrence and his mademoiselle?" asked Charles earnestly, studying her expression.

"I do know Mr Lawrence quite well," she answered, blushing crimson at the recollection of all that he meant to her, and could hardly look Mr Carey in the eye. What must he think of her? Margaret managed to stammer that she was unacquainted with Mademoiselle de Fontenay, before she became aware that she was being observed from across the room.

Henry was staring at her. As she looked over to give him her fullest attention with a smile, his eyes moved to that of her partner. He looked him up and down, looked back at Margaret, and nodded. Margaret smiled again but Henry made no such effort to do the same, returning to his partner and resuming their conversation.

Everyone was being encouraged to join or re-form new tables for cards. Margaret did not particularly enjoy cards but she hoped there might be some opportunity for her to join Henry in a game. There they might be able to be converse more easily and she hoped to distract his attention from a certain quarter. Mrs Jennings was doing her best to make sure all her guests were accommodated, steering Sir Edgar and the Comtesse onto a table with Marianne and Robert Ferrars and asking Lucy to join her with Lady Lawrence and Colonel Brandon. Margaret was delighted. Henry had still not sat down, but then it occurred to

Mrs Jennings that her evening party had not been formed with due consideration.

"Dear me, we are fourteen and we have only enough tables to play three games. Never mind, we'll soon amend that."

"Do not worry, Mrs Jennings," Henry spoke up. "I never was much of a card player myself; I would sooner sit out."

Margaret's heart swelled. Here was a chance to sit with Henry. She opened her mouth to speak.

"I will keep you company, Monsieur Lawrence," Mademoiselle de Fontenay declared, before Margaret had a chance to utter a word. "Perhaps I could play the pianoforte for our general amusement. If you could turn the pages for me, I would be most grateful."

Mademoiselle de Fontenay took her seat, made her selection of music, and started to play. Showing no hesitation, Henry soon joined her. His studied contemplation of the manuscript and his full concentration on his companion was evident to all.

"How lovely," cried Mrs Jennings, "we shall have a musical accompaniment to our games. Now then, Miss Dashwood, Miss Steele, it would seem there are only these two young men left. I'm sure you will not mind entertaining Mr Carey and Mr Mortimer. Indeed, Miss Dashwood, you have already been most helpful in making Mr Carey feel at home here amongst us. Let the games begin!"

At that precise moment, Margaret became aware of Henry's scrutiny again. She tried to give him the benefit of her most winning smile but he simply turned to his partner, speaking so closely into her hair that Margaret could not watch. Charles led her to the table. Sitting down, she perceived the misfortune of placing herself opposite the pianoforte. Mademoiselle

Antoinette was stifling a laugh and giving Henry the benefit of her large sweeping lashes.

"Is anything the matter, Miss Dashwood?" asked Anne Steele. "You look awfully pale and your eyes have turned red."

This observation led to the gentlemen's close examination of Margaret's countenance. Biting back the tears, she told herself not to be silly, whilst assuring everyone else that she was perfectly fine.

"Oh, it is nothing, I think an eyelash might have lodged itself," she cried, furiously wiping her eyes.

Mr Carey immediately pulled out a pocket handkerchief and as he was sitting in closest proximity, suggested he might be of assistance. Whilst Anne held a candle as close to Margaret's face as she dared without setting her coiffure on fire, Mr Carey instructed the invalid to drop back her head in order to fully inspect the eyes of his patient. Suddenly, everyone in the whole room had turned to observe them; even the pianoforte was no longer to be heard.

"Mr Carey has such a gentle touch, he would have made an excellent doctor, I think," declared Miss Steele. "Just look at the way he is holding Miss Dashwood's chin, like a true professional!"

Margaret felt most disturbed by her comments. How it would appear to Henry, she did not want to guess. Mr Carey was being too particular, especially when she caught his returning gaze by accident. She struggled to sit upright, saying that she was sure her eye was feeling much better.

"My dear, I will have some water and linens brought to you," Mrs Jennings began. "Lord! But your eyes look very sore. Now, come along, Miss Dashwood, I think it best to take you to my chamber and we will see what can be done. I insist!"

There was nothing to do but follow Mrs Jennings out of the room and upstairs. Margaret felt so stupid. Why had she let herself become so upset? For heaven's sake, she scolded; after all, Henry was just being polite. Was she going to react in such a manner every time a young woman spoke to him?

"I have a little ointment which will just do the trick, my dear, sit down there and let me see."

"My eyes feel much better now, Mrs Jennings, I think whatever it was has washed itself out."

"I'll be just a moment, do not fret, I'll soon have you back at Mr Carey's side, not to worry." She manoeuvred Margaret along to the chaise longue at the end of her bed and busied herself with a basin of water, all the time talking without a pause. "I am pleased to see that you and he have made friends again. And, from what he's been telling me, he's made a little fortune in the war. He'd make someone a very good husband."

Margaret held her breath to stop herself from sighing. All she needed was Mrs Jennings to interfere. Her fingers clenched the fabric of her gown and it was all she could do not to say that she couldn't care less how much money Charles had and that she was in love with Henry.

"I know you have a soft spot for Mr Lawrence," Mrs Jennings said quietly, as she bathed Margaret's eyes, "but I would hate to see you have your heart broken."

Margaret was all attention. Her instinct was to sit up, yet she managed to will herself to stay put. "Whatever do you mean?"

"Well, my dear, perhaps I have said too much already, but I think his family's hopes lie in another direction. It's no good to pretend, I've seen the look in your eyes as I once did in your sister's, and I would do anything to spare you the hurt she endured."

Margaret had heard enough. "Thank you, Mrs Jennings, but you are quite wrong. I do not know where you can have gleaned any ideas about my feelings for any gentleman, let alone those for Mr Lawrence. Thank you very much; my eyes are quite restored. I will return to the drawing room now, I beg you."

Mrs Jennings had hardly turned to dry her hands, when Margaret excused herself and disappeared. The old lady shook her head. One thing was absolutely certain. Miss Margaret Dashwood was head over heels in love with Mr Henry Lawrence.

Chapter 25

AS SHE ENTERED THE room, Margaret saw she was responsible for the card parties having broken up altogether. Everyone expressed their concern and asked how she did; all except the very person she was longing to hear from. Mr Carey soon commandeered her again and before she knew it, she was sharing the sofa previously occupied by Henry and his friend.

Mrs Jennings came rushing through the door, begging forgiveness from them all. "I wonder if we might continue with the delightful musical diversion," she exclaimed. "Mademoiselle de Fontenay, would you do the honour of leading the young ladies?"

Once more, Margaret was forced to watch Henry attend his friend. The young lady gave a faultless performance to resounding applause.

"How about a duet, Mademoiselle Antoinette? Would you join me in a song for two?" Henry asked, placing the music and clearing his throat.

Antoinette looked up at him adoringly, Margaret noticed, their eyes never leaving the others for a moment as they trilled in perfect harmony. There was rapturous applause at the end.

Colonel Brandon rose to his feet. "May I compliment you, Mademoiselle de Fontenay, on an exquisite recital? I declare I've not heard such delightful singing since I was last at Covent Garden."

"Hear, hear," all the gentlemen cried with one voice, rising to their feet, as everyone clapped again enthusiastically.

"What a delightful picture you both make, sitting together at the pianoforte," cried Lady Lawrence, turning for approval to all who looked in her direction. "They played together as babes, you know, Mrs Brandon, and have scarcely ever been apart."

Margaret saw Marianne glance over, her expression almost enough to have Margaret in tears again. She knew exactly what her sister was thinking. It would not have escaped her notice how Margaret had been ignored by Henry.

"Miss Dashwood," Mrs Jennings pronounced above the subsiding applause, "shall we hear from you next?"

How she wished the floor would open and swallow her up. The whole room had silenced, as if awaiting her answer. Margaret stood up but she felt quite unsteady on her feet. Taking a deep breath, she ventured a step toward the pianoforte but had to hold onto a chair. Her head felt light and her ears were buzzing. "I'm sorry, Mrs Jennings, but I have a headache and am feeling a little unwell."

Hardly were her words uttered, when she fell. Charles Carey, anticipating her distress, leapt to his feet and caught her in his arms. Holding her aloft, he carefully laid her on the sofa.

Marianne rushed to her sister's side with smelling salts and decided that now would be a good time to leave. Whilst Mrs Jennings fussed over Margaret once more, with Mrs Ferrars and Anne Steele proffering their advice in the background, Marianne was able to have a word with her husband.

"Dear me, Miss Margaret seems to be of a very sickly constitution," announced Lady Lawrence. "In one so young, it does not bode well. I remember my school friend, Miss Thackeray, a large girl like Miss Dashwood. She looked as strong as an ox, but went to bed one night and didn't wake up again."

"I hope it's nothing serious, perhaps you should take her home, Mrs Brandon," said Sir Edgar kindly. "I will have the carriage sent round immediately."

"As I am sure you all know," his wife went on, "I suffer quite dreadfully myself, but I never knew a single malady in my youth. I do not remember you ever knowing a day's illness, Mademoiselle Antoinette. You are such a delicate-looking girl, yet like myself, you come from good, stalwart stock."

"'Tis a good thing you were there to catch her, Mr Carey, I saw there wasn't a minute's hesitation," murmured Anne, looking on with envy, "and you picked her up as though she were a little doll. If ever I were to faint, I hope I should be caught by some gentleman half as gallant as you. What say you, Mr Mortimer? Are you a valiant catcher of ladies?"

Mr Mortimer seemed somewhat taken aback by Miss Steele's forthrightness and blushed crimson to the roots of his hair. It was apparent he could not think of a ready answer, so surprised was he by Miss Steele's openly coquettish manner.

Colonel Brandon made his apologies, saying how sorry he was to be breaking up the party so early. "We will all meet again soon, I am sure."

"Oh, yes, William, it will not be too long," exclaimed Lady Lawrence. "I shall call on you tomorrow."

Marianne received this news with dread. Why was it that she looked forward so much to coming to London, she wondered?

When they had first been married, everything had seemed so exciting about the London season. But they had not had to share their experiences with anyone but themselves, if they so wished. The Colonel had shown her all the historical attractions, taken her to the best shops, as well as the theatre and they had chosen only the soirées and balls they wished to attend. Marianne had to admit that the absence of William's sister had probably also contributed to her sense of freedom and happiness.

The disappointment felt by them all was expressed with much reiteration on the subject of seeing one another again soon. Henry and Mademoiselle Antoinette came to shake Margaret's hand and wish her well.

"I am so sorry, Miss Dashwood, that we have not had a chance to form a more intimate acquaintance, especially as Henry has told me so much about you," said Mademoiselle de Fontenay. "He is so grateful to you for keeping him company; it is so very kind of you to put yourself out."

Margaret looked toward Henry, who smiled, but she could detect no real warmth in his eyes. He said he hoped she would feel better soon.

"I hope you will keep your promise and take me to Hyde Park," she said before she knew she had done it.

Henry cast his eyes to the floor. "I'm sorry, Miss Dashwood, but I am unsure of my engagements at present. Unfortunately, my life is not my own when in London; my mother makes many demands. Besides, I am sure Mr Carey will be more than willing to oblige."

Margaret could not believe her ears. This was not her Henry speaking. This Henry could barely look at her; his eyes and expression were cold. What could have happened to produce such a change in him? Reluctantly she turned away, looking to her sister, who on seeing her distress, immediately took charge and escorted her out of the room.

With enormous relief, Margaret settled into the coach. Her symptoms were real enough; she was feeling most ill. Tears threatened once again; she could not remember ever feeling so miserable in her life before. To go home was her greatest desire.

Colonel Brandon broke the silence first. "Mademoiselle de Fontenay is a very charming and beautiful young woman, is she not?"

Neither of the sisters spoke. Marianne made a gesture of a half smile but she could do no more. William's sister had treated Margaret abominably, she felt, in order to make the mademoiselle appear to advantage.

"Charles Carey seems to be as much your admirer as he ever was, Margaret," the Colonel continued. "He would make an excellent husband for you. Fifteen thousand pounds, Mrs Jennings told me he has won in the war. Besides, he is clearly a very caring and thoughtful gentleman, apart from all his naval honours."

"But you must know that Margaret's hopes lie in another direction," Marianne blurted out before she could stop herself. "And I think if it were not so obvious that your sister has been plotting against those expectations, then Margaret might have been congratulating herself on an engagement this very evening."

"Marianne, I know my sister can be trying at times but I am sure she would have no such schemes as you describe. You are being a little fanciful, you know. In any case, I must admit that I am not altogether surprised by Henry's attendance on Mademoiselle Antoinette this evening. She is an old friend; the families have known one another since the old days in France. Henry is a responsible boy, brought up to do his duty."

"Well, if that is the case and he is inclined to do everything his mother tells him, perhaps you would be better off with Charles Carey, Margaret."

"Marianne, that is unfair. My sister has done an excellent job of bringing up Henry; he is a most delightful boy."

"Fortunately, he takes after his father," Marianne retorted, her dark eyes flashing wildly. "I thought Hannah was unforgivably rude about my sister, who is an angel and far superior in looks and accomplishments to that French madam!"

Margaret sank back in her seat. More than anything she did not want her sister to argue with her husband again. "Marianne, please, it does not matter. Lady Lawrence did not mean to be rude, I am sure. I am sorry to have caused such a fuss. As for Henry, do not worry, I could never tolerate knowing that I was considered second best. If he prefers Mademoiselle de Fontenay, then so be it."

Marianne turned her head to look out of the window. If the Colonel was to defend the behaviour of both his sister and his nephew, she could not continue the conversation without revealing her true feelings. Time had helped Marianne learn the necessity of curbing her strongest emotions, but at this moment she felt in great danger of exposing herself.

Chapter 26

PART OF THE FOLLOWING morning was taken up with callers, Mrs Jennings in the first instance and Lady Lawrence in the second. Mrs Jennings called on an errand of sincere concern for Margaret, who did not make an appearance due to her further indisposition. Lady Lawrence had no enquiries to make after Miss Dashwood's health and came only to gratify her vanity, expecting to be congratulated on having such fine friends as the Comtesse and her daughter. Marianne was not in a mood to receive either of her callers, was civil with Mrs Jennings, but was as blunt with Lady Lawrence as she felt it possible to be without being overtly rude.

As soon as they had gone, she went to find Margaret. It was very clear that her sister had spent most of the night awake and upset. Her eyes were swollen with crying and her nose red.

"Oh, Margaret, do not despair," Marianne cried, sitting on the bed and taking her sister's hands in her own. "Something is not quite right about this whole affair and I think I know who is to blame."

"There is no mystery, Marianne," whimpered Margaret, blowing her nose and dabbing at her eyes. "It is perfectly plain what has happened. Henry has not seen Mademoiselle Antoinette for a long while and now that he has, all sorts of feelings, long buried, have come to the fore!"

"Hannah Lawrence is at the root of Henry's apparent doting on that girl. She wishes him to make a wealthy alliance," Marianne insisted, shaking her head, "and if I am wrong I will jump off London Bridge!"

The idea of Marianne uncharacteristically leaping off the well-known landmark into the freezing Thames water brought a smile to Margaret's countenance.

"But, Marianne, whatever the case, I do not have the power to change anything. What is more, I am so sorry to be causing further trouble between you and William. You have not fallen out with him on my account, I hope."

Marianne pretended she had not heard this, smoothing the cover on Margaret's bed before looking into her sister's eyes with a smile on her face. "I thought if you were feeling a little better that we might take the air this afternoon. Walking is so good for the soul and the spirits. And when we have done with fresh air, I will take you to Hookham's and you can choose a book and then perhaps we shall take a stroll to Burlington House to look at the paintings. William is out and about on some business or other and we have no one to entertain but ourselves. What do you say?"

"I fear I look an awful fright, but I should like to go out. I have been thinking. Henry has never really professed any particular partiality for my company. It was wrong of me to think that his friendship was leading somewhere else."

"No, I will not have that, Margaret. I think it was obvious when the two of you were together that he was singling you out for more than mere friendship. Consider all the hints he made to you about his feelings. Well, I don't know how his mother has turned him against you, but I am determined to find out."

Just then, there came a knock at the bedchamber door. It was Sally, Marianne's maid, with a card in her hand. "Forgive me, my lady," she said, "but are you at home to the Comtesse de Fontenay and her daughter? They are waiting downstairs in the hall, ma'am."

"Indeed, we are not," came Marianne's emphatic reply. "Be so good as to tell them that we are out and you are uncertain when we will return. As quickly as you can, Sally."

"Thank you, Marianne," Margaret said, breathing a sigh of relief as soon as Sally left the room. "I am in no mood for being pleasant to Mademoiselle Antoinette! I daresay she has called with the intention of rubbing my nose in her triumph."

"Come along, get up now. Let's have no more talk of conquests and victories, especially since we do not know which campaign will win the day. You are looking brighter already and a frosty day will put a blush to those pale cheeks."

"Not to mention my nose," laughed Margaret, who was feeling ready to face the day at last.

Bond Street was teeming with the London crowd. Marianne made one or two purchases along the way, treating Margaret to some wildly expensive faux cherries for her bonnet, which the latter declared made her feel better just to look at them.

They soon turned into Hookham's to spend a quiet hour in search of a novel or two, but on entering the library, immediately ran into Lucy Ferrars and her sister Anne.

Margaret was particularly ill-disposed, from the state of her spirits, to be pleased with either sister, especially in light of their behaviour the previous evening. She had not been amused by their thorough want of delicacy and had no wish to spend time in the company of a pair who joined insincerity with ignorance and whose conduct she felt was particularly thoughtless. But there was nothing to be done; a conversation must be endured.

Miss Steele began by enquiring particularly after Margaret's health, but managed within the same sentence to divert the subject onto that of the gentlemen with whom they had conversed at Mrs Jennings's house.

"There now," said Miss Steele, affectedly simpering, "I have endured such teasing from Lucy this very morning. Everybody is laughing at me about Mr Mortimer, and I cannot think why. My sister says I have made a conquest; but why she should say so, I do not understand. 'Lord! Here comes your beau, Nancy,' Lucy said when she saw him approaching the house to pay us a call. Said I, 'I cannot think who you mean.' 'Why,' she answered, 'it is he who played you a pretty hand last night.' 'I am sure Mr Mortimer is no beau of mine,' I declared as he knocked upon our door. And, I beg you will tell me if you ever hear such a thing talked about."

"Mr Mortimer stayed for a full fifteen minutes," added Lucy. "If that is not the behaviour of an ardent beau, then I am an actress on the Drury Lane stage."

Marianne considered that this last proclamation was not very far from the truth; acting was an occupation that seemed to come far too easily to Mrs Ferrars.

"I daresay she'd have me secretly engaged to Mr Lawrence as well," Anne went on, "but if you ask me, it's far more likely that's done already. He and the Mademoiselle de Fontenay called not five minutes later. We were quite a merry set, until they left for an outing to Hyde Park. You never saw such looks between them; smouldering hardly covers it!"

"Mr Carey singled you out for a lot of attention, Miss Dashwood," Lucy interrupted, talking almost before her sister had finished. "I think he's still holding the torch for you and if I'm not mistaken we'll have a wedding in London before summer. Mrs Jennings says that your beau has ever been constant and that he has waited years for this chance to be reconciled. It is so romantic!"

"Why does everyone think I have the slightest inclination for getting married to anyone, when nothing could be further from the truth!" Margaret was seething with indignation. "I have no wish to be married by summer or even by next Christmas, so I would be very grateful if you would inform your friends and relations of this fact forthwith. If you will excuse me, I have come to select a novel or two, and as yet, have not opened a single book for perusal."

Margaret turned on her heel, cross that she had lost her temper in front of the sisters, but glad to have escaped their company. She soon lost herself amongst the bookshelves, striding up and down, convincing herself that she was engaged in a purposeful mission for some reading matter.

"Goodness me, Mrs Brandon, is your sister quite well? That was quite an outburst."

Marianne had also had enough of the sisters' company. "Excuse me, Mrs Ferrars, Miss Steele, I must go to my sister. Goodbye."

Without a backward glance, Marianne set off in pursuit of Margaret, only to find her distractedly pulling one novel after another from the shelves. Her face was pale and wan, wearing an expression that showed a determination not to give in to her real feelings. It was obvious to Marianne that Margaret was not reading a single word of any of the books she picked up, despite her studied contemplation of every one.

As if reading Marianne's thoughts, Margaret addressed her sister directly. "I am fine, Marianne. Please do not be concerned. I am perfectly happy and just wish to select a book. I suggest you do the same."

Sensing that Margaret might wish to be alone with her thoughts, Marianne went in search of some music manuscripts. When feeling at odds with the world, her remedy was to lose herself in melodious harmony. Nothing soothed so well as a piece of composition. Although she had not confided in Margaret, the truth was that relations between her and William were strained once again. Criticising Brandon's sister had been an ill-judged censure but she had felt it necessary, nevertheless. Her fierce and protective love for her sister and perhaps for a part of herself she now thought lost had been at its root, but how she was to make her husband understand, she could not decide. However, all that could be forgotten at the present; Marianne selected a large sheaf of music and finding a seat in a cosy corner, determined to lose herself for a pleasant half hour.

Margaret busied herself with a variety of books, stacking them on a small table beside her; unable to decide whether she wished to read of gothic horrors or maiden's fortunes in love. She opted for the former, a tale of terror bound in leather, as the prospect of happy endings filled her with more dread than the most ghostly tale. Determined to find a seat where she would not be disturbed or observed, Margaret worked her way past several rows of bookshelves until at last at the very back of the library in a quiet, but dimly illuminated spot from the lack of natural light, she found an unoccupied chair set against a tall but empty bookcase. The chair was a comfortable-looking seat so she sat down, convinced that the lack of any reading matter at hand would mean that she would be left alone. Closing her eyes, she tried to blot out the thoughts that persisted in haunting her. Everywhere was quiet, only the clock ticking on the wall and the occasional scrape of a chair leg or a person coughing could be heard. As Margaret tried to relax, to clear her head of unwelcome thoughts, her ear was caught by the low voices of a couple, a man and woman, talking in whispers, quite intimately on the other side of the high shelving. It was impossible to see them but her attention was duly fixed when the agitation and accent of the lady rose to a pitch, making her curious to hear more. There was no mistake. The possessor of the genteel voice, which kept lapsing into French, was a lady. Margaret held her breath, longing to hear the answering speech of the gentleman. His voice was deeper and it was more difficult to hear him. But she could hardly believe her ears nor stop the trembling, not only of her hands, which shook so much that she feared she would drop her book, but also of her entire being. For his was a voice she knew and she could not hear it without emotion. Henry Lawrence's mellow tones were detected and from her quiet spot on the other side, she was petrified and riveted all at once. Margaret clasped her hand over her mouth as Mademoiselle de Fontenay started to speak again.

"But how is it to be accomplished, Henry? I dare not hope that we will be together at last," cried Mademoiselle de Fontenay. Her voice was strained and anxious. "If anyone were to see us, all will be undone!"

"You must not worry," Henry replied in a soothing manner. "True love always finds a way; you must believe me, Antoinette, my dear girl. Have I ever let you down yet? I promise I will not fail you."

"If I could only feel that what we are to undertake will not be seen as folly or despicable behaviour. I do not wish to upset my mother, but I cannot see what else we are to do. Our happiness is at stake."

"I have told you, Antoinette, my dearest one, I will think of a way and with luck, all will be resolved in time. I have a plan. All I ask is that you trust me."

"Oh, Henry, of course I do. I trust you with my life; I always have, ever since those days, so long ago in France, when we were only playmates. If we had known then how the fates would join us…"

Margaret involuntarily and audibly drew in her breath. A moment of terrified suspense followed, there were scuffling noises and fretful whispering on the other side, as the couple recognised that they might have been overheard. Seconds later, as Margaret hardly dared to let go her breath for fear of discovery, she heard their footsteps retreating, until they were distinguished no more. Her own emotions still kept her fixed to the spot. She had much to recover from before she could move, she had heard a great deal to disturb her. What on earth could they be planning and why were they being forced to act with such secrecy? The more she thought on the matter, the more she puzzled on a conclusion. It didn't make any sense.

As soon as she could, she went after Marianne, and having found, and walked back with her to their carriage, felt some consolation in being together. London was as crowded and noisy as ever. People thronged the streets in profusion. But despite the comforting reassurance of her sister's company, Margaret had never felt quite so lonely or dispirited.

Marianne had once thought that she never wished to see London again. Her discovery of Willoughby's duplicity and consequent marriage to Miss Grey with her fifty thousand pounds, several years ago in this very town, had been quite enough to resolve upon a disinclination for the metropolis. However, marrying William had changed this perception. London had been a splendid backdrop to their mutual discovery and blossoming love for one another. So, it was with some surprise that she found some of her old feelings of agitation and apprehension returning as she stared out of the carriage window at the familiar streets. Her disappointment for Margaret was partly to blame, her heart ached for her sister as she recollected those emotions which loomed out of the past, lingering like the swirling fog which rose from the river, cloaking the city. But most importantly, her beloved William seemed aloof and distant. Since her outburst, there had been no further dispute or disagreement between them. On the surface, everything appeared to be perfectly fine, but Marianne felt the want of inti-macy, which prevented them from being as close as was usual. She knew in her heart that she should apologise to Brandon for speaking so ill of his sister, but she also felt she had been right to do so. Marianne could not bring herself to say sorry, but also knew that in order to feel at peace with the world, the situation must be dealt with sooner or later.

On their return from Hookham's they discovered that Mr Carey had called in their absence and that they had received an invitation from a lady who was a complete stranger to them all.

Marianne did not recognise the name of Lady Denham and was just informing Margaret that they had been invited to this lady's house for a ball, when Brandon walked in.

"Lady Denham is a friend of the Comtesse," he explained. "I believe they were neighbours for a time in Paris. Mademoiselle de Fontenay called again this afternoon when you were out, to bring the invitation on Lady Denham's behalf. It is a pity that you were out this morning and were not able to receive her and her mother."

Marianne felt herself turn crimson under the Colonel's scrutiny. He did not have to say anything for her to know that he was completely aware that she had been here in the house. Margaret got up and went to study the scene out of the drawing room window, in the hope that Brandon could not observe her flaming cheeks.

"That is very kind of the Comtesse to use her influence to procure an invitation, but I am not sure if we can accept," said Marianne, immediately thinking how painful it would be for her sister to have to witness Henry and Antoinette dancing together.

"I am afraid it would be seen as a great slight if we do not attend," answered Brandon. "I understand that you might not wish to go, Margaret, and if that be the case, we can easily think of a reason why you are not able to accompany us."

Marianne smiled. There was no man as understanding or so thoughtful as her husband when he needed to be, she thought. He had obviously been considering Margaret's position.

Margaret thought over the matter for only a moment. Perhaps if Henry saw her again at a ball, as he had in Delaford, she might persuade him that he was making a dreadful mistake by her charms alone. "I would like to go," said Margaret, turning from the window, wearing her bravest expression. "I'm sure a dance would be the very activity to cheer me up. I have always longed to attend a ball in London after hearing Marianne's glittering descriptions. When is it to be?"

"On Friday, so there is enough time for you and Marianne to buy every satin in London town for the occasion."

"That is already done," Marianne announced with a laugh, relieved that William's mood was so jovial and that Margaret appeared to have rallied so quickly. Perhaps everything would be fine after all.

Chapter 27

ON REACHING GROSVENOR SQUARE and Lady Denham's residence, the size and importance of the whole event was brought home as they saw carriages queuing around the whole of the square, three abreast, blocking the easy progress of any oncoming traffic and causing a complete jam.

Torches lit up the edifice of the great house, and an army of footmen guided their steps to a grand ballroom, where the guests were assembling, already wilting in the heat caused by the glow of wax candles and the close proximity to their numerous, fellow human beings. Such splendour and magnificence was enough to make all the party more than a little subdued, as they looked around in search of a familiar face. Margaret, who had tried to equip herself with a firm resolve not to be upset by anything that could possibly happen, was still unprepared for the intense feeling in the pit of her stomach when first she encountered Henry and Mademoiselle de Fontenay standing together with an air of complete intimacy. The entire room seemed to be plumed by tall feathers of ostrich and egret waving above the ladies' heads; but none were more splendid or profuse as those combined into a coronet on Mademoiselle de Fontenay's gleaming coiffure. Her slender frame was swathed in sheerest muslin, set with sewn pearls in motifs, graduating in size toward an embellished hem. Margaret thought her rival looked like a princess and though delighted by her own appearance in a simple, tamboured muslin, felt she must appear as a country bumpkin in comparison.

Henry and Antoinette were chatting with Sir Edgar, Lady Lawrence, and the Comtesse. A meeting was unavoidable, so Margaret steeled herself as best as she could, taking deep breaths as she weaved her way through the braying crowd who were all talking in such loud tones as to make the strongest constitution take on an immediate headache.

Marianne and William were soon absorbed in conversation with the elders of the party, which left Henry, Antoinette, and Margaret all looking at one another.

"I have never seen such a splendid ballroom," Margaret began, wishing to say something to cover the silence that ensued. "And so many people in one place, parties in Devonshire are such small gatherings by comparison."

"It is very beautiful," agreed Mademoiselle Antoinette, regarding the room about her. "Do you enjoy dancing, Miss Dashwood? We both love to dance, don't we, Henry?"

Margaret felt her cheeks flush. "Yes, I do enjoy a dance very much. At home I love going to the assemblies above everything else. I particularly enjoyed a ball my sister gave a few months ago at Delaford. Mr Lawrence was there also."

"Charles Carey and his friend have been included in the invitation," interrupted Henry, "I expect they will be here in a moment. I hope that is to your liking."

Margaret looked at Henry's countenance. He was staring at her with such a blank expression that she wondered how she could ever have thought there was anything more between them than polite civility. "It will be pleasant to see Mr Carey and Mr Mortimer again," she answered, looking down at the floor. She wanted to move away, the silences subsisting seemed to be growing ever longer.

"Here you are at last!" cried a voice behind them and for once, Margaret was pleased to see Mrs Jennings, though not so thrilled to observe her companions, Mr and Mrs Robert Ferrars and Anne Steele.

"Are Mr Mortimer and Mr Carey anywhere to be seen yet? I should not say it, but I know those gentlemen will be on the lookout for us if they are in the vicinity," said Anne to Margaret, as she giggled behind her hand. "Mr Mortimer is so brazen in his addresses that Lucy's teasing is mortifying, but I know Mr Carey is very particular about you, Miss Dashwood." She turned toward Henry and his companion. "Do you not think so, Mr Lawrence? Have you noticed how much Mr Carey seems to enjoy Miss Dashwood's company?"

Margaret could have died, especially when she felt Henry's eyes on her countenance. How could Anne have said such a thing to Henry, above all people? She instantly blushed and looked down; she could not meet his eyes. Fortunately, Mr and Mrs Ferrars now took over the conversation and in the ensuing exchange of gossip, where Margaret could not bring herself to utter a single word; she managed to manoeuvre herself away from Henry and his companion, to place herself between Marianne and the Colonel. Everyone was talking at once, Henry and Antoinette seeming to have eyes only for one another. Therefore, she was quite relieved when a tap on her shoulder and a friendly hello announced Mr Carey and Mr Mortimer. Margaret was made the centre of attention, which was quite enough to restore her spirits a little, especially when she noticed Henry looking over.

"Oh, let him think what he wishes," she thought. If he really didn't realise where her true affection lay, what could she do? In any case, she thought it was very clear where Henry's heart's desire tended. Determined not to give him the satisfaction of revealing her true feelings, she endeavoured to be as bright, sparkling, and witty as she could.

"We are just in time, Miss Dashwood," said Charles Carey, "I hope you have not promised the first dance yet. Please say that you will honour me with your company on the dance floor."

"Mr Carey, I would be delighted to accept," she declared at once, immediately linking her arm through his and smiling up at him.

"I will show Mr Lawrence that I do not care for him," Margaret thought. "Yes, stare at me, Mr Lawrence. See, I do not even wish to dance with you." Turning her back on Henry, Margaret proceeded to talk animatedly to Charles, who looked down at her face with admiration. The orchestra were tuning their instruments; it was time to take their places. Gradually, the hum of voices, punctuated with peals of laughter, dwindled to a whisper. The swishing and rustling of satins and silks of every hue became the dominant sound, as scores of lavender scented girls made their way across the floor with their escorts. The first notes were struck and the dance began.

Marianne watched from the side. It was impossible not to have noticed the almost cold manner in which Henry had regarded Margaret. At least her sister did not appear to be too upset. Perhaps her feelings were not as strong as Marianne believed; she hoped it would all blow over soon as a matter of course. Brandon was still talking to his sister and Sir Edgar, with Lucy and Anne attentive to every word that passed. Then, just as she was thinking what a charming couple Margaret and Charles made, a couple dancing in another set on the other side of the room caught her attention. His dark head was unmistakable and as her eyes followed him, watching his athletic form move gracefully around the floor, her heart involuntarily missed a beat. It was Willoughby: handsome, impeccably groomed in black, his shock of ebony curls framing his face. He was dancing with his wife, partnering her with grace and all due attention. They were both laughing and Willoughby had an expression of true affection on his countenance. As the dance came to a close, he stepped up to kiss his wife's hand with a flourish. Marianne saw him tuck a piece of her hair that had escaped from her headdress back into place, before tenderly stroking her cheek. She could look no longer. But despite turning away from the scene, her mind's eye was filled with an image from long ago. Marianne was in a Devonshire lane, sitting next to Willoughby in his curricle where they sat sheltering under some trees, waiting for the rain to stop. He teased out the wet autumn leaves caught in the brim of her bedraggled bonnet, before catching a curl that kept being blown across her eyes, tucking it into place behind her ear. His fingers didn't stop there, moving down to brush her face and throat. Tilting her chin, clasping it firmly, he leaned forward and she felt his lips on hers.

"Marianne, shall we dance?"

She came to with the sudden awareness that her husband was speaking to her. Managing a nod and a smile, she slipped her hand inside William's arm. How reassuring it felt to be touching him. Towering above her, he covered her small hand with his large one and for the first time in days, she felt their confidence and closeness return. Any thoughts of the past faded rapidly into insignificance. With luck the Willoughbys would not be seen again. There were so many people and they were bound to be with their own party. In such a large assembly there was little chance that they would meet. Looking about her, Marianne was thankful that they had disappeared from view.

The dance began. Brandon took her hand, escorting her with care. William's eyes held hers during the entire dance and once, when they came together, he whispered so gently, that she wondered if he had really spoken, saying that he loved her. Making up had to be the most wonderful part of being estranged, she decided. Falling in love all over again with an even greater intensity was the usual outcome. Marianne chuckled.

"Why do you laugh so?" William asked.

"You will think me a very wicked and licentious creature if I tell you," his wife answered.

"I could never think anything other than that I am the luckiest man in the world, even if my wife does have a fiendish streak," he teased.

Marianne looked into William's eyes. "I feel an overwhelming urge to lie down," she said quietly, squeezing his hand surreptitiously, "with you."

William returned her touch, with a firm pressure. "That is an invitation which I regard as binding as a promise. The very moment we can get out of here and go home, I intend to have you fulfil your pledge immediately, Mrs Brandon," he whispered.

"It will not be too soon, my love."

Brandon tightened his grip on Marianne's hand. Pure happiness seemed to flow through her veins. At last, everything was as it should be.

For all Margaret's gaiety, she was feeling most despondent. Mr Carey had claimed the first two dances, then looked no further for a partner, giving her the impression that he was perfectly happy to stand at her side all evening without wishing to dance with anyone else. Whilst she was grateful for his attention, she did not really think she should give him any reason to hope that she wanted to spend her time with him exclusively. Thankfully, Mr Mortimer came to her rescue. They took to the floor, Margaret aware that Charles was watching their every movement.

"Charles is thrilled to be acquainted with you and your family again," he said, steering her down the set.

"I am pleased to see him again; he is an old friend."

"When we were at sea, he often talked of you. I feel I know you as well as my own sister for all that he told me of you, your interests and ambitions. He said you wish to travel some day."

"Yes, Mr Mortimer, I would love to see the world. How I envy you and Charles; to be in command of my own ship, now that would be something!"

"I hope you don't mind me saying so, Miss Dashwood, that I think Charles's hopes for his future happiness lie with you. His dreams involve you both sailing into the sunset, I know. Perhaps your own desires to travel the world will come true."

"Oh, Mr Mortimer, I wish you hadn't told me that."

"Do you mean to say that Charles's hopes are in vain?"

"Yes... no, I don't know," Margaret muttered incomprehensibly. "I love Charles dearly, I truly do, but I have only ever thought of him as a sister thinks of a brother."

"I see. Then there is no hope for a match between you."

"I should hate to hurt Charles's feelings, but I cannot lie about what I do not feel. I could only marry for true love. But, in any case, Mr Mortimer, how can you be so sure that Charles's wishes are as you say?"

"He is planning to propose to you, Miss Dashwood."

"Oh dear, I should hate to break his heart, Mr Mortimer. I would hate to lose his friendship over this, especially as we have only just become reacquainted. Whatever can I do?"

"Leave it with me, Miss Dashwood. With your permission, I will inform him of your wishes. All I know is that Charles has only ever wanted you happy. He will be disappointed, of course, but he will want to remain your friend, I know."

"I hope so, beyond anything. But what shall I do now? I cannot bear to see his face, knowing that you are to enlighten him of my sentiments."

"I shall take my friend off to the card room this instant, Miss Dashwood. Supper is not far off now and we shall be mingling in a larger set. Everything will be fine, do not worry."

As the dance came to an end, Mr Mortimer excused himself and left the floor to join Mr Carey. Margaret stood, not wishing to move. Charles would despise her, she thought, after his friend had divulged her thoughts on his idea of a proposal. Henry clearly disliked her, too. Her spirits sank further. The recollection of her arrival in town, with feelings of excitement and happiness, depressed her further. All she wanted was to return home to Devonshire. London was a horrible place, she decided.

"May I have this dance?"

With enormous surprise, Margaret turned at the sound of the familiar voice belonging to the young man she most wanted to dance with in the whole world. Bowing before her, stood Henry Lawrence.

Chapter 28

MARIANNE WAS FEELING HOT and bothered. William had left her in Mrs Jennings's company whilst he caught up with the news from an old General he had known in the East Indies. The ladies were watching the dancing.

"Lady Lawrence is in good spirits this evening," observed Mrs Jennings.

"Yes, I cannot remember ever seeing her so animated," Marianne answered as she watched Hannah dancing with her husband.

"Well, I am glad to see Miss Margaret has her turn with young Henry at last. I hate to see her looking so disappointed, but now look at her, so happy and carefree. I wonder where Mademoiselle de Fontenay can be. I am surprised she has let go her companion's arm."

"I'm sure she's not far away," snapped Marianne. "She is like a limpet, hanging onto Henry's arm. From the way she clings, anyone would imagine they are engaged. I cannot think why Henry wants to spend so much time with such a needy person."

"I think, my dear, Mrs Brandon," the old lady hesitated, "you had better prepare Margaret for the worst news. Lady Lawrence confided in me this evening. Although it is not yet common knowledge, everything is set for an announcement by the end of the month."

This news was not completely unexpected, Marianne thought. But how could Henry be so cruel? He must have seen that Margaret was becoming attached to him and whilst she was grateful that their relationship had not reached the level of intimacy that she and Willoughby had known, she knew, without a doubt, that Margaret's heart would be broken when his wedding was announced.

Marianne wanted to get away before she could be prompted for any more information. "We have been left to shift for ourselves, Mrs Jennings," she said, rising abruptly from her chair. "I will go in search of some refreshment. Would you like a glass of something cooling?"

On the lady's ready acquiescence, Marianne set forth, glad to have escaped Mrs Jennings's society for a while. A room just off to one side had been arranged for the purposes of refreshment. Marianne joined the throng that jostled and pushed their way to an inadequate table, where glasses were being filled with a wide variety of wines and other drinks. Managing eventually to procure a glass for herself and one for Mrs Jennings, she eased her way back through the great crowd, which pressed on either side. She was just feeling thankful that no mishap with two glasses filled to the brim had yet befallen her, when the sound of a voice she recognised nearly had her dropping both glasses in shock.

"Yes, that lady is the beautiful Mrs Brandon," she heard Mr Willoughby announce to an unseen audience, who, judging from their appreciative murmur, were all gentlemen.

Marianne's heart was pounding; she had no wish to turn her head and tried her hardest to manage her nerves. Keeping her eyes forward, she slowly progressed through the crowd.

"No, I will not hear that Lady Hamilton is the standard by which all beauty should be compared. On the contrary, in my eyes, none bear comparison with Mrs Brandon and there is an end on it," Willoughby protested.

Marianne wished she were invisible but, determined to act as if she had not heard him, kept her vision fixed directly in front, holding the glasses aloft as well as she could. Such was the crowd that it was impossible to move without being nudged and more than once did she spill the orgeat.

"May I help you?"

A voice from behind, in her ear, so close that she could feel the warmth of his breath on her neck, alerted her to Mr Willoughby's presence.

"Thank you, but I can manage, Mr Willoughby."

"Here," he insisted, "it is no trouble, let me take them."

Before she could protest again, he had moved around and was standing directly in front of her. The multitude pushed and bumped them ever closer, it seemed to Marianne. Her hands were full; another push from the rear had her careering almost into his arms. She felt his fingers enclose hers, reaching to take the glasses from her grip and in doing so, Marianne was so astonished that she nearly dropped them. However, she kept her composure, even though her heart was beating wildly.

"Allow me to escort you back to the ballroom, Mrs Brandon."

Moving through the sea of people with ease, Marianne had no choice but to follow Mr Willoughby. What Mrs Jennings would make of it, she did not even want to contemplate. The old lady's eyes were out on stalks as they approached, but fortunately, before the situation could be made even more embarrassing, Willoughby immediately took his leave. He did not linger, merely greeting Mrs Jennings and presenting her with a glass.

Marianne was mortified. Despite her best intention, she felt most discomposed, berating herself for being so unfortunate as to have the kind of complexion which betrayed her feelings so easily.

"I didn't know Mr Willoughby was here," said Mrs Jennings, regarding Marianne closely.

"Yes, I believe he is here with his wife and a party of friends. I bumped into him in the refreshment room."

"He's still a handsome rogue, is he not, Mrs Brandon? And with his wife, you say. Well, by all accounts that is most unusual. Does the Colonel know he is here? Though perhaps it might be a good idea not to mention him; that gentleman's presence only seems to upset your husband. Old wounds take a long time to heal!"

Marianne felt her confusion most pertinently. To her great relief, she saw Margaret coming off the floor after dancing with Henry. Excusing herself, she moved off to greet them both. To her great dismay, Margaret did not look at all happy. Perhaps Henry had told her of his forthcoming engagement. It was impossible to talk now; she would have to wait until they were at home before she could even broach the subject and even then, she thought, it might be necessary to wait for Margaret to speak on the matter.

Colonel Brandon appeared at her side, only to tell her that he was in request for a game of cards after supper with an old

friend he had known in the East Indies. He apologised, promising her the last dance, but Marianne felt most disappointed.
He always revelled in the company of men, she mused, and her
own dislike of cards, particularly whist, meant that she was often
left to find some other amusement whilst he entertained. He
was not really a man who loved to dance as she did, although he
usually tried to please her by partnering her often. However, on
this occasion she felt most upset that he was choosing to leave
her alone.

Alas, the supper bell rang out at that moment. She really
did not feel in the mood to sit with anyone and was worried
that Mrs Jennings, or worse still, Lucy Ferrars, might mention
Willoughby. Marianne was sure William had not yet seen him
and hoped it would remain so, as she knew nothing would alter
his mood quicker than the knowledge that his old rival was in
the vicinity.

Margaret's dance with Henry had been a disaster from her point
of view. Although she had been delighted that he should have
asked her to dance at all, the outcome could not have been
more upsetting. Henry had not spoken a word; there had been
no familiarity, no ease of address, and certainly no feeling that
he was going to repeat his request. She felt he was simply going
through the motions out of a sense of duty. Margaret wished he
had not bothered. But by the time she returned to her seat she
began to blame herself, thinking perhaps that she should have
made more effort to speak to him. The activity had been such a
strain on her nerves that in a way she was glad it was over. Henry
would not have to ask her again; he had behaved in a polite if
cold manner and could now return to his Mademoiselle.

Supper was a trial. Margaret imagined that Mrs Ferrars and Miss Steele only sat on her table to amuse themselves by her reactions to the behaviour of Henry and his ladylove, who were seated further down the table.

"Look at the lovers now, Lucy," cried Miss Steele. "Did you ever see such a public display?"

Margaret did not want to look down the table but could not help herself. Henry was whispering to his lover with urgent intent. Never had two people looked more confidential to her way of thinking.

"I expect Lady Lawrence is thrilled," answered Lucy. "Mademoiselle de Fontenay's fortune will mean there will be no delay to their marriage."

Margaret tried hard not to listen as the sisters talked of weddings, with hints of naval ceremonies and nudges in her direction. Her eyes perused the lower end of the table; she could see Marianne seething with indignation as Lady Lawrence regaled her with tales of nuptial expectations and stories of ill health, whilst piling her plate high with pastries and cake, managing to consume every last morsel.

Charles Carey and Mr Mortimer did not make an appearance at supper, and on looking about, Margaret could not see any sign of them. She wondered briefly if they were still in the card room, but decided that this was not very likely. It was more probable that they had left, especially if Mr Mortimer had explained Margaret's position. This idea did not please her and her spirits sunk lower. The last thing she wanted to do was hurt her old friend, but she could not go on giving him the idea that there could be any hope of her accepting a proposal. It was best this way, but she hoped he would forgive her in time.

With most of the eating accomplished, tables were breaking up and new groups forming. Margaret observed Henry greeting Mr Willoughby and his wife, introducing Mademoiselle de Fontenay, who curtsied prettily. Looking at Henry made her feel more miserable than ever. How soon could they go home? Looking across at Marianne, their eyes met. It was clear that she was thinking the same.

"Where has your beau gone off to, Miss Dashwood?" came Anne's irritating voice to break her reverie. "Mr Mortimer promised me the first dance after supper and now I can't see either of them. Mind you, we were behaving a little particularly after having danced two together. Maybe he doesn't want to set tongues wagging against us. If you are about to tease me about him, Miss Dashwood, I do not know what I shall say in return!"

"I have no intention of doing anything of the sort," retorted Margaret, who could not bear Anne's company any longer. "Excuse me."

She got up, leaving the room immediately in search of quiet and solitude. Out in the corridor she did not know which way to go. In such a large house it was easy to lose oneself. Heading off the main corridor, she turned, mounting a few steps into a smaller walkway. On spying a door left slightly ajar with a glimpse of bookshelves and an easy chair, she slipped into the room. Flopping down on the seat, she gave in to her feelings at last. Having tried so hard to rein in her emotions, they got the better of Margaret now. Tears filled her eyes and spilled over her cheeks at the recollection of images too painful to recall, her small frame convulsing with racking sobs, which nothing could prevent. After a few minutes, willing herself to stop, she brushed at her damp cheeks with the back of her hand. This would never do. The last thing she wanted was to give Henry the satisfaction of seeing that she was upset. Any feelings of concern and affection for him were rapidly giving way to other sentiments. "He is no better than a libertine," she thought, "dallying with my heart." Fetching out her kerchief from her reticule, she wiped her eyes and blew her nose.

With a determination to triumph over her emotions, she opened the door to set off back to the ballroom. As she turned the corner into the main corridor, she was arrested by the sight of Mademoiselle de Fontenay engaged in conversation with a young man whom Margaret did not recognise. They neither of them appeared to notice her, so engrossed were they in animated dialogue. Margaret managed to pass them undetected; only the agitation in the young man's voice was discernible. A good-looking gentleman, but with the appearance of one who had known better times, Margaret could not distinguish enough of what he said to make sense of his speech. His voice was low and his French dialect so strong that she could not make out a single word, although it was very clear that he was greatly upset. She was most curious, wondering who he could be. Mademoiselle Antoinette was clearly disturbed by what he was saying. Margaret looked about but could see no sign of Henry. As she reached the end of the corridor, she looked back. Antoinette turned to regard her but as Margaret lifted her arm to salute in recognition, the other young lady turned her back as if she did not see her. Margaret was sure that she had been observed. Mademoiselle Antoinette's behaviour was more than a little puzzling.

Chapter 29

IN THE BALLROOM, MARIANNE had sat out the first three dances after supper, sitting between Mrs Jennings on one side and Lady Lawrence on the other, who for the most part talked across her and at length on the merits and disadvantages of every match in the room. William had abandoned her to their care, leaving for the card room with what seemed to Marianne to be indecent haste. She could not blame him nor could she easily forgive him. If she were a gentleman, she mused, forced to sit with the likes of these ladies, she would be as anxious to escape. Indeed, it was hard enough to bear but Marianne disliked cards so much that she was prepared to admit that half an hour in the company of her sister-in-law was almost preferable to a game of chance.

So she was thrilled when Sir Edgar stepped up to claim her for a dance. Willingly, she took his arm to join the set for a country dance. The dancers lined up on either side, forming a long chain. Sir Edgar was very gallant, complimenting her on her grace, telling her what a pleasure it was for him to stand up with her. As usual, Marianne delighted in his attentions. Although quite a portly figure, her partner was very light on his feet and made her feel as if he would not have treated a queen with any more distinction.

Gaining the top of the room, to her dismay, she encountered Mr Willoughby.

"How charming to see you again, Mrs Brandon," he said, as they both turned to promenade down between the dancers together.

"Good evening, Mr Willoughby."

Marianne could not look him in the eye. It was enough to feel the pressure of his thumb on her hand, his fingers underneath brushing her palm as he reached out to hold it. She felt his hand against the small of her back as he steered her round in the dance. Her body immediately responded to his touch; she was unable to prevent the feelings that quickened her breath, making her head pound with the surge of blood. Struggling against it, she determined to give him no inclination of her bewilderment. Fortunately, his power was supreme for only a moment before she managed to subdue her emotions, angry that her innermost feelings had betrayed her.

"You always were the most beautiful woman of my acquaintance," he went on, "but I have never seen you looking quite as wonderful as you do tonight."

"I do not think that you should be talking to me in this way, Mr Willoughby," Marianne said, able at last to look directly into his eyes. "Think of your wife, to whom you should be paying such compliments."

"I never can think of my wife when I am with you," he murmured. "Indeed, it is hardly possible to think at all. You must be aware of my regard."

"You are clearly drunk and talking nonsense, Mr Willoughby. I think you are not in your own mind at present. All I know is that I do not wish you to speak to me of such things again. If your unfortunate feelings are such as you confide, I beg you will show your true regard by leaving me alone."

As Marianne moved on to the end of the dance, meeting Sir Edgar once more, she felt such a cheerful sense of release from the anxiety she had been suffering that she felt her countenance must give her away completely. As he escorted her back to her seat, she was surprised to see Colonel Brandon. From his expression, she surmised that he must have witnessed she and Willoughby dancing together, though she felt certain that he must have seen them talking, he could not have had any idea of the subject matter.

"Will you dance with me, Marianne?" He held out his hand.

"I thought you were playing cards."

"I was..." he hesitated, "but my thoughts kept turning to you. I am sorry to have left you alone for so long, Marianne. Please forgive me and do me the honour of accompanying me."

"I can think of nothing I would rather do at this moment, than being joined with you in the dance," she said, taking his hand. She stood on tiptoe to whisper in his ear. "Then again, if I might refer to our earlier promise, perhaps there is just another form of union that I might consent to with more than a little pleasure."

William looked lovingly into her eyes to whisper in return, "I can assure you, Mrs Brandon, I never break a promise and am duty bound to our pledge."

"Must we wait until the last dance before we go home?" Marianne implored, returning his stare with an expression that spoke of her greatest desire. More than anything she wished to go home, to renew the close bonds between them that she felt wanting these last weeks. Marianne desired to show her husband how much she loved him and to feel him loving her in return.

William stroked his chin thoughtfully, catching his wife's regard with a bemused glance. "Of course there are the vast numbers of carriages to consider which might impede any expeditious progress. Perhaps it might be deemed wise to take our leave now."

"Colonel Brandon, I insist upon it!" Marianne declared with a laugh and, taking his arm, marched him toward the door.

To be a woman with a passionate nature had its most favourable advantages, Marianne decided, pulling the pins from her hair that fell about her pale shoulders in a mass of dark, luxuriant waves. Such was her anticipation of the promised meeting with William that her hands shook and trembled as she struggled to remove the flowers from her tresses. When they had first married, Marianne had been quite anxious about that aspect of married life that she knew nothing about. Her love for her husband was not born of a grand passion in the way it had been for Mr Willoughby. The feelings of love that had developed from becoming more acquainted with Colonel Brandon and having a thorough knowledge of the man and his character had grown over a long period of time. He had courted her in the truest sense. Marianne's mind had first consented to the emotion that she believed was as near to being in love as that she had ever felt for Willoughby. The feelings were not so zealous, but the love she bore for William flourished slowly and with such intensity as she had never before known. He tended their affection with as much care as a gardener over a sick plant, and Marianne blossomed, blooming like a rose from one of his hothouses, her petals unfurling with every sonnet and poem of love that he read to her and with every attention that he paid. She had wished to be married. Colonel Brandon was the man she knew would make her happy; his temper and understanding were exactly what she wished for in a husband, but to say that she did not feel apprehensive about the expectations her husband might have when they were married would be to write a false history. Again, she need not have worried. No such demands were made. Indeed, her husband sought so little physical attention, keeping to his own quarters in the first days of their marriage, that Marianne was surprised to find that she was the one to crave his notice. The more he ignored her, the more she pursued William with relentless fervour. To her great delight, her mind and body soon met as one. Before the week was through, she was astonished to find not only did she want Colonel Brandon to love her but that she was pleading with him to make love to her over and over again.

Dabbing perfume on her wrists and throat, she hoped her appearance would have the desired effect. She tied a single, red silk ribbon about her throat and, thus satisfied with her appearance, arranged herself against the propped pillows on her bed. Marianne did not have to wait long before she heard a discreet knock at the door and her husband's voice call her name. Marianne was so thrilled to see him, draping her arms around his neck as he sat at her side, that she did not at first realise that his expression was sombre or that his countenance bore all the marks of one troubled by anxiety and worry. After peppering his face with kisses but not receiving one back in return, she pulled away.

"What is wrong, Brandon?"

"I have some bad news, Marianne. I came to tell you that I am unable to keep our appointment."

"Whatever do you mean? What could possibly be more important at this hour of the night than of our being together?"

Taking his hands in hers, she kissed them both before employing his fingertips to her pleasure, easing herself as she did so onto his lap. He could not resist her, his hands caressing the softness that pressed against him, his mouth seeking hers with an urgency that thrilled her. Whatever it was that had threatened to separate them had vanished: Marianne knew that for the time being he was in her power and that he could do nothing to free himself. But as Marianne's yearning for her husband's love increased to a pitch of fever, William suddenly withdrew from her arms, concern etched on his features.

"It is no use, Marianne," he said, kissing the top of her head before standing to adjust his dress. "I have come to say goodbye. It is imperative that I leave for Lyme immediately. Word has been sent that little Lizzy is dangerously ill again. Indeed, I have been informed that she may not see daylight tomorrow, and even if I leave now, I may be too late."

Marianne could not believe what she was hearing. How could this happen now when she was beginning to feel that they might be resolving their differences, rekindling the love that she knew was threatened by misunderstandings?

"It will be a trial for us both to be separated again, my darling," he murmured, sitting down again to take her hand in his own, "but you must understand there is nothing else to be done."

"But Lizzy recovered last time and she will be sure to again. You do not need to be there. Stay with me, William. Wait and see; if she is not better in a week, then you may go."

"I cannot delay. If anything were to happen to the child, I would never forgive myself. Please, Marianne, you must see I have no choice."

Marianne reached for her peignoir, wrapping the muslin tightly round her slight form. She was shivering now; all warmth seemed to have evaporated from her body like the dying embers in the grate. "Why must you always put their welfare before mine?" she cried. "When will you consider that my needs are as important? I want you here, William; I shall be ill if you go, and if you leave me again, I shall not answer for the consequences. I am certain this is just a ruse to take you away. Eliza cannot bear the thought of you being happy with your own family!"

Marianne knew that she must sound like a jealous harridan, but she could not help herself. Was she always to come second or third in importance to Brandon? All her jealous insecurities came rushing forth in a torrent of words.

"There are times, Marianne," he answered in grave tones, "when you astonish me. I do not think you are recognisable at this moment as the woman I married, and I must admit that I am finding it difficult to understand you. How you can imagine that I do not consider you is beyond all comprehension. That you do not appreciate my position, or that of others who do not enjoy your fortunate situation, is very clear. A little girl may be dying and all you can think of is yourself and your own selfish wants. Think for a moment, I beg you. Please understand that I have no choice."

Marianne regretted her outspoken tirade in that moment but could not find the words to apologise. Her anger still seethed inside. William stood before her with his arms crossed, looking most displeased. "I will leave now but I need not go alone.

Perhaps you would care to accompany me; then you will see for yourself that it is impossible for me to act in any other way. Come, let us leave for Lyme together."

Marianne knew that she could not accept William's invitation. There were unspoken reasons. "How can he ask me to nurse Willoughby's child and consider making me stay with the daughter of his first love? His one, true love," she thought bitterly. What was William thinking to even consider putting her in such a position? No, she did not appreciate nor understand him, she realised, sitting with her arms hugging her body and her feet tucked under her. Perhaps it was better if he left. Some time apart might do them good.

"I cannot leave Margaret," she said finally.

"Then I will say goodbye."

Colonel Brandon paused, as if to add something else. He took a step toward the bed. Marianne simply turned her back and lay down, pulling the coverlet almost over her head. She did not move nor speak, even when she heard the door open and shut with a soft click. The departing sound of carriage wheels and horse's hooves had only the effect of increasing her agitation, as she bitterly contemplated their angry exchange.

Chapter 30

WITH WILLIAM BRANDON GONE under such unhappy circumstances, a feeling of gloom and oppression settled on the house and its occupants. Margaret could easily perceive that Marianne was not in a mood to discuss the difficulties that she and the Colonel were having at present and found as a result that any conversation was problematic. Marianne was silent and uncommunicative. Excuses were readily found for the endless piles of unanswered invitations that came to the house, and a whole week passed by before Marianne decided that she was not looking after her sister's entertainment as well as she might. To make matters worse, she had only received two brief notes from William to say that he had arrived safely and that he had no real improving news of Miss Lizzy to give. In return, Marianne sent a single sheet of similar brevity.

Margaret was beginning to wish she could go home. She tried hard when writing letters to her mother to give the impression that she was having the time of her life, but several missives from Mrs Dashwood revealed that lady's concern all too readily. She wanted

JANE ODIWE

to know why Margaret did not seem to be enjoying London society and was anxious to hear if she had seen much of Henry.

Therefore, when Margaret heard that Charles Carey had called and was awaiting her company in the drawing room, she almost skipped along in anticipation to see him. Gone were any feelings of trepidation about what he might have to say or how he might react toward her; she was so relieved that at last she had a chance for some cheerful company. To her enormous relief and surprise she discovered he was not unaccompanied. James Mortimer was standing at his side, along with two very pretty girls, one of whom Margaret recognised as Emma Carey, Charles's sister. Margaret rushed forward to greet her old friend.

"Miss Carey, what are you doing here? How delightful to see you!" she exclaimed.

"Miss Dashwood, I am thrilled to see you, too. When Charles wrote with an invitation from Mr Mortimer to come and stay for a few weeks before Easter, I could not refuse." She paused to indicate her companion. "Please allow me to present my host's sister, Miss Caroline Mortimer."

"Dear Miss Dashwood," said Miss Caroline with a beaming smile, "I am so pleased to make your acquaintance. I have been away from home visiting my married sister in Cheltenham, but I have heard so much about you from my brother in his letters that I couldn't wait to meet you."

"Miss Mortimer, the pleasure is all mine," Margaret answered, gratified that there would be someone else in the party to divert Charles's attention away from herself. Caroline Mortimer was a beauty with her fair curls and green eyes.

Miss Carey continued. "Charles has promised that he will take us around to see the sights, which will be a pleasure I shall enjoy. But I must admit that as soon as I heard that you were here, my first wish was that I should call upon you. It is so long since we met. It must be last summer, I think, before I was sent to school. Well, my mother could hardly spare me, but she did want me to enjoy my brother's society and that of his friends."

"Miss Dashwood, how pleasant it is to see you again," Charles joined in, if a little hesitantly. "I declare we have not seen you for a week at least. I am glad to observe that you are in striking health; I had begun to think that you and the Brandons must be ailing."

"Oh no, Mr Carey, we are very well, but the Colonel has been called away on business and we have not had the leisure to be accepting as many invitations at present as we would like."

"Well, I hope you will accept our invitation to accompany us on a jaunt out to Hyde Park. It is a most enjoyable drive and the weather is very mild for this time of year."

"Please come, Miss Dashwood," begged Miss Carey. "Charles has hired a chaise for our use whilst I am in London. It will be such fun."

Margaret did not hesitate. Charles seemed as affable as ever and showed no signs of any suffering as a result of being informed of her sentiments by Mr Mortimer. Besides, she was quite wild to get out of the house.

Marianne was on the point of quitting her London home and heading back to Devonshire. Three weeks away from little James was too much to bear, she decided, and even though she knew he was probably having a wonderful time with his grandmother, aunt, and cousins, she ached to see him. She also needed the comfort and counsel of her mother and sister Elinor respectively, because she was finding it impossible to think clearly about the whole situation. In moments of reflection she wished that she had agreed to travel to Lyme with the Colonel, but there was nothing she could do about that now. Besides, she was still cross with Brandon. Though in her heart she knew her sentiments toward Miss Williams were bordering on her own misguided jealousy, she was still convinced that she had been right about her husband's lack of duty to his first family. She questioned his love for her and decided that she was no longer secure in his affections. By the end of the second week of his absence she was reconciled to what she imagined would forever be her lot: a marriage without true love and tenderness. Marianne was not ignorant of other marriages where the husband and wife, tied by alliance and fortune, carried on their lives as if the other person hardly existed. The wife surrounded herself with children; her husband took a mistress, setting her up in town where she generally enjoyed a freer if not better life than her counterpart. But she did not want to think of William taking such a woman or acknowledge her dark thoughts about Miss Williams in the dead of night. And however ridiculous her fears might seem on waking, when she thought about the Brandon she had married, Marianne was apt to spend long intervals in debating the probabilities of his constancy.

At least Margaret was enjoying herself at last and was going out and about looking more cheerful than Marianne had seen her for a while. The days out in Hyde Park or visiting museums would do her good. Even though the season was just starting, she would be sure to see enough to interest her and Marianne was glad that she had friends to share their pleasures.

On one such morning Marianne had waved goodbye to Margaret as she and her friends set off for a visit to the Tower of London to see the wild beasts. Marianne was just deciding what to do next when her reverie was broken by the sound of loud knocking upon the front door. Looking out of the window down onto the square, she could not imagine who her visitor might be; she did not recognise the smart equipage below. The servant came in proffering a card upon the salver. Taking it up, she read its owner's name with surprise.

"A Mr Willoughby is downstairs, ma'am, and begs me to inform you that it is on a matter of great urgency that he wishes to speak with you."

The violence of the knocking on the door had been enough to make Marianne exceedingly curious to know why he had presented himself. Thinking of their last exchange made her hesitate momentarily before she gave the instruction for him to be sent up.

His entrance into the room had none of its usual elegance. Mr Willoughby's dark capes flapped from an equally dark coat, giving a sombre yet agitated picture. His cheeks were flushed like raspberry stains on a damask cloth and his black hair lay in damp tendrils against his furrowed brow, emphasising the expression he bore of great concern. Marianne could not help but be moved by the sight of him.

"What on earth is the matter, Mr Willoughby?" she demanded, indicating a seat with a wave of her hand.

Willoughby remained standing, choosing to ignore Marianne's invitation. "Tell me, Mrs Brandon," he cried, "I have just heard and am anxious to know. Is the child out of danger?"

Marianne did not immediately answer for she was so shocked. There was only one child that he could be referring to, but how could he possibly know of her predicament? Her first thought was to deny him the knowledge he craved and send him away. But as he stood before her with an expression of sincere distress upon his face, she could only give him the news that the child was in a stable condition to her knowledge, if not out of grave peril.

"Lizzy is under the best care and with those that love her, which surely must be the best medicine any child could receive," she said with as much equanimity as she could muster.

"Thank God!" Willoughby cried. "I beg your forgiveness, Mrs Brandon, but when I heard the news that she was dying, I had to hear it from those who know the true facts."

"From whom did you receive this news?" asked Marianne, perturbed and puzzled about the source of his information. To her knowledge no one in London knew anything about the Williamses apart from Mrs Jennings. She hoped the old lady had not been indiscreet.

"I have my informants, friends near Lyme who bring me intelligence and news about those in which I have an interest."

Scarcely able to disguise the surprise on her face, Marianne was mute, unable to speak for a moment.

"I realise that my coming here like this will probably be a shock to you," he went on, "and I can imagine what you must think about my past misdeeds… You of all people know that I was a young man only capable of folly and imprudent behaviour."

"And a total disregard for the effects or outcome on those for whom you had little consideration," Marianne answered immediately.

"I cannot tell you how truly I regret my past conduct," he pleaded, "not only to Miss Williams, who did not deserve such reprehensible treatment at the hands of the scoundrel that I was then, but also because the woman I loved above any other was lost to me forever as a result."

"Come now, Mr Willoughby, do not pretend that you were in love. As I recall your true devotion was a predilection for the finer things in life. Your material satisfactions far outweighed any devotion to another human being."

As soon as the words were out she could have bitten her tongue. To show him how much she was still affected by his actions after all this time was not her intended purpose.

"I have regretted you ever since and I will to the end of my days, you know that," said Willoughby. "You were so gracious as to grant me forgiveness for my actions against you, but it will never entirely assuage my guilt, all that I suffer."

"But why wait until now to show your concern? And what of your child? As far as I know you abandoned Miss Williams to her fate and have never once tried to make reparation to little Lizzy."

"Believe me, Marianne," he murmured, using her name in the old familiar way, "I have wanted to, but I knew Brandon would sooner kill me than agree to let me anywhere near the child. Do you remember when we last saw one another at Whitwell?"

Marianne felt the blush painting her cheeks with spots of colour that Anna's doll would have been pleased to sport. Mr Willoughby was looking at her intently.

"I tried to tell you that evening. I wanted to ask you to intercede on my behalf," he continued. "I realised that I was asking too much and that to put you in such a position with your husband might make matters difficult for you, but please believe me when I say that I wish to atone for my sins. If I could be allowed to see the child, help provide for Lizzy and her mother, I hope I might feel some of my misdemeanors eradicated."

"Brandon will never allow it!"

"Ordinarily, perhaps, but if you were to speak on my behalf, I think anything might be accomplished. If you were my wife, I should not refuse anything you asked of me."

"But I am not your wife, Mr Willoughby," said Marianne, regarding him with distrust, remembering all his crimes with a sickening lurch of her stomach.

"If I could change the hands of time, you would be my wife. Forgive me; I have broken my promise not to talk to you of those feelings I once had for you. All I ask is that you help me persuade Colonel Brandon to let me make amends; to little Lizzy, at least."

In spite of herself, Marianne was very touched to hear the tender way in which he spoke his child's name and moreover, she could not really think why he should now be denied a chance to repair the past.

"Please, Marianne, I will never ask anything of you again."

"I will certainly consider the matter, but I have to tell you that I am not at all sure that my influence will count for very much. I do not know if I shall be able to change the Colonel's mind."

"Thank you," he managed to utter, stepping forward to take her hand between both of his, before bending his head to plant a kiss. "I will be forever indebted to you."

Marianne watched his carriage move off from the window. Shivering at the sight of the fog descending on the square, she pulled her shawl tighter about her shoulders. The fine weather of the last few days was turning; the temperature was dropping, changing the unseasonable warmth into winter again. After she watched the carriage disappear from view, Marianne sat down to compose a letter to her husband, but although her promise to Willoughby had been heartfelt, she did not think she could broach the subject in a letter. She fully intended to keep her promise, but she would have to wait until Brandon came home. How long that might take she had no idea.

When Margaret returned from her outing, Marianne saw at once that her sister was upset despite her denials and protestations to the contrary. Far from enjoying the day, Margaret had had the misfortune of running into Anne Steele, who had taken great delight in informing her of Henry Lawrence's forthcoming engagement. Margaret insisted that she was resigned to the idea, declaring it was no more than she expected, but Marianne was not blind to the truth of her real sentiments expressed behind her blue eyes in sadness. As soon as Margaret retired to her room, Marianne sat down to write a letter to her mother telling her of a change of plan. She and Margaret would be cutting their holiday short and coming home as soon as arrangements could be made.

Chapter 31

MARGARET AWOKE NEXT MORNING to the sense that somehow the world was different to the one she had known the day before. Her bed chamber was not suffused with the glorious sunshine of the past week, but as gloomy and dark as it ever was in winter. The windows were spangled with frosty ferns and ice blossoms, and the familiar sounds of London outside seemed muffled with a curious resonance. Carriage wheels and horses' hooves were barely audible, and the customary calls of the milk-maids and muffin sellers echoed as though they were calling out of a long tunnel. She got out of bed to pull back the muslin from the window, shivering with the cold as she did so. The sky, dark as a woodpigeon's breast, was filled with floating crystal feath-ers swirling down to earth to alight on grey rooftops swathed in swansdown, icy pavements and the cathedral tracery of dark boughs. Looking up at the leaden skies, she watched the snow's twirling progress from the heavens, blinking as each sparkling flake hurtled into her line of vision. Margaret wondered if Henry was looking out at the snow, too. The remembrance of yesterday's news came to her in sudden recall. At least she now under-stood why he had behaved in such a cold manner. Pulling the coverlet off the bed, she arranged herself on the window seat to watch London turn white and sort out her thoughts. There was something so underhand about the whole affair with Henry that she could not get out of her head, which, combined with the memory of their last outing together, puzzled her exceedingly. Perhaps Marianne was right. Lady Lawrence must be implicit in his change of heart. But if that was the case, then surely she was better off without a man who could be so easily persuaded to marry someone else. She couldn't deny that she had seen admiration in Henry's eyes for Mademoiselle de Fontenay. No, more than that, she had seen true love between them. It made her angry to feel how she had been duped, deciding there and then that she would never trust a man again, nor give away her heart so readily.

Marianne awoke late. When she eventually sat up in bed to observe the state of the weather, her spirits sank. The snow was drifting up to the railings and settling like thickly folded cotton sheets blanketing every surface, making the street outside look more like a scene from a country landscape. There would be no chance of travelling today, and she would be very lucky to even manage to send a letter to tell her mother of delays. And what of the weather in Lyme? Brandon would not be able to travel if the roads were bad. In any case, he did not seem to be in any hurry to return to London if the contents of his last letter were anything to go by. Perhaps the snow would be descending on Delaford also. She knew Mrs Dashwood would understand and wait for news. But if Marianne could not send a letter home, then surely none would be delivered in London either. However, at that very moment, as if the fates decided to prove her wrong, a knock at her door brought a pile of post and a mysterious parcel, which she was informed had been hand delivered. A quick perusal of the handwriting on each revealed that she had received news from her mother, Elinor, and William. On examining the parcel, the recognition of the script had the effect of disturbing her mind with sensations she could hardly describe. It was put aside; she did not want to unwrap it immediately. Marianne opened her letters first, saving Brandon's until last.

> *February 4th*
> *Wolfeton Fitzpaine*
> *My dear Marianne,*
>
> *I write with good news. Lizzy has turned the corner at last and we believe she is on the road to a full recovery. Eliza wishes me to thank you for your kind letters—they have been a true source of comfort. She is quite worn out with tending to the child; I have rarely seen such tender devotion or such capability. I wish you had made up your mind to travel with me; for I am sure if you could meet them you would hold them in the same esteem as I do. I have tried to make their home as comfortable as is possible whilst I remain here, but Eliza has a very independent streak and there are only so many gifts and offers of help as I am able to bestow upon them. But despite their lack of riches and their humble way of living, I have never witnessed such a harmonious household with boundless love, joy, and laughter to make me quite envious of their situation. I think you would be very taken with their cottage, Marianne. Eliza's talent for making*

something special out of the most unpromising materials have produced a warm and cheerful home, from the fashioned drapes at the windows to the carefully tended kitchen garden, her accomplishments with so very little would astound you, I am certain. Now the child is out of danger theirs is the happiest abode you can imagine. I wish you could see little Lizzy; I am sure you would love her as I do. She is growing into a very pretty girl; her hair has become quite dark and has a natural curl. Her manners are unaffected and she is unspoiled, making her quite the little heroine of the village. Despite their situation, the people round about have taken them to their hearts, and since I have been here they treat me with equal cordiality. Never a day goes by without a visit from some kindly neighbour bringing a posset of herbs or a mustard plaister. It gladdens my heart to see it and to know that when the time comes for me to leave I shall be able to do so in the sure knowledge that they will be well cared for when I am gone.

If all goes well, it will be in my power to return in another week. Of course I must be satisfied that my charge is truly recovered; there is a danger of a relapse and it would be pointless for me to make a journey too soon only to find that I am required to come back again.

I trust you and Margaret are enjoying yourselves in London. I suppose the delights of all the city has to offer would always be preferable to life in a cottage.

I remain,

Your loving husband,

William Brandon.

Marianne tossed aside the letter in frustration. All her jealous suspicions surfaced with a greater resentment than she had ever felt before. "It is clear," she thought, "that Eliza intends to beguile and captivate my husband with her charms and talents." To what ends, she did not want to envision. Miss Williams and her daughter had seduced him as surely as she believed the first Eliza had done so and Marianne could only feel animosity toward them. She hated William at this moment, for choosing to spend his time with Eliza and more so for loving her daughter with a tender affection he did not seem to bestow on his own child. Besides his obvious infatuation of the Williams family, Marianne was disturbed by the apparent lack of feeling or any sense of true devotion toward herself. His final words were deficient of any real sense of passion or love, she thought. Suspecting that he had transferred his affection, she reasoned that it was only too apparent that this was the case. But what she would do about it, as yet, she could not decide. Venting her feelings of frustration in a single cry, which echoed in the empty silence of her room, did not assuage her emotions. As the snow fell out of the sky her anger turned to bitterness.

In her fury she had almost forgotten the package, tightly bound in string and brown paper. Her trembling fingers could not untie the knots, so gummed were they with red sealing wax, and her stomach churned with anticipation. She hardly wanted to acknowledge her excitement and eagerness to discover its contents. Climbing out of bed, she fetched her scissors from the drawer of her dressing table and with a satisfying scrunch the string was cut. Marianne tore at the paper and found within the layers a slim volume, a book of poetry. Her fingers stroked the leather cover and traced the embossed name on the spine of her favourite poet, William Cowper. Skimming the pages to find her best-loved poems, the book fell open at the place where a piece of folded paper had been inserted. She read.

February 5th
My Dear Mrs Brandon,

Words cannot express my gratitude to you for your kindness to me yesterday. I think I have probably asked too much of you and will understand if you feel you cannot help me. I hope you know that my intentions have only been to right my mistakes; though I fear I shall never truly be able to reverse every wrong I have inflicted, especially those crimes committed against the dearest and loveliest creature I ever had the good fortune to know.

I wished to send you wildflowers, which I recollect were always your favourite, as a symbol of my gratitude, but as there are a scarcity at this time of year and are hardly to be found in London at all, I hope you will accept this "Winter Nosegay" which so eloquently laid down in this tome provides all the sentiment I could wish to express.

I am yours ever,
John Willoughby.

Marianne read the poem, one she knew well but with a sense that she was reading it for the first time. It was the last verse that she read over and over again.

See how they have safely survived
The frowns of a sky so severe;
Such Mary's true love, that has lived

Through many a turbulent year.
The charms of the late blowing rose
Seem'd graced with a livelier hue,
And the winter of sorrow best shows
The truth of a friend such as you.

Folding the paper, she replaced it between the pages and, clasping the book to her breast, smiled for the first time that morning.

Chapter 32

BY THE MIDDLE OF the week the snow had stopped falling, and grey skies were replaced by bright blue, making everywhere glitter in the sunshine. Visitors started to call again. Mrs Jennings and Sir Edgar visited as soon as their carriages could be dug out of the snow. Marianne did not feel equal to such gadding about herself, but received all her guests with cordiality. Mr Carey and his sister came with an invitation for Margaret to go skating with them in Hyde Park on Thursday. The Serpentine had frozen to a solid thickness, they reported, adding that Mr Mortimer and his sister were to be of the party also. Their excitement at the scheme soon infected Margaret with the idea that this venture might be as fun as it was proclaimed and so she accepted.

The following afternoon, as good as their word, the party called. Marianne greeted them in the hallway as they arrived.

"I do hope that you will consider joining us, Mrs Brandon," pronounced Charles.

"Oh, Mr Carey, that is very kind of you," Marianne answered, "but I am sure you young people won't need me to chaperone you."

"Marianne, please come," entreated Margaret, who thought the change of scene would do her sister good. Moreover, she considered that another person added to the party could only be of benefit, although she was glad to see that Charles spent all his time observing Caroline Mortimer when he thought no one was looking. Indeed, his behaviour toward that young lady was becoming very particular, she surmised.

Everyone declared how much they would all enjoy Mrs Brandon's company. Before she could make any further protest against their entreaties, Margaret summoned a warm pelisse and fur muff for Marianne to face the chill outside.

The main roads were quite clear so that the carriages made steady progress, arriving at Hyde Park in a very short while. All were astonished to see the great crowds of people intent on trudging through the snow for their amusement. Children with sledges slid down any likely hump in the landscape, their faces bright with laughter. Snow figures lined the roadways and a crowd of rowdy youths pelted one another with snowballs. As they approached the frozen lake, Margaret craned her neck to see the wintry scene. She had heard of famous frost fairs in London when the great River Thames had frozen over, but nothing had prepared her for the sight of the Serpentine Lake fringed with glowing lanterns in the dim afternoon light, the branches of trees dipping their lacy fingers into the polished, black ice. Crossing and re-crossing the vast expanse skated a myriad of figures in a stately ballet, silhouetted against ribbon streams of sunshine in tints of rosy pink to gild the clouds. There were icemen sweeping and burnishing the lagoon to a gleaming finish, hiring out skates for those intrepid enough to try them. Several booths had been set up from which hot ginger wine, ale,

or brandy could be purloined. The costermongers were setting
up shop by selling fruit, their wives tempting weary skaters
with oysters and hot meat pies. The noise of people shouting,
cheering, and laughing echoed in the still air to the accompaniment of cracking ice, loud as a firing musket.

They soon had their skates on and were taking their first
cautious steps upon the ice. The frozen water was very thick;
leaves imprisoned in layers within the depths gleamed like
amber jewels in Venetian glass. Margaret linked arms with her
sister and before long Miss Carey and Miss Mortimer joined
them. They kept up a swift pace to skate behind the gentleman
and were soon out of breath, Marianne begging them to stop so
that she could rest for a while.

"I cannot go any further," she cried. "I will stop awhile and
watch if you will excuse me."

"Then I will sit with you," added Margaret, holding onto her
sister's arm.

"That is quite unnecessary," Marianne insisted. "You go on
or the others will disappear. I am quite happy to sit on this bench
until you have exhausted yourselves. Go and have fun!"

Marianne sat down, watching her breath in little puffs
on the cold air gradually slow to a normal rhythm. Margaret
disappeared from view. It was very gratifying to see her laugh
again, thought Marianne. Miss Carey and Miss Mortimer were
clearly intent on making her feel most welcome into their circle.
Skating had lifted her spirits, too. It was only now that she began
to wonder about Brandon again. There had been no more post
since last week, but she knew that the weather was responsible
for that.

"Will you take a turn with me, Aunt Brandon?"

Henry Lawrence's voice brought Marianne out of her reverie. She looked up to see not only Mr Lawrence standing before her grinning from ear to ear, but also Mr Willoughby at his side, regarding her with an air of study.

"Good afternoon Mr Lawrence, Mr Willoughby," Marianne managed to say. She was shocked enough to see Henry here at all, but the recollection of Willoughby's gift was enough to emblazon her cheeks the same hue as the setting sun. But she was cross with Henry. How dare he stand there as though he had nothing to be reproached for, as if his behaviour had not been reprehensible?

Henry held out his hand. "Please, Aunt Brandon. I wish to speak to you on an urgent matter."

Marianne saw that the laughter had died from his eyes and that he was in earnest. "Very well," she replied, rising unsteadily, "but I warn you, skating is not my forte."

He took her arm and, leading her around the edge of the lake, they moved slowly along hardly skating at all.

"I must say, Henry," Marianne began, "that I can hardly bring myself to speak to you at all. I am sorry to say this when I am aware that I should be congratulating you on your forthcoming engagement, but I believe you have behaved very badly toward my sister. I am quite astonished that you appear to have no remorse or that you can address me in such a manner that belies any sense of guilt. There, I have said what I think on the matter and am not in the least sorry for it. Perhaps you would rather find someone else to go skating with than an aunt who expresses such displeasure in your company."

All this was said before Henry managed to utter a word. He stopped. "How is Margaret? I see that she is very happy in the company of other friends and in one gentleman in particular."

"Margaret is happy, but it is no thanks to you."

"Anne Steele says Margaret is on the verge of becoming engaged. Is it certain that Charles Carey has proposed?"

"I have no idea," Marianne replied. "It is true that Mr Carey is very attentive, and I believe he may make her an offer but whether she will accept, I cannot say."

"Then she is not in love with him?"

Something in Henry's expression made Marianne wish to tell the truth, however angry she was with him. "No, I do not believe Margaret is in love with Mr Carey. Unfortunately, some other scoundrel has stolen her heart, someone most unworthy!"

"Please believe me when I say that I have never wished to cause any suffering to your sister. I would like the opportunity to explain myself. May I gain your permission to call on Margaret the day after tomorrow?"

"I do not know that your calling on Margaret to explain yourself will make matters any better. Indeed, I am certain it will not be of any help at all." Marianne remembered the effect Willoughby's calling on her sister Elinor had made all those years ago when he had tried to explain why he had married for money. Should Margaret have to suffer knowing those same reasons?

"Please, Aunt Brandon, I beg you."

Marianne hesitated. What good could come of it? Margaret would only be made more upset. "I don't think it is a good idea, Henry," she said at last. "I'm sorry, but I think it would be better if you left Margaret well alone." They had turned in the course of their conversation and were now moving back towards the bench. Mr Willoughby rose from his seat to acknowledge them.

"I have to go now, Aunt Brandon," said Henry. "I have a matter of the greatest urgency to attend, an assignation which I cannot be late attending. Forgive me, I must go, but I will leave you in the very capable hands of my friend here, Mr Willoughby."

Before Marianne could protest Henry was gone, skating at great speed, weaving his way through the throng. She watched him until he was almost out of sight, coming to an abrupt halt before a young girl. It was impossible to see exactly whom the creature was that he took into his arms, but she thought she could guess. Mademoiselle de Fontenay linked her arm into his before they disappeared completely from view.

Marianne did not know what to say to Willoughby. She felt embarrassed, especially when she remembered the gift of poetry that he had sent and the sentiments behind the winter nosegay.

Mr Willoughby spoke first. "Forgive me, Mrs Brandon, but I hope that the book did not cause you distress. I wanted to express my heartfelt thanks. I think I see by your expression that my gift was not welcome. Perhaps it was, after all, a silly idea on my part. I am sorry."

"No, Mr Willoughby, do not apologise. I should be the one to say sorry for not thanking you immediately for your thoughtful present. But nevertheless, I do not think I should accept it, however sincere your motives."

"I quite understand; it was wrong of me to put you in such a position. Return it to me at your leisure, Mrs Brandon."

"I must rejoin my party," Marianne entreated, hardly wanting to meet his eyes, which had never left hers from the moment they met.

She took a few tentative steps on the ice, anxious to leave him yet aware that her sister and friends were nowhere to be seen.

"Here, let me help you," Mr Willoughby said, skating with precision to her side in a second.

"No, no, I assure you, I am well able to skate on my own, thank you," Marianne stated as convincingly as she was able as she tottered uneasily on the ice. He caught her arm and as he did so the sharp lemon scent of his fragrance assailed her senses with an onslaught of memories.

Shrugging away his arm, she staggered for a few steps more, but as she began to feel more confident took longer strides, sliding out across the polished surface as skillful as any dancer. She looked back momentarily to wave before the inevitable happened. Without quite knowing how she became entangled with another skater, the collision was one of great force, her feet skidding on the glacial surface until she fell with great indignity to her pride, humiliated that Mr Willoughby had witnessed her fall.

The pain that seared through her foot was immense. Mr Willoughby rapidly skated to her assistance. She had raised herself from the ground, but her ankle had been twisted in the fall, and she was scarcely able to stand. Marianne could hardly look him in the eye as he offered his services. Too many were the memories and the feelings that rushed in upon her as he loosened her boot before taking her up into his arms without further delay. There was little choice but to drape her arms about his neck and allow him to take charge. Marianne shut her eyes in agony for the pain was unbearable. She didn't open them again until she was aware that she had been seated in an unfamiliar carriage. Mr Willoughby closed the door behind them and bade Marianne not to distress herself as she started to protest.

"I think you might have a break," he said, unlacing her boot and easing it from her foot with careful fingers. His touch was very gentle though Marianne winced with every pressure she felt. It was with some relief that she heard on his greater inspection that her ankle was only twisted, there were no bones broken. He would bind her foot and arrange to take her home. A glass of hot mulled wine was instantly procured, which she was made to drink, being assured all the while of its medicinal properties.

"My sister," whispered Marianne through her suffering, "Margaret will wonder what has become of me."

"Do not worry," he replied, "I have sent word already. I will take you home and have the doctor sent for immediately."

Unwinding the stock about his throat, she watched him wrap the fabric around her swelling ankle. His expression was serious, his bottom lip bitten in concentration. Her eyes wandered to the gaping neckline of his shirt, where the pulse throbbed in his neck. He looked up suddenly as if he felt her contemplation, catching her expression. He smiled, looking deeply into her eyes.

Tears misted her eyes as she winced again. Willoughby held the cup of warm liquid to her lips and she drank the remainder of the spiced wine. Fetching out his pocket handkerchief, he handed it to Marianne. Dabbing at her eyes, his perfume and the images of a hundred autumn days threatened to overpower her.

Marianne returned his smile as Willoughby took the seat next to hers.

"I hope you feel more comfortable," he said. Marianne could no longer look into his eyes and turned to regard the world outside. Her head felt woozy from the wine, but she felt a glow of warmth within. The sun was setting, a huge crimson ball of fire reflected in slivers of rose and silver across the lake. Outside the gaiety continued in noisy effervescence. Torches were being lit against the dimming light. It was growing dark and the carriage was filling with velvet shadows creeping over her like a mantle.

Marianne suddenly sensed that it might be dangerous to turn her head to look at Willoughby. The tension in the air was great and the only sound was their breathing, rapid with emotion.

"Marianne," started Mr Willoughby in a low voice.

"Yes, Mr Willoughby," Marianne answered, turning her head slowly. Her heart was beating so fast that she thought he must hear it.

He was staring at her mouth. His eyes penetrated hers with such a look of intent that she knew he wanted to express his desire. She felt lost in the depths of those dark pools, which drew her in with such a power that she knew she would need all her strength to thwart it. He moved in silence, carefully tucking the blanket he had provided around her. Too aware of his close proximity, his breath stirring the curls around her face, she felt the quiet strength of his hands and was ashamed when she acknowledged to herself that she wished to feel those fingers on her skin. Forcing herself to turn away again, she gazed out at the torchlit procession.

"Marianne..." Willoughby softly persisted.

Marianne knew before she turned her head again that something was going to happen, and though she wished she could prevent it, knew as her eyes met his once more, the certainty of the moment.

Willoughby leaned over her in the darkness. Everything was blotted out as his lips brushed hers. As if propelled by attracting forces, their lips sought one another. Willoughby's touch was as gentle as she remembered, his kiss awakening the ardour of a time she thought long over. For a moment Marianne felt her mouth disobey her inner commands and her lips seek his as hungrily as he sought hers.

"Please God, Marianne, forgive me," Willoughby cried when she pulled away in some distress, "I could not help myself."

Marianne was trembling, partly with the feelings of aroused passions she could not control, but also with the knowledge that she had behaved just as badly as he. For in that split second when she might have turned her face away from his, she had decided to meet him on equal terms. She had known that he was going to kiss her and she had acted accordingly. Just once more she had wanted to feel his desire, acknowledge her yearning for lost love with a craving to feel alive again. If Brandon didn't want her, then why shouldn't she satisfy her longing for affection, she had reasoned in a split second. In her moment of madness Marianne had believed that she was the wronged wife and was thus justified in her conduct. She collapsed into a fit of sobbing, averting her countenance and indeed her whole body away from Willoughby, who frozen into inaction by his own misdeeds, sat helpless and remorseful.

"Please, Mr Willoughby," she managed to say at last, "will you take me home?"

Willoughby instructed his coachman to fetch the servant as soon as they reached Manchester Square and left as soon as Marianne had been carefully removed from the carriage. The doctor soon arrived to make her comfortable, swiftly followed by Margaret, who could see from her sister's countenance that she was in no mood to discuss her escapade. As Marianne lay back upon her propped pillows, her foot throbbing with pain, she tried with little success to blot out the memory of Willoughby's kiss, refusing to acknowledge her own part in the fatal conspiracy. Willoughby alone was to blame, she decided at last. He had taken advantage of a situation where, completely powerless against him, she had surrendered. Having trusted him again, he had ruthlessly broken her faith. Marianne cried for Brandon, weeping for the man she felt lost to her forever. What a fool she had been to let Willoughby kiss her and kiss him in return. But wishing that nothing had happened was not going to alter the fact that it had. Marianne knew she would have to live with this truth and with the consequences, whatever they may be.

When Margaret questioned her about the accident the following day, Marianne could hardly meet her eyes, relating the briefest details of Willoughby's rescue, choosing instead to turn the conversation round to that of her sister's recollections of the day. Marianne's own thoughts on the matter had shifted slightly. She did not blame John but acknowledged that her own part, fuelled by unhappiness and Brandon's neglect, had been partly responsible. The combination of so many factors had led to her disgrace. Finding herself in so intimate a situation with Willoughby had brought back so many emotions from the past. Acting instinctively by following her heart had led to a second of selfish desire. It had been a gross mistake but she could not pretend that Willoughby was entirely to blame. Marianne could not think about what she should do but knew beyond a doubt that she would never allow such a dreadful episode to happen again. But for now, in order to preserve her sanity, Marianne decided to put the whole affair out of her head.

Chapter 33

MARIANNE'S THOUGHTS TURNED TO her sister, deciding that she would not tell Margaret about the conversation she had had with Mr Lawrence. He was another gentleman of whom she was extremely wary; she was not clear about what he had meant and wanted to spare her sister from further harm if she could. But an incident that morning not only puzzled her exceedingly but also was enough to divert any misgivings she had had about the events of the previous day.

Mrs Jennings called with a report of such astounding news that neither Marianne nor Margaret quite knew what to make of it. She almost burst into the room, her agitation clear for all to see.

"Well, my dears," she started, "this is a to-do and no mistake. I have just called upon my friend Mrs Clarke and she informed me of a most alarming report." The old lady paused to catch her breath, puffing as she lowered herself onto the sofa. "God bless me, I am quite out of sorts," she laughed, fixing her eyes with such intent upon the two sisters that their first thought was that she must be about to tell them a huge joke. "You will never guess what has happened!"

Marianne and Margaret waited to hear the momentous news.

Certain that the sisters were completely engaged and anxious to relate her gossip, she announced the terrible event with much gesticulation and nodding of her head.

"Mademoiselle de Fontenay has disappeared!" she declared at last.

This information was quite enough to produce audible gasps from the two young women. Margaret's first thought was that she was certain Mademoiselle de Fontenay had not vanished on her own and waited with dread to hear that Henry had quit London also.

"Not only has she gone, no one knows where, but she has run away with a good-for-nothing fellow, as I heard tell of it!"

Margaret was so shocked she blurted out, "Who on earth can you mean, Mrs Jennings?"

"Apparently, Lady Lawrence has taken the news very badly, for you know she had such hopes that her Henry was going to marry the French miss. It appears that she has run away—nay, eloped—with a penniless Count by all reports. Unfortunately, Mrs Clarke didn't have any more details; she had only just heard it from her friend Mrs Harris, but I thought you would be interested to hear of it. What do you make of it, Miss Margaret? Didn't we all think that a wedding was about to be announced between Mr Lawrence and his mademoiselle?"

Margaret was so shocked that she couldn't speak. The more she puzzled about the affair, the more entangled her thoughts became. She kept returning in her mind to the day at Hookham's library when she had overheard the whispered conversation between Henry and Mademoiselle de Fontenay. Nothing made sense.

"I only saw Henry yesterday," Marianne said at last, not quite knowing what to make of the news. "I am sure I saw him with Mademoiselle de Fontenay, although it is true they were quite a distance away from me."

Mrs Jennings now rose to take her leave, having divulged her gossip to great effect. "I daresay you will have to call on your sister-in-law, Mrs Brandon. She is by all accounts in a terrible state, a relapse, I have heard, of her old ailments. Lord knows what Brandon will say when he hears about this. I do hope he comes home soon. You are looking a little peaky, my dear. I daresay he will put the colour back in your cheeks soon. Well, I had better be going. I am sure Lucy will want to hear my news!"

Then her eyes alighted on the stick at Marianne's side. "My dear, what on earth has happened? Are you lame?"

Up until that point the offending foot had been hidden underneath Marianne's skirts, but it was impossible not to give some account of her accident. Margaret filled in most of the details, but Marianne noticed that she gave no hint of Mr Willoughby's implication in the whole affair, for which she was really grateful. After expressing much commiseration and recommending ice for the swelling, both girls were relieved when Mrs Jennings called for her carriage.

No sooner had Mrs Jennings left than Henry Lawrence called. He stood at the door looking almost bashful, Margaret thought. He came in at Marianne's invitation and sat down.

"I expect you have heard the news by now that Mademoiselle de Fontenay has left town," he said.

Margaret could not speak. She stared at Henry, who looked so handsome in his blue coat, she decided. Almost overcome by her feelings, she could not think how to answer him and sat staring, quite mute.

"Mrs Jennings called not ten minutes ago," Marianne said eventually.

There was silence for a minute after this last statement, broken at last by Henry, who appealed to Marianne and Margaret at once.

"I wondered if I might persuade you to accompany me to Gunter's once more, Miss Dashwood. That is, if I may gain your permission, Mrs Brandon. Of course, Miss Dashwood, I will quite understand if you do not wish to come. Perhaps you are engaged elsewhere. You might have other plans and be expecting other callers this morning who may wish to take you out." He stood up as if he could not decide whether he should stay or go. "But I should like it above all things if you should come. I must speak to you and explain everything."

Margaret could hardly contain herself; she didn't know whether to feel pleased or be cross with Henry. But she knew she was quite prepared to hear him out and if necessary was ready to give him a piece of her mind. "I should like to come with you, Mr Lawrence," she answered, taking the arm he proffered.

Marianne was unsure whether she was doing the right thing by allowing her sister to go off with Henry. It was indeed a puzzling affair, but she hoped everything might soon be settled one way or another between them so that they could both go home to Delaford. Wanting to leave London was her priority, but she wanted to depart from town with her husband. Where was he? Would he ever come home? There was still no news from

Brandon, but she reasoned that the weather had no doubt made delays in the post. In her thoughts the Colonel seemed such a remote figure. Whenever she tried to think of him, the image in her head depicted scenes that she did not want to acknowledge. Haunted by the idea that he was happier in Lyme with Eliza and Lizzy, she imagined him with the child on his knee, kissing her ebony curls. How did he occupy himself in the evenings? Did he read poetry to Eliza as he had once read it to her, sitting by the fire in a cosy inglenook with the curtains drawn against the storms outside? Did he sit in the parlour watching her nimble fingers and swift needle weave their magic? How did Eliza look in candlelight? Like her mother, Marianne had no doubt. Her dreams entwined the pair, Eliza and Brandon joined by the passion of love lost long ago. Marianne, jealous and resentful, felt her solitude and loneliness increasing. She faced the future with dread.

Chapter 34

MARGARET COULD NOT HELP feeling a mixture of emotions as she stepped into Sir Edgar's coach. She did not know what to think; anger, excitement, and fear trembled over her in waves. Henry seemed like a stranger; she could not think when last they had really spoken to one another and as yet, Henry had not uttered a word.

"Miss Dashwood, I realise I have a lot of explaining to do," he began from his seat on the opposite side, "Would you mind if I change our plans very slightly? I have so much to talk to you about and I do not think I can relate it all to you in so public a place as Gunter's. I have my father's permission to take his coach for the afternoon, and I wondered if I might take you first for a drive through Hyde Park as I promised all that time ago."

There was something so gentlemanly about his request and he put her so at ease by the kindly way he addressed her that she raised no objection. Henry gave the command and they set off, soon finding their way down Oxford Street in the direction of the park.

Neither of them spoke for a moment or two. Margaret looked out at the melting snow turning to slush along the highway, dripping iced water from tree branches of black lace silhouetted against a sky of storm clouds.

"I saw you with Charles Carey and his sister yesterday," said Henry.

"They have been very good to me whilst I have been in London," Margaret answered. "James Mortimer and his sister have been very kind also."

"Mr Carey admires you very much, I know," Henry ventured, watching Margaret's countenance closely.

"Mr Carey is a friend of long standing. Whether he admires me or not is another matter." Margaret felt her confusion in a warm glow spreading upwards from her neckline.

"But Anne Steele told me he wishes to marry you and that everything is set for an engagement between you."

"Mr Carey has no such expectations. I have no desire to marry him. He is like a brother to me and as such could never be anything else."

Margaret turned her gaze to look at Henry. "Appearances are not always as they seem, I do not think."

"No, indeed," said Henry with a smile. "One should never rely on outward show alone or the confidence of others. Miss Steele and her sister Mrs Ferrars were very convincing. I was assured that you were to be married before Easter."

"I would like to be able to pardon them, to say that they mean well, but unfortunately I cannot in truth come to their aid. Those sisters have always enjoyed a gossip and if there is none to be had, they simply make it up," Margaret declared with a shrug of her shoulders. "Getting wed is all they talk about. Perhaps that is their ambition, but I have never had any intention to get married to anyone."

"I am sorry to hear that," Henry replied. Margaret noted that Henry had such an expression of sadness on his face that instead of feeling any animosity toward him, she felt rather sorry as she remembered that his heart must be broken and his pride more than a little bruised. It was impossible to feel anything but compassion for him.

"Henry, I am so sorry about Mademoiselle Antoinette," she said. "I know you were engaged. It must have been a huge shock."

Henry raised his eyes to hers, shaking his head before bursting out with laughter. "Margaret, forgive me, but as you said yourself, outward show is not always as it seems."

Margaret felt quite cross again. He was laughing at her, she was sure. She stared at him incredulously, deciding she should ask him to take her home instantly.

"Listen, Margaret. My engagement with Antoinette was all pretence and façade, you know. There has never been anything other than a deep friendship between us; we have known each other since we were small children. I do love her but as one loves a sibling, the sister I never had. Our mothers are great friends and they always cherished a hope that we might marry some day. Antoinette met her Count several months ago in the Assembly Rooms at Bath and fell in love whilst dancing."

Margaret was stunned into silence. She was remembering the young man she had seen at Lady Denham's ball. "I do not understand," she said at last. "Surely there could be no objection to her marrying a French Count."

Henry sighed. "I feel very sorry for the fellow. He has unfortunately lost all his money so it was considered a most imprudent match. He has always nurtured hopes that his house and land might be returned to him in France, and Antoinette told me that he is to come into an inheritance some day in the future. Regrettably, this information was not enough to satisfy her mother and why everything was set for a match between us. You may imagine that my mother and the Comtesse are most displeased. Happily, they are unaware of my involvement in the whole proceedings."

"Did you help Antoinette run away?" asked Margaret, certain of the answer.

"I did, and was prepared to take the blame also, but she would not hear of it. Fearing the wrath of both our parents and more particularly of my mother, she insisted that I should not give myself up to their questions. Nevertheless, I have still endured a dreadful interrogation, but I am happy that the lovers are far away."

"Will you tell me where they are gone?" Margaret knew she shouldn't ask, but she thought she had an idea that they might have undertaken a long journey.

"Can I trust you, Margaret?" Henry looked into her eyes. Margaret held his gaze steadily, so earnestly did she wish him to divulge his secrets. "You can trust me with your life," she answered truthfully.

"I believe I can. They have gone to France where Jean has many friends and relatives to help them. Perhaps it might be seen as a dangerous step, but Jean is adamant that his claims to his land may yet be fulfilled and his home recovered. I do not know if they will stay, but Antoinette did not want to risk remaining here. After all, she might have had to marry me!"

"Did she consider that to be such a bad thing? Antoinette is a very good actress, I think. I was completely fooled. She looked as if she adored you."

"And may I ask, Miss Dashwood, what you thought about that?"

Henry's eyes were staring into hers again. Margaret fixed him with a bold glance. "I must admit that I did not like it."

"And I must admit that I was ready to run Charles Carey through with a sword!"

"Oh, Henry!"

"Will you forgive me, Margaret?"

"Of course I will, Henry."

The coach had come to a standstill under the trees in a deserted spot at the edge of the park. Margaret felt the impropriety but could not have cared. To be sitting so intimately with Henry gazing at her with adoration was all she could wish. He sat forward on the edge of his seat and put out his hand to take hers.

"I love you, Margaret," he said softly. "I have since the moment I met you and never did stop loving you, though I am certain that is not how it must have appeared. The risk was too great. Not that I couldn't confide in you, but I had to convince others that there was no hint of any relationship between us. I had to make you hate me and make my mother and the Comtesse believe that I loved Antoinette in order for our plan to succeed."

"I understand, truly," Margaret whispered, delighting in the touch of his fingers entwined with her own. "But in any case, I could never have hated you, Henry, whatever happened. I love you too much."

Suddenly, the sound of dripping water pattering down upon the carriage hood rose with a crescendo, drumming with the rhythm of a sharp shower of rain. Water ran in great rivulets down the panes of glass at the windows, making it impossible to see out. Margaret felt cocooned in a little world of her own, marooned with the only man she ever felt she would love. Henry stroked her gloved fingers, raising them to his mouth. He turned her palm over, brushing the soft flesh of her wrist just above the edge of her glove with his lips.

"Margaret, forgive me," he said, clasping her hand to his cheek with great affection, "I must ask you something of importance, but I have to tell you that I am so afraid of your answer that I do not wish to ask it of you."

"Oh, Henry, am I so fearsome?" Margaret declared, thrilled by the sensation of her hand against his face, "Please ask me anything at all!"

Henry shook his head. "No, I do not think you fearsome, Miss Dashwood. On the contrary, you are the most delightful person I ever met and that is why I am wary of speaking to you on a matter which will decide my future forever."

Margaret attempted to cover her feelings with a flippant retort. "Henry, you are so funny. I should think you didn't like me from the way you talk."

Henry moved from his seat to sit next to her, still clasping her hand in his own. He looked down, smoothing the leather as he spoke. "I know that you have no wish to marry anyone ever, but I am hoping that if one day you should change your mind that you would consider becoming my wife."

"Henry, I should be honoured to be your wife, whenever you wish it," she answered, moving her head to arrest the gaze of his wandering eyes so that she could show him her sincerity with a look of pure love. "I didn't know it before you asked me but I am very sure now that I should like it above all things."

Henry bent down on one knee, looking up at her imploringly. "Margaret Dashwood, will you marry me?"

"Yes, Henry Lawrence, I will!" Margaret answered eagerly.

Margaret watched Henry rise to be seated at her side again, only this time he was so close that her breath quickened in response. He lifted his eyes to hers again, as he removed his gloves, revealing his long, tapered fingers. She felt the tug on her bonnet ribbons as they slipped undone between his fingers and made no movement as he removed her bonnet. Henry touched her hair softly. "You are so beautiful," he whispered, reaching to clasp the tender skin at the base of her neck where the curls fell down her back. Pulling her toward him, Margaret anticipated him, raising her lips to his own to enjoy the sensation of his mouth caressing her in a sweet kiss.

"We have just one small problem to overcome," Henry began as they reluctantly broke apart.

"Your mother will do everything in her power to oppose the match."

"I would not be telling the truth if I were to contradict you, but that is not the immediate problem. I have not yet told my parents of my desires. As it is, Antoinette has only just fled from London and I hope you will understand when I say that I wish to keep our engagement secret for a while. My mother thinks I am heartbroken and for the present I do not wish to disillusion her. I think it safest if Antoinette and Jean are given as much time as possible to secure their own marriage and livelihood. I am so sorry, Margaret, if I disappoint you. I hope you understand."

"Henry, I do not care how long we have to wait to tell others about our engagement," she said, regarding him almost shyly. "All that matters is that I know you love me and you want me to be your wife some day. Do not worry, I shall not tell a soul, not even Marianne, though how I shall manage that under her scrutiny, I cannot quite imagine. But I will, I promise."

"Margaret, I have a little something for you, a token to express my love and, I hope, secure our secret engagement."

Henry pulled a small, hinged box from his waistcoat pocket. Hesitantly, he offered it to Margaret, who gasped with delight.

"I was not expecting a gift, Henry," she cried, sliding back the hook on one side. Within the box she found the most perfect ring she could imagine. An emerald, surrounded by diamonds, twinkled like a daisy in summer from its velvet cushion. "Thank you, Henry," Margaret cried as he placed it on her finger. "Of course I shall hide it until we can make our announcement official. I do hope you will be able to persuade your mother and father that we might marry."

"My father will be very happy, I know, and I am sure it will just be a matter of time before my mother will be brought round. No one could help falling in love with you, Margaret. We shall be the happiest pair that ever lived!"

Indeed, no two people could have seemed happier at that moment as Henry Lawrence and Margaret Dashwood took a turn around the Park once more, clasped in each other's arms.

Chapter 35

MARIANNE WAS DISAPPOINTED THAT Margaret did not have any interesting news to divulge on reaching home. She had been sure that Henry's explanation of everything that had happened might mean that he wished to make amends to her sister, but all her questions proved in vain. Margaret was being highly evasive. The most her sibling would admit was that it had been good to see Henry, going so far as to say that she hoped they might be very good friends again. But Margaret's behaviour was very worrying, Marianne decided, especially on further observation over the next few days. Her sister kept choosing to go out alone, spurning the company of all her friends. It didn't seem natural. Perhaps Henry had told her of his broken heart. How selfish men could be.

"I just like to go walking, that is all," Margaret insisted after Marianne's curiosity got the better of her later on in the week.

"Forgive me for asking this, Margaret, but did you and Henry quarrel that day?" Marianne asked, forgetting all her resolution to remain silent on the subject of Henry Lawrence.

Margaret looked at her sister with exasperation. She had known it would be difficult trying to meet Henry in secret, but she had at least credited Marianne with having some discretion. "I've told you, Marianne, it was lovely to see Henry and we are friends again."

"But did he not give you any indication of anything else?" Marianne started, realising instantly that she had probably said far too much and had communicated her enquiries very ill.

"Marianne, I think your questioning of me in this manner a great impertinence," declared Margaret before deciding to assuage her sister's inquisitive nature by attempting to silence her on the subject of Henry Lawrence permanently. "Henry has yet to recover from Mademoiselle Antoinette's duplicity, he told me. He wished to speak to me and confide in me as his friend; that is all. Besides, I do not want any romantic attachments, Marianne," she said, turning away from her sister as she spoke the words so that her face and expression were averted. "My heart was broken quite cruelly and I do not know if I can trust any gentleman ever again. I am happy to be on friendly terms with Henry and Charles, but I do not wish to marry either of them! That is all I am prepared to say on the subject. I am going out now. The fresh air restores my spirits and if you do not mind I would prefer to walk alone."

"We will go home to Delaford, Margaret. I think you will be much happier if you can see Mama," soothed Marianne. "The weather is much better now and I think it will be for the best."

"I do not want to go home; I wish to stay here. Goodbye." Margaret ran from the room, fearful that Marianne might stop her. On reflection she realised that she had not conducted her side of the conversation very skillfully. Marianne would be even more determined to find out where she was going and what she was doing. But she couldn't help that now. All she wished was to meet her love in secret.

Another week passed by and there were no more letters from Brandon. When people made their enquiries, Marianne was finding it difficult to provide explanations. Her husband's "business" in the West Country was taking an inordinately long time and with everyone expecting his prompt return as soon as the snows thawed, it was a problem knowing how to answer their questions when he didn't arrive. As for Mrs Brandon herself, she had no such eagerness to know what was delaying her husband. She tried not to dwell on bleak contemplation. At least she had seen nothing more of Mr Willoughby. Fortunately, the memory of that fateful wintry day, too terrible to dwell on, like the bruising on her ankle, was fading fast.

An invitation arrived from Sir Edgar on Tuesday to attend an evening party in Portman Square. His letter begged that Marianne and Margaret should be present as they all needed cheering up, what with a certain young lady not being amongst them anymore. He added that the party would be large, Lady Denham, Mrs Jennings, Mr and Mrs Ferrars, Miss Steele, the Mortimers, and the Careys having all accepted. To her great surprise, Margaret seemed eager to go and as Marianne reckoned it would cause more gossip to decline than to go and suffer interrogation, she opted to accept the invitation. Though she was not looking forward to the questions and examination that she knew Mrs Jennings's conversation would entail, it would give Margaret a chance to be out in society again with a group of young people. All this walking around on her own was not entirely healthy, Marianne knew, and besides, there was always the chance that Henry might fall in love with her again or that Margaret might finally fall for Charles.

The party was considerably larger than either of the young women had anticipated. There were many faces that Marianne did not recognise, and she was grateful to Sir Edgar for introducing them to many of his friends so that for an hour at least Mrs Jennings could not get near them.

Finally, it could not be avoided. Mrs Jennings appeared, regaling them with all the gossip she had heard.

"It seems Lady Lawrence is reconciled to the fact that Henry has missed his chance with Miss Antoinette. She thinks he has had a lucky escape now she has learned of the elopement. I notice the Comtesse is not amongst us this evening; I daresay she must still be distraught at what has happened. I don't believe they have yet tracked down the rascals."

"Either that or Lady Lawrence has omitted to invite her, which would not surprise me," Marianne declared, the words out before she could stop them. "I expect the Comtesse has fallen down the social ladder somewhat after this escapade."

"Mrs Brandon," said Mrs Jennings at the volume of an actor's stage whisper, "I hate to be the one to tell tales, but Sir Edgar did let it slip that Lady Lawrence and the Comtesse have become quite estranged as a result. He has been quite out of his mind with worry about his wife; I believe she has been very ill. Sir Edgar says he is only thankful that Henry has come out of it reasonably unscathed. Broken hearts and young people are ever twinned, are they not, Miss Dashwood? Have you broken Mr Carey's heart irrevocably? Look, over there, he is gazing at you with such admiration, poor fellow. Give him a little more encouragement this evening and if you are not engaged to be married by the end of it, I shall not know my own mind!"

Margaret followed her pointing finger to the other side of the room where Charles, James, Emma, and Caroline were standing. It had not escaped Margaret's attention that Charles and Caroline seemed to have become very easy in one another's company. She noticed with glee that he was not staring in Margaret's direction after all, only into Miss Mortimer's eyes, which pleased Miss Dashwood exceedingly. Emma Carey was waving at her to join them. "Excuse me, Mrs Jennings, I must go to my friends," she said and left before anyone could make any attempt to stop her.

"Where is the spurned suitor?" questioned Marianne, looking about for Henry.

"Sir Edgar said he's been out with friends all day. I expect they are trying to cheer him up. I don't know what the world is coming to, Mrs Brandon. I never saw a pair so in love and now look at what has happened. I don't understand these young people nowadays with their fickle hearts. Not like their elders, steadfast and true, eh, Mrs Brandon?"

"No, quite," muttered Marianne, who could not bring herself to look Mrs Jennings in the eye.

"When is Brandon coming back to London?" Mrs Jennings was scrutinising Marianne very carefully, waiting for her response. She lowered her voice again. "How is the little girl? Is she gaining strength? I have not heard from the Colonel lately but I daresay he has been keeping you informed of her progress. I do hope he comes back soon. You are still not looking yourself, my dear."

Marianne did not have to answer any questions after all, it seemed. Mrs Jennings was quite happy to provide what she surmised were the answers herself. All Marianne had to do was nod in the right places. It was true; she was not feeling quite right, though she would never admit it to Mrs Jennings. She felt tired and lacking in energy. Her spirits were not high and she was worn down with trying to appear as if all was well in her world. There was a gnawing tension in the pit of her stomach, which increased every time her thoughts turned to Mr Willoughby. When she saw him standing by the door with Henry Lawrence, her fears increased.

Margaret was delighted to see Henry even though she knew she could not give away her feelings. It was almost too much to bear pretending to be civil with barely a smile for him and having to pass on in the crowd, talking to others with whom she had no wish to converse. So she was delighted when she received a message from Henry delivered by Mr Willoughby. Taking her to one side, he whispered into her hair that Henry wished to meet her on the floor above at the top of the stairs towards the other end of the house. She looked up at Willoughby in surprise but a simple gesture raising his finger to his lips was enough to keep her silence. Almost running out of the room with excitement, Margaret forced herself to walk slowly away. With such a crush of people, it was easy to disappear. Out in the dim corridor she rushed forward into the darkness of the upper staircase filled with anticipation and longing. Henry was waiting, stepping out of the shadows to take her hand. They ran, laughing as they went, secure in the knowledge that everyone was downstairs.

Henry stopped before a door. "This is my room," he whispered, turning the handle to reveal a spacious chamber, and ushered Margaret inside.

Marianne did not know what to make of the scene she had just witnessed. Indeed, her astonishment was turning into incredulity. Watching Mr Willoughby whispering into her sister's hair and witnessing the exchange of cognisant looks between them had given her quite a shock and much cause for concern. Now they had both disappeared. Marianne's mind searched for an answer, but the only possible scenario she could devise was not one she could clarify. Her thoughts kept turning to Margaret and her solitary walks and those confessions made long ago of an infatuation with the man Marianne alone had thought possessed her soul. No, it was too ridiculous. There must be some other explanation. All she had to do was find Margaret and everything would be understood.

"Mrs Brandon, how charming you look this evening, does she not, Mr Ferrars?" Lucy asked her husband. Barring the way with firm resolution stood Mrs Ferrars. Marianne would have liked to pass by, but it was impossible and she certainly did not want Lucy to know that her sister was nowhere to be found.

"You must be missing your dear husband so much. Didn't I say, Mr Ferrars, how much Mrs Brandon must have been pining for her spouse?"

"I cannot recollect anything of the sort, Lucy. But then I daresay I don't attend to half of what you say. Were you just talking of Colonel Brandon?" Marianne watched him preen himself. Without casting an eye over either lady, his full attention was on his reflection in the looking glass on the opposite side of the room.

"Yes, of course, Mr Ferrars," Lucy cried in exasperation. "I do wish you'd pay attention. Colonel Brandon has been away on business but he has been gone for three weeks; or is it more like a month, dear Mrs Brandon? You must be so lonely. And especially with him not being here to help you when you sprained your ankle. It's a good job you have other friends to keep you company."

"I am fortunate indeed," Marianne managed to say but did not fail to catch Lucy's expression.

"Mr Willoughby has been a friend of your family for a long time, has he not, Mrs Brandon?" She lowered her voice before announcing, "It must be of some comfort to you and your husband that difficult scenes from the past have not stood in the way of true friendship. But I see what you are thinking, Mrs Brandon. Perhaps not everyone might understand your carrying on such a friendship whilst your husband is away. Be assured, my dear, I am as silent as the grave." Patting Marianne's arm as if to reassure her she added, "Well, I daresay I am very discreet but I cannot talk for others. Take care, my dear, I should not like to see gossip and false talk come of such a harmless episode. Come, Mr Ferrars, you promised me a dance and I'm jolly well going to get one." They left, leaving Marianne staring after her, quite ready to burst into tears.

Chapter 36

HENRY AND MARGARET WERE sitting on the window seat hidden between wooden shutters and long velvet curtains.

"This was such a wonderful idea, Henry."

"I could not spend all evening without speaking to you or touching you," Henry whispered, taking her hand to plant a kiss. "Besides, I have something I must tell you. I don't know what I am to do about it yet; or even if I can find a way out but…"

Henry broke off with such a look of concern on his countenance that Margaret was instantly alarmed.

"What is it, Henry? Oh, please do not look like that, you are truly frightening me."

"You must promise not to be too upset when I tell you. There are more problems for us to face, but I hope I can find a way to overcome them."

"Tell me, Henry, I can endure anything so long as I can be with you."

"That is part of the predicament I find myself in, dearest Margaret. My mother's attempt to cheer me up involves plans to have me sent away to further my education. We will no longer be able to see one another."

"Oh, Henry, where does she wish to send you?"

"To the continent. She reasons that as people are heading over to France once more that I should take advantage of the present climate and embark on a grand tour, taking in the sights of France, Germany, Italy, and Switzerland."

"I see," Margaret whispered quietly, trying to keep every hint of sadness at the prospect of Henry leaving out of her voice. "What a wonderful opportunity."

"They are places I know well enough, I assure you. We spent so much of my childhood travelling from one health spa to another for a cure for Mother's ailments. And splendid though some of these places may be, I have no wish to go gallivanting abroad at present. At least I do not wish to go alone."

"So what will you do?"

"I don't know what to do, Margaret. I do not think I have the power to refuse. I am entirely dependent on my parents at present, and I have no desire to be the cause of family argument. My father suffers quite enough at the hands of my mother without me adding to his burden. In any case, it is all arranged. I will be gone for a year at least, I imagine."

"You have no choice but to go, Henry," Margaret said bravely. "I daresay your mother thought she'd best remove you just in case we struck up our friendship again. But I hope you will come back to me. Please do not forget me."

Henry pulled Margaret as closely to him as was possible. "Margaret, I love you, do you understand? I will not forget you. We are engaged! And one day you will be my wife, I promise."

Margaret felt certain that Henry's declarations were sincere, but she thought him already lost to her. He would go abroad to far off exotic places where he would no doubt be introduced to Italian heiresses and German princesses. She could not imagine him running back to marry plain and penniless Margaret Dashwood. "I can't bear the thought of not seeing you for a whole year," she murmured, "but I shall endure it for your sake, Henry."

"And when I come back we will be together, forever. I'll come into my money then and Mother will have no say about what I do. Wait for me, Margaret."

"I will, Henry. When do you have to go?"

"There is a boat sailing next week. We have only a few more days together."

Henry reached down to lift her face to his own. He kissed away her tears so tenderly and with such endearing protestations of love that Margaret could only smile and kiss him back.

"How I wish I could stay in your arms forever, Henry."

"One day you shall, my love."

A sudden rapping at the door had Margaret almost jump out of her skin. They froze, their hearts hammering together behind the heavy drapes. The door handle creaked as they listened to it slowly turn. Margaret imagined that her breathing was so loud that it must be heard all over the house. The door opened with a noise like a low groan. Margaret had never felt so frightened. She clung onto Henry and buried her head in his chest. When the door closed and she heard footsteps across the floor she nearly screamed out loud.

"Henry, where are you?" a voice hissed in the darkness.

Henry laughed. "What is it, Willoughby? You are not wanted here, you know."

"Listen, I thought I'd better warn you that I've seen Mrs Brandon wandering about the place. I think she's looking for you, Miss Dashwood."

"Thank you, Mr Willoughby," Margaret managed to say behind the curtain. She was far too embarrassed to show her face.

They heard the door open and shut once more. It was time to go, but surely they could find a moment for one last, sweet kiss.

Marianne left the room as soon as she was able. If it were possible she would find Margaret and they would return to Manchester Square. Her impatience to be gone from London increased with every moment. She sighed for the air, the liberty, and the quiet of the country, and fancied that if any place could give her ease, Delaford must do it. She would be reunited with little James, and the world would be set to rights again. They would go home in the morning. Out in the corridor she walked along, looking into rooms where cards were being played, and people stared at her as if they wondered why they were being disturbed. At the end by the staircase she decided she would take one quick look upstairs. Mounting the steps, she felt rather nervous, almost as if she were snooping. It was very dark as she looked down the length of the corridor and deciding she would not venture far she took a few steps before she was struck by the sight of a figure coming out of a room. In her haste to get away, she turned quickly on her heel. The pain that seared through her ankle was enough to make her cry out. She stumbled but before she hit the ground with a thump she had been caught, righted on her feet, and swept up into the arms of Mr Willoughby.

"Put me down at once, Mr Willoughby," she started in distress. The gentleman, ignoring her protestations, opened a door to his right and carried her in. He promptly put her down as she requested, on a striped sofa at the foot of a large four-poster bed.

"I will get help. Stay there; do not move or you will do untold damage."

"I must go and find Margaret," she said as she struggled to get on her feet. "She has disappeared and I am a little worried about her at present."

"Miss Dashwood is quite capable of looking after herself," he answered immediately in a stern voice. "Stay where you are."

The authoritarian tone of his voice had an immediate effect. Marianne allowed him to take charge for a moment before the recollection that she had seen him looking most intimate with her sister made her instantly speak out.

"I saw you with my sister earlier this evening," Marianne began in an accusing tone. "I'd like to know what you think you are doing."

"Forgive me, Mrs Brandon, but I have no idea to what you allude."

"You were whispering into her ear, I saw you," she started, not quite knowing how to go on.

"What do you accuse me of doing, Marianne? Am I guilty of having an exchange of words with your sister?"

"I saw the way you looked at one another, an expression so conspiratorial that I do not know what to think."

"Ah, I see. I think I know now what you have assumed. You think I am carrying on a liaison with your sister, am I correct?"

Willoughby was kneeling next to her, with his face inclined toward her and very close. In the dim light his eyes were laughing, his expression one of mockery. Marianne wanted to move; at least she told herself that she did. She struggled to sit up but realised that by doing so his countenance was brought ever closer.

"I do not know what to imagine, Mr Willoughby."

"I think you have imagined the very worst of me," he said, all the amusement gone from his face. "How could you believe that I would even look at your sister, let alone make love to her, when the only woman I want to take in my arms is here with me now."

"Mr Willoughby, you must not say those things. Please, you said you would get help." Marianne made a great effort, rising to her feet. The pain was not so strong now and she made a move toward the door, only to be caught by Willoughby, who grasped her arms tightly, forcing her to stop.

"I should not say these words, I know, but I want you to listen to me, Marianne. I love you and I know that you love me. Deny it if you will, but I do not think you can if you search your heart for the truth. If you would admit your own true feelings, you would remember we are as twin souls, Mrs Brandon. Whosoever and whatever may separate us will never destroy that bond. We will always love one another forever, that is our burden."

Marianne opened her mouth to speak. "John, this must stop. Please let me go." Willoughby had backed her against the wall, and he began to stroke her hair. His touch was gentle as a single finger traced a line down her cheek and over her lips. She gasped as he murmured into her hair, whispering of his love.

"Shall I stop?" he taunted, his eyes fixed on hers with an expression so artless, so appealing that Marianne felt she was lost. As if in a hypnotic trance, she felt powerless against him. Willoughby's mouth enclosed hers, he held her face in his hands and kissed her with such passion that she couldn't even think. Every instinct, every nerve in her body responded to his touch.

"Come away with me, Marianne," he whispered, brushing her neck with his mouth.

She felt his lips on her skin, his fingers flickering like feathers over her flesh, making her ache to be loved by him. Willoughby's embraces were tender and his skills as a lover so expert that Marianne began to feel that she was losing the battle. She started to cry.

"Please let me go," she pleaded. "I cannot come away with you, nor do I wish to."

"But we love one another, Marianne. That cannot be fought. We were meant to be together, and we can be if you come away with me now. Deny that you love me."

"I will deny it," she pronounced forcefully, pushing him away with all her strength. "I do not love you. I love my husband, and you are wrong to love me like this. I beg you, Willoughby, it must stop now."

"You are lying to yourself, Marianne. I know you better than myself. Besides, everything denies your protestations. Your looks of love, your tender kisses, all betray your real feelings. We both recognise the truth. Come now, am I really to believe that you love your husband as passionately as you pretend when it is clear that he has his interests elsewhere? Where is he tonight? Lying in the arms of his lover, the spitting image of her mother before her, no doubt."

This was too much for Marianne to bear. She raised her hand and struck him a blow across his face; immediately regretting her action, she put out her hand to soothe the red mark she had left. "I am so sorry, that was unforgivable, but the truth is that I have made a life without you; for better or for worse, it is the life I have chosen. It is the life I want with a man who truly loves me as you never could love me, John Willoughby. You have your obligations, responsibilities that were chosen, decided upon, and made of your own free will. We both know that what you propose is shamefully wrong. You say you love me, but if you really loved me you would leave me alone. Let me go, John. If you truly love me, let me be."

John Willoughby gazed down at Marianne and knew he was defeated. He knew she was right, and the appeal in her eyes touched him to his heart. "Very well," he said, his voice soft and quiet, "if that is your wish, I will go, even if every instinct in my soul tells me that we are meant to be together. I only ask this, that you will give me your assurance: that if you ever change your mind or find you need me, that you will come to me."

Marianne looked into his eyes, sincere with his request, and hesitantly nodded her assent before turning away from him for the last time.

Standing alone in the dark after he had gone, shivering with shock and remorse, she considered how thankful and relieved she was that it was finally all over. Whatever madness had existed between them she knew was finished for good. Reason told her she could never have been happy with Willoughby, even if free to be with him. Her heart and her soul belonged to one man, however uneasy their present predicament. William Brandon was the love of her life, even if he loved another.

Marianne managed to escape to the safety of her carriage with little fuss or notice from anyone after all. Everyone else was so intent on enjoying themselves that the departure of Mrs Brandon and Miss Dashwood passed with barely a comment. Mrs Jennings, who always liked to be the first fount on any gossip, assured anyone who asked that Mrs Brandon felt out of sorts due to being parted from her husband for so long. Only Lucy was disappointed that she had not seen anything pass between Mrs Brandon and Mr Willoughby to talk about. Having found Margaret, who seemed to be equally eager to leave the party, they travelled the short distance home in silence. Both were consumed with their own thoughts, Margaret upset that she had only a few days left to spend with Henry before he was to disappear for a whole year and Marianne determined to put the recent past behind her.

Unable to sleep, Marianne sat up in bed, a single candle glowing at her bedside. They would travel back to Delaford in the morning; she did not want to stay in London any longer. Thank heaven this whole business with Willoughby was over. It had been a kind of insanity, but it was over for good. All that mattered was trying to win her husband back, but how she might manage that she did not entirely know.

Just before her candle finally guttered for the last time, she heard a knock downstairs at the front door. There it was again, loud and insistent. Who on earth could it be at this hour of the night, she wondered? She did not have to wait long to find out.

Sally appeared at the door, an express letter in her hand. "I'm so sorry to wake you, madam, but I think it might be urgent."

Marianne undid the seal and read.

Wolfeton Fitzpaine
February 23rd
Dear Mrs Brandon,

   Please come as soon as you can; the Colonel is very ill.
He has been unwell for more than a week but, not wishing
to alarm you or have you change your plans, he would not
let me write before. I am very sorry and worried out of my
mind. Make haste,

   With sincere wishes,
   Eliza Williams

"Oh, heavens, Sally," Marianne cried. "Will you help me pack? The Colonel is ill and I must leave at once."

Sally started packing efficiently whilst Marianne darted round the room selecting any object she deemed necessary to her travelling arrangements. She tried not to think about her husband who lay ill, or how dangerously sick he had become to necessitate an express letter from Miss Williams, but tried instead to focus on practicalities. What would Elinor do, she asked herself? And what was she to do about Margaret? Perhaps Mrs Jennings would take her in whilst she was away.

Entering Margaret's room, Marianne proceeded to wake her. "Margaret," she said softly, trying to make the shock of waking in the middle of the night less great, "I am sorry to have to tell you but I have some bad news."

Margaret struggled to sit up, rubbing the sleep from her eyes.

"I have to go to Lyme. William is very ill and I cannot delay a moment longer. I am to take the coach immediately; Reynolds and Bertram will accompany me, so you do not have to worry. I want you to go to Mrs Jennings, do you understand? You cannot stay here on your own. Write to me in a couple of days and let me know that all is well. I am so sorry to leave you, Margaret. Indeed, I am sorry that you have had such a miserable time in London and that all I am doing is prolonging the agony. I meant you to have the time of your life."

"Marianne, I have had a wonderful time, truly," Margaret answered sleepily. "Do not worry about me, I shall be fine. Kiss William for me and do not fret, Marianne, I am sure he will be on the road to recovery as soon as he hears that you are on your way."

"Yes, I must send a note immediately, so that Miss Williams will expect me. Goodbye, Margaret and don't forget to write."

As her carriage moved away, the horses galloping down the dark streets, Marianne was filled with a sense of dread now that she had time to think about the situation. It was now easy to see why she had not heard from William. If he had been ill he could not write. It was typical of him not to want to distress her, and she reasoned that he had probably thought he would be set to rights within a day or two. Eliza had not specified what sort of illness he had contracted, but Marianne thought she could guess. Having spent so much time nursing little Lizzy had brought him into close contact with the little girl. Marianne did not want to think about the possibilities. She felt consumed by guilt that as her husband had lain unwell she had been conducting herself disgracefully. "How could I have been so stupid?" she asked herself. "How could I have jeopardised my marriage, my home, and the love of my husband and child for a moment of folly?" Swept up by her emotions, she decided she had behaved as badly as Willoughby had ever done. The kisses she had bestowed on that gentleman were as reprehensible as any act of love they might have indulged upon. Marianne prayed to be forgiven. She prayed, as she had never done before. All she wanted was to see Brandon and see him well again.

Chapter 37

ON THE THIRD DAY Marianne entered Lyme, weary but
thankful she was nearing her destination. She had made occasional visits to the watering hole in the past with her sister Elinor
and the children on hot sunny days and remembered them with
happiness. The splendid situation of the town with the principal
street almost rushing into the water looked very different in the
winter light. Everywhere was shut up; only the fishermen were
to be seen on the Cobb, their boats bobbing on the water, their
nets prepared for fishing. In warmer weather the pleasant little
bay would be lively with bathing machines and company in the
season. Her eye sought the beautiful line of cliffs stretching out
to the east of the town; they passed through Charmouth, backed
by dark escarpment, trotting down narrow lanes and past Pinny,
finally entering the village of Wolfeton Fitzpaine where the
forest-trees and orchards waved bare, skeletal arms as if to hasten
the warmer winds of summer.

They were soon stopped outside a cottage in the centre of the
village, a neat-looking house with mullioned windows to either

side of a canopied doorway over which was trained an old rambler. There was a small garden to the front behind a wicket fence with a bench under a window and a stone path winding between the flower beds, where the first signs of spring were starting to sprout in the form of green shoots. Now she was here, Marianne felt very apprehensive. With anxious fears attending every step, she was assisted down from the coach and took a deep breath as she looked toward the house. Before she took another step, the door was flung back and a young girl, her dark hair framing her pretty features, rushed down the path to take Marianne's hands in her own.

"Mrs Brandon, thank heaven you are here. William has been calling for you since breakfast. I know he will feel better the moment he sees you."

Marianne was touched by her warm reception, her worries subsiding as she entered the house, following Eliza into the parlour. A fire roared in the grate, which made the dark room appear quite cheerful. William, a diminutive bundle, lay on the sofa, which was doubling up as a makeshift bed complete with pillows and blankets. He was sleeping, lying so still that Marianne rushed forward with a cry. He looked like a small boy, she thought, his sweet countenance lost in dream and his hair tousled. Then his eyes opened.

"Marianne, you've come," he said weakly. "I prayed that you would." He started to sit up until Marianne scolded him to lie back down.

"I'll leave you together if you'll excuse me," said Eliza, bobbing a curtsey. "I'm so glad you are here, Mrs Brandon. I am honoured that you could come."

"Thank you, Miss Williams, for writing to me and allowing me to intrude upon your household."

"It is the least I could do…" Eliza faltered before leaving the room.

Now she and Brandon were alone Marianne felt awkward, unable to look at her husband with all the expression of love she hoped to endow. How she wished she could erase the recent past, strike it from her existence and her memory. "How are you, William?" she managed to say at last.

"I am all the better for seeing you, my darling. Come here, let me look at you." Marianne stepped forward, glowing under William's scrutiny. "I thought I might never see you again."

"Oh William, I wish I had known sooner."

"Even so, I did not imagine that I would see you here." His eyes held hers for a moment but she could only look away. "Come here, my darling."

Marianne rushed to his side and sat down on the small stool at the side of the sofa. She put out her hand to stroke his face and felt alarm at the touch of his fevered brow and pallid complexion. "Why did you not let Eliza write sooner?" she asked with fear in her voice. William's breathing was shallow; he appeared a shadow of the man she knew, as he lay languid and low.

"I did not want to worry you, my darling. Besides, I wanted to be sure."

Marianne took a wet cloth from the bowl on the table at her side, wringing out the cool water before applying to William's forehead. His eyes were closing again as he grew restless and feverish.

"I wanted to be sure you came because you wished to be with me," he muttered faintly before he fell into a slumber.

Marianne did not move, keeping watch over her husband's disturbed countenance as he slept. A half hour passed, during which William's repose became more and more troubled. Marianne, who steadfastly watched his continual change of posture and heard the frequent but inarticulate sounds of delirious murmurings which passed his lips, was on the point of rousing him from his sleep when William, suddenly awakened by some accidental noise in the house, started hastily up, and with feverish wildness, cried out, "Marianne is lost to me. Fetch Marianne, if she will come. Tell Willoughby I need her."

"William, I am here; Marianne is with you, my darling," she cried, concealing her terror, and assisting the Colonel to lie down again.

Marianne recognised with anxiety that he was not himself, and whilst attempting to pacify him, eagerly felt his pulse. It was very low and so fast as to give real concern. William was still talking incoherently so that her alarm increased rapidly. She quit the scene, running to find Eliza to ask her advice. Miss Williams was in the kitchen attending a small girl that Marianne knew was Willoughby's child the instant she saw her. The shock was great and for a moment she could not speak. Lizzy had her mother's dainty frame and pretty countenance, but the dark eyes that looked at Marianne from under arched brows were Willoughby's, with the same intensity of expression.

"Miss Williams, Brandon seems quite delirious. He only spoke to me for a moment before he slipped away into a deep sleep during which he has become most agitated. I cannot wake him. He doesn't see me. I think we should send for the doctor."

"Of course, Mrs Brandon, I will have Doctor Oliver sent for at once. Perhaps William needs a new dose of the cordials that he made last time."

Mr Oliver had still something more to try, some new medicines, of whose success he was almost as confident as the last, and his visit concluded with assuring the ladies of his confidence in the efficacy of the treatment. Marianne tried to remain calm, but William showed no signs of improvement. His restlessness was gone but he lay very still and his breathing was imperceptible. Marianne felt hopeless, and in this state she continued, scarcely stirring from her husband's bed. She was convinced that she would not see Brandon's eyes open again, and her thoughts reflected on images of grief, and her spirits sank. Marianne was certain she was being punished for her wickedness, felt persuaded by the idea that her husband was ill because of her conduct, and it gave fresh misery to her reflections.

About midnight, however, she began to hope once more, to fancy that she could perceive a slight amendment in William's pulse. She waited, watched, and examined it again and again; and at last, with an agitation more difficult to bury under exterior calmness, than all her foregoing distress, ventured to communicate her hopes to Eliza. Miss Williams, though forced on examination to acknowledge a temporary revival, tried to keep her companion from indulging a thought of its continuance; and Marianne told herself likewise not to hope. But it was too late. Hope had already taken over and feeling all its anxiety, she bent over her husband to watch. An hour passed away, and she saw with increasing anticipation a change take place. William's breath, his skin, his lips, all thrilled Marianne with signs of improvement. Brandon's eyes looked into hers with a flicker of recognition though he could still not rally enough to speak. Anxiety and hope now afflicted her in equal measures, and left her no moment of tranquillity till the arrival of Mr Oliver at two o'clock in the morning, when his assurances on a recovery in her husband even surpassing his expectation gave her belief, consolation, and tears of happiness. With each passing minute his recovery seemed certain. Marianne's joy knew no bounds and when for the first time he whispered her name, her joy was complete.

Eliza had prepared a hot meal: vegetable broth with home-baked bread. Marianne fed William small mouthfuls of soup from a spoon. He could manage only a little, but seeing him looking more like his old self was more than enough reward. It was only when the dawn light broke as William fell into slumber again that Marianne sought out Eliza's company. The two women sat together on a settle in front of the fire, keeping a watchful eye on their invalid.

"I do not know how to thank you for alerting me to William's illness. He always did have a stubborn streak. I suppose he thought he had a cold and would soon recover."

"Mrs Brandon, I have been racked with guilt and worry, but whenever I requested that you be sent for, he would not hear of it. He was not right in his mind and he rambled on about all sorts of nonsense in his sleep. I knew he was not entirely well when he kept saying that you were gone away to Allenham. He appeared to have everything so mixed up in his mind that I did not know what to do. I decided I must send for you and the doctor thankfully agreed with me."

Just at that moment Lizzy came into the room. "I cannot sleep, Mama," she said in a quiet voice. "Will Uncle William still be sick in the morning?"

"I am sure he will be much better, do not worry," said Marianne kindly before Eliza managed to speak.

The little girl walked over to her with an engaging smile. She looked so appealing that Marianne swept her up and onto her knee. Lizzy allowed herself to be cradled, leaning back into Marianne's comforting arms. The smell of freshly washed hair and the innocence of childhood moved Marianne to silent tears. This was Willoughby's child, a sweet and precious little girl who had never known what it was to be loved by her father. And then Marianne realised with an enlightening acknowledgement the part that her husband played in the life of this child, acting in selfless kindness since Lizzy had been born. Marianne felt more ashamed than ever and mortified that she could ever have thought the worst of her husband. His only crime was to have wanted to protect those that he loved and make a little girl understand what it was to enjoy a father's love. She did not know if she would ever forgive herself for making such foolhardy assumptions about William. Would she ever earn the right to reclaim his love as her own? She thought that might now be impossible. If he knew the truth he would surely disown her. One day she would have to tell him about what had happened between her and Willoughby. Only then would he be able to decide her future and restore or put an end to their marriage. Despite the warmth of the fire Marianne shivered as she pulled Lizzy ever closer into her arms.

Chapter 38

BY THE FOLLOWING TUESDAY, Colonel Brandon was feeling stronger and looking more like the man Marianne had married. He wanted to be out of bed and up and about. Eliza and Marianne had a great deal of trouble trying to keep him to his bed, but were very encouraged by his hearty appetite and the return of lively spirits. The very next day he appeared at the breakfast table, washed, shaved, and in his clothes, much to the consternation of the two young women.

"I have trespassed upon your kindness long enough, Eliza," he said, sitting down and helping himself to a hearty bowl of porridge. "I cannot thank you enough for your pains, but it is high time my wife and I left you to yourselves. Now Lizzy is coming along so well I would hate to be the very reason she has a relapse."

"Your home is my home, William, you know that," Eliza answered. "It has been a pleasure to have you here. You know full well I could never have nursed Lizzy on my own, and I am certain that if you had not been here, I might have been telling a different story now. And, Mrs Brandon, I have so long wished to make your acquaintance; it has been a delight to have you here, too. I only wish I could have made your stay more comfortable. It has been an enormous honour for me to have the company of William's beloved wife; I hope you do not mind when I say that although I never had a sister, I now feel as if I had gained one!"

Marianne felt very humbled at this little speech. Indeed, every day she had been in the cottage had taught her something more about true humility and humble modesty. Eliza was entirely selfless, which made Marianne only remember her own pride and shameful attitudes towards the Williamses with regret and sorrow.

"Well, I have been thinking," said Colonel Brandon, "that if you approve, Marianne, we shall repair to the Three Cups Inn in Lyme for a few days before making the journey home to Delaford. If I am to convalesce, I have a fancy to do it whilst watching the sea through my window."

"I should like it very much if you are sure you are strong enough to make the journey," answered Marianne, rather nervous at the prospect of being alone with her husband at last. But she had known this time would come, she reminded herself, and was prepared for whatever lay ahead. And besides all this, she had another problem pressing on her mind. Having written to Margaret twice and having received no reply on either occasion, she was starting to worry. Marianne could not think what to do; she did not want to alarm her mother, Elinor, or William, who was looking so much better. Perhaps she should write to Mrs Jennings. After all, Margaret was young and forgetful. It had most likely slipped her mind to reply and she would not even consider that Marianne might be worried. Even so, her mind was disturbed by Margaret's lack of correspondence. There had not even been a single enquiry asking after William.

The Brandons left shortly after breakfast for the short journey down into Lyme. The town wore a cheerier prospect this morning with a pale sun glittering on the water and the bustle of townsfolk about their business. As soon as they had secured a room, the Colonel expressed a desire to walk. Marianne tried to protest against such a scheme, saying that he should lie down and rest, but Brandon would not hear of it. He could think of no exercise to do him better on such a fine March day with a fresh breeze to blow away the cobwebs than to enjoy a walk on the Cobb. They set off down Broad Street and turned onto the Walk, neither of them saying very much. Marianne was feeling very tired, the last few days had taken their toll. But even putting aside the effort it had taken of looking after her husband day and night, she admitted to herself that she was not feeling quite well.

At last they turned onto the Cobb and, exclaiming at its treacherous height, encountered fresh, salty winds, which buffeted them along, so that they were forced into a trot. They laughed into the wind and were caught by salt spray dashing over the high walls; it was a heady mixture of elation and fear. Marianne felt she might be blown over the edge at any moment and clung onto her hat and William's arm for dear life. They were nearing the end, where on both forks of the harbour wall, they could see the waves leaping and crashing over onto the stones to trap the unwary. Despite the sunshine, up here on the highest level, the gales from every compass point squalled and stormed. They were blown from side to side by the wind. Teetering on the edge, Marianne wondered what it would be like if she were to be blown right over and onto the treacherous rocks to meet with death down below. It would be so easy to slip and trip down into the glassy depths of the bottomless sea.

"Come away from the edge, Marianne," William cried, as his wife let go his arm to stand swaying on the brink, watching the waves crashing on the rocks, drawn by the mesmerising mass of water, breaking and foaming incessantly. A wave of nausea swept over her as she looked down. The wind was blowing so hard it took her breath away. Marianne looked up to regard William's anxious face. Dear, sweet William, she thought, how could I ever have doubted him? As she watched him walk towards her, she was stopped again by another sensation, which almost overpowered her. She really was not feeling very well, her stomach was churning, and she felt so light-headed she had to stand still to try and compose herself. Another gust almost blew her off her feet and as Brandon reached her side she gave in to the consciousness that she was slipping away. William seemed to be somewhere at the end of a dark tunnel where she could not reach nor hear him. Marianne slumped in Brandon's arms much to his great alarm; her eyes were closed, she did not breathe, and her face was like death. The horror of that moment to Colonel Brandon, who caught her up, kneeling with her in his arms, looking on her with a face as pallid as her own, in an agony of silence.

"Marianne, my darling, please open your eyes. Whatever is the matter? You do look most ill!"

Marianne lay in his arms, still and pale. Brandon laid her down to determine whether she still breathed and was immediately rewarded by the sight of her eyes opening.

"Thank God, Marianne," he called, as she struggled to sit up. "I thought you were lost to me!"

"I have not been feeling quite well all morning. I think I fainted," Marianne managed to say.

"Come," William said picking her up in his arms, "I think you need some rest."

As they reached the start of the Cobb, the sight of the Colonel carrying Marianne had the fishermen rally round, eager to help. A messenger was sent and a chair fetched to convey Mrs Brandon back to the inn. Brandon insisted upon fetching the doctor immediately and Marianne was put to bed. The doctor was with Marianne for a short while and, having assured Colonel Brandon that his wife was in good health and that there was nothing to be unduly concerned about, he left after giving orders that she have plenty of bed rest for the next few days.

Colonel Brandon could hardly wait to see Marianne. He entered the room, rushing to her side to plant a kiss on the top of her head. Marianne sat up in bed, her colour restored, but she was looking rather grave.

"How are you, Marianne?" William asked, taking up position on the side of the bed. "Please forgive me, I should never have suggested a walk; you must be worn out with looking after me. I was very thoughtless."

"No, William, you are never thoughtless," said Marianne quietly. "Only your wife has that distinction."

"Come now," said Brandon, tucking the covers carefully around her, "you are overwrought and not yourself. I think a little sleep is in order."

"No, William, I cannot sleep. I must talk to you, though I fear the outcome. I must tell you what happened in London, knowing that as soon as it is told you will despise me forever. Especially now, I must tell you the truth."

William took her hand in both of his with such tenderness that Marianne could not think how to begin to tell him the horror of all that had taken place. How could she spare him?

"I do not wish you to tell me anything, Marianne. All I desire is that you love me, and I know that to be the case. I have a very good idea what may have happened to you, but I do not blame you, nor do I blame Mr Willoughby, you will be surprised to learn."

Marianne stared at her husband in shock. She could hardly believe what he was saying.

"Men are foolish creatures, Marianne. They think all they need do is set up a wife with a home, a child, and a pocketful of pin money. They think that is all there is to marriage. They go about their own concerns without giving a thought to the lives of the women they leave behind. I have been guilty of neglect. Eliza told me as such, though I did not want to listen."

"You have not neglected me."

"On the contrary, I am guilty as charged. You were merely nineteen when I married you, a girl with no experience of the world who was thrust into the life of hostess, wife, and mother, with a large house to command before you were ready. Small wonder that you seemed desperately unhappy at times. I had lived your life span twice over by the time you came to Delaford and had many experiences to draw on in times of difficulty. Eliza reminded me of her mother's fate. My brother's cruelty and disregard made his wife turn to another for solace, and though he was the truly guilty party, she paid the ultimate price when he divorced and abandoned her. If she had been loved, as she ought to have been, she would never have suffered as she did. I too am as culpable as he. I have not taken such care of you as I should and have been guilty of spending too much time on matters of business and on matters of duty. I am sorry for it, but I only have myself to blame."

"William, you don't know what happened."

"But I do. I left London when you most needed me. I had seen the way Willoughby was behaving toward you and I was still determined on going to see Eliza and Lizzy. If I had chosen to leave in the morning instead of rushing off in the middle of the night, or if I had asked you to come with me in any way that might have tempted you to accompany me, I am certain we would not be having this conversation. If I had loved you as I ought to have done, or half as much as you have loved me, you would not be lying there so ill and forlorn. Eliza made me see how difficult it must be for you to have her constant presence in your life. I want you to know I have never loved anyone as much as I love you. Can you ever forgive me?"

"William, can you ever forgive me?"

"Hush, Marianne, all that matters is that you came back to me. All I wish is for your happiness, and having you returned to me I can only say has made me the happiest of men."

Marianne, unable to contain her emotions a moment longer, burst into tears. How would she ever deserve this worthy man? How would she ever be able to love him enough to return the devotion he lavished upon her?

"Please do not cry; you will become ill again. I cannot bear to see you ailing," he began, reaching out to brush away her tears.

"Oh my darling," she said, raising her eyes to his with a look of adoration, "I am not ill, on the contrary."

William looked at Marianne, who was now smiling, almost laughing at him. She took his hand, holding it against her body as she watched his expression change. "I have some news, which I hope will please you. William, my love, you are going to be a father again."

Colonel Brandon's joy knew no bounds. Throwing his arms about his wife, he cried, "Is it really true?"

Marianne nodded. "The doctor just confirmed it. I wondered why I had been feeling so strange of late. And then I remembered the delectable afternoon we spent before Lady Jennings's evening party."

She blushed. Colonel Brandon was gazing at her with love in his eyes. "Which puts me in mind," she whispered in his ear as he bent to kiss her. "You are looking very tired, my darling. I think it is time for your afternoon rest."

Chapter 39

NEVER HAD MARIANNE FELT happier or more contented. Reunited with her husband and with the promise of a new life to come, a sister or brother for little James, Marianne thought she must be the luckiest woman alive.

They were sitting at dinner looking out through the window at the stunning views over the sea. The evening sunshine sparkled on the ruffled waves and on the fishing boats bobbing in the harbour. Lyme and its environs presented such a simple, good way of life that Marianne felt quite envious of the fisherfolk who sat chatting or mending their nets. Marianne had not stopped thinking about the little cottage they had just left and felt most anxious that Miss Williams and Lizzy should not be neglected in the future.

"Why cannot they come to live at the Park, William?" she asked her husband.

"Marianne, that is a most generous thought, but Eliza has made it very plain that she has no such ambition. She has her own life and simple though it might seem to our ideas, she is happy enough."

"I am very ashamed when I think how I thought about Miss Williams," Marianne admitted. "I have been very selfish and jealous without a proper cause. I am sorry, William, but I could not bear the thought of sharing you."

"Let us not talk of the past but look to our future. We have a wonderful life ahead of us, my darling. I must admit, though Lyme has had a tremendous effect on my spirits, I am looking forward to going home to Delaford. We will return to London tomorrow to collect Margaret on the way."

"I must confess I am a little worried about Margaret," admitted Marianne. "I haven't had a letter from her since I came away. Well, I expect she has been busy with Mrs Jennings. I do hope she is having a better time of it."

"We must send a letter," said the Colonel, "and thank Mrs Jennings for her pains. Why did you not tell me of this before?"

"I did not wish to worry you, and I imagined it was just thoughtlessness on Margaret's part," said Marianne, wishing she had spoken earlier.

As the Colonel called to the servant to bring him writing materials, the landlady approached, two letters in her hand. "These have just come by express, ma'am, I hope it's not bad news."

Marianne scrutinised the handwriting on the first but could not distinguish its owner. She eagerly undid the seal with impatient fingers.

Russell Square
Thursday, March 3rd
Dear Mrs Brandon,
  I hope this letter finds you and Colonel Brandon well. When I first learned that Margaret had been left in London

quite alone, I must admit that I was somewhat surprised. Mrs Jennings, I'm sure, has done her best to keep Miss Dashwood entertained, but I have to say that to my mind at least, leaving a young girl in the charge of an old lady who may not always have her wits about her was perhaps ill-judged.

I do not wish to alarm you but I happened to be in town very early this morning when I saw Miss Margaret getting into a carriage I did not immediately recognise. On closer examination, I ascertained that she was not alone. I daresay there is a completely innocent explanation as to why she was sharing a carriage with Mr Willoughby, but I thought it might be prudent to inform you, as on relaying the information to Mrs Jennings, it appeared that she had no knowledge that Margaret was even out of the house.

I think it a shame that Mrs Jennings has been put to so much trouble looking after an ungrateful girl who has not the courtesy to tell her protector whither she is bound.

I hope to see you in London shortly,

With all due felicitations,

Mrs Lucy Ferrars

Passing the letter to William, she hesitated, waiting for the curious landlady to leave before opening the second. "Oh, William, I should not have left Margaret on her own. What can it mean?"

Marianne could not imagine that the latest letter contained any better news, but it was worse than she could possibly have imagined.

Upper Berkeley Street, March 3rd
Dear Mrs Brandon,

You must return to London at once and bring the Colonel
with you if he can make the journey. I do hope he is feeling
better. I am so sorry to be the bearer of such bad news, but
I have to tell you I am very frightened for Miss Margaret's
well-being. Mrs Robert Ferrars saw Margaret get into Mr
Willoughby's carriage early this morning, and she has not yet
come home. I hope all will be resolved before you return but I
am most anxious to see you,

Yours ever,
Mary Jennings

"We must leave for London immediately," Marianne cried, unable to remain calm. "What on earth can have happened? Oh, William, I knew Margaret was not in her right mind when I left, but I can hardly credit this behaviour."

"I can credit Willoughby with almost any behaviour," Brandon said grimly. "Come, we must leave now. I only hope we are not too late."

Marianne could not voice her fears. It all seemed to make perfect sense. The balance of Margaret's mind had not been right. When Marianne thought about the outings that Margaret had been making on her own, everything suddenly seemed clear. Henry Lawrence was to blame, she thought. If he had not broken her sister's heart, none of this would have happened. Margaret had always been in love with Willoughby, an infatuation that had now brought her to ruin. But what had been his motives? What did he want with a young girl? That he might wish to take his revenge in some dreadful way for having been spurned by

Marianne was a thought which immediately crossed her mind. She shuddered to think of the possibilities.

Their journey went off well. Colonel Brandon decided it would be quicker if they travelled through the night, only stopping for refreshment at a roadside inn and for the purpose of changing the horses. On the second day they arrived in town at five o'clock and travelled straight to Berkeley Street to find Mrs Jennings. However, they were dismayed to discover that she was not at home and, not knowing what else they could do for the moment but see if there were any more news in Manchester Square, they directed the coachman to return to their home. As the carriage came to a standstill, Marianne looked up at the house with a sinking heart. How they were to find Margaret and discover what had happened to her she had no idea. What was she to tell her mother? How would Mrs Dashwood react when she heard the news?

As they entered the hallway, Marianne was stunned and surprised to see Margaret running down the stairs toward her, followed not far behind by Henry and Mrs Jennings.

"Margaret, you are safe! Thank goodness! We were so worried about you," Marianne cried, throwing her arms about her sister with a mixture of relief and genuine affection at seeing her. She looked toward Mrs Jennings, who smiled conspiratorially.

"Miss Margaret was in safe hands after all," the old lady said.

"Yes, I am safe and it is all thanks to Mr Willoughby. Look, Marianne, I am engaged to be married and with the blessing of Lady Lawrence, too. We are to be married next week!"

Neither Marianne nor the Colonel could understand what Margaret was talking about, but there on Margaret's wedding finger sparkled an emerald and diamond ring for everyone to see.

"Speak up, Henry, what is the meaning of this?" William Brandon declared in a stern voice.

"It is true, Uncle William. Margaret and I have been secretly engaged for some time now."

"But what has Mr Willoughby to do with it?" asked Marianne, who could make neither head nor tail of any of their story.

"Henry was leaving for the continent, but he wanted me to go with him, as we could not bear to be apart for a year as Lady Lawrence wished. We were to run away. Mr Willoughby pretended that he would help us when all the time he was plotting against our elopement," cried Margaret.

"Mr Willoughby persuaded my mother that we should be allowed to marry," Henry interrupted. "He has quite a way with the ladies, you know, and especially with my mother. He told her that he had once loved someone that he should have married, though he was comforted by the fact that she is married now to a better man than he. Mr Willoughby even extracted a letter out of my mother giving her consent. He was determined to do what he could before he went away."

"Where has Mr Willoughby gone, Henry?" asked Brandon.

"He has taken his wife abroad to the continent. Willoughby had a hankering to see Switzerland and the Alps. He gave me this letter to be entrusted to you, Uncle Brandon."

Marianne could not believe what she was hearing. She was so relieved to find Margaret so happy and glad to think that Willoughby was not such a villain after all. "My hearty congratulations to you both," she cried. "Although I must admit that you completely fooled me, you dreadful pair."

Marianne stopped when she saw the expression on Brandon's face as he read the letter. "Miss Williams is to be provided for whilst Willoughby is out of the country, which may be for some time. He is bestowing a very generous allowance upon my ward and her daughter. I am utterly astonished."

Marianne knew that the possibility of Willoughby ever seeing his child was remote, but she was gladdened to think he had considered them enough to make financial provision. His departure from England could only mean that his sentiments of love for her had, after all, been real. It was impossible not to think of him without a certain affection; she had loved him once, and he had proved that his love for her was genuine.

Marianne observed Henry and Margaret standing next to one another and thought how wonderful it was that they were to marry, but how such a feat could be accomplished in so short a time she could not begin to think. "I am genuinely delighted for you both," she addressed Margaret and Henry, "even though I cannot imagine how a wedding can be arranged next week!"

"Do not worry, Mrs Brandon, it is all in hand. Your mother is on her way with Elinor, Edward, and the children." Mrs Jennings lowered her voice to a whisper. "And I hope you do not mind me adding that I really feel that in your condition you should not be worrying your pretty little head about it, but sitting down."

Marianne could only laugh. As she looked around her at the happy scene, her eyes met William's as he gazed back in sheer adoration. "Come along, Mrs Brandon," he said, sweeping her off her feet and picking her up in his arms before she could protest, "Mrs Jennings's advice must not be ignored." He kissed her cheek tenderly as he mounted the staircase, whispering into her ear. "Doctor's orders, Mrs Brandon. Lots of love and plenty of bed rest."

THE END

About the Author

Jane Odiwe is an artist and author. She is an avid fan of all things Austen and is the author and illustrator of *Effusions of Fancy*, annotated sketches from the life of Jane Austen, as well as *Lydia Bennet's Story*. She lives with her husband and three children in North London.

Lydia Bennet's Story

A Sequel to Jane Austen's Pride and Prejudice

JANE ODIWE

"A breathtaking Regency romp!"
—Diana Birchall, author of *Mrs. Darcy's Dilemma*

How does impulsive, high-spirited Lydia turn out?

Lydia is a girl of untamed expressiveness and vulnerability, and all she can think of are pleasure and marriage. She's convinced George Wickham is the man of her dreams, but quickly discovers her hero is not the man she believes him to be.

In this spicy sequel to Jane Austen's *Pride and Prejudice*, Lydia is reunited with the Bennets, Bingleys, and Darcys for a grand ball at Netherfield Park, where she'll have to face down the greatest scandal of all, and in the process, might just find the key to true happiness.

"An absolute delight to read."

—*Historical Novels Review*

"Odiwe emulates Austen's famous wit and manages to give Lydia a happily-ever-after ending worth of any Regency heroine."

—*Booklist*

978-1-4022-1475-2 • $12.95 US/ $13.99 CAN

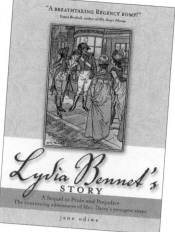